NOUVEAU RICHE

B. E. BAKER

For Tessa
May you never have to sell your "Hottie"

EMERSON

My mom always forgot things we needed when she went to the store. She sometimes forgot to pay the utility bills as well. As a result, they cut off our power on several occasions, including once during a snowstorm. Mom also never had what we needed when we traveled, no matter how minor the trip.

As I got older, the problem was clear. She never made lists.

I became somewhat obsessed with them.

Throughout school, my teachers mocked me for always having them, but I always remembered to bring projects, homework, and everything else I needed. Lists work when used properly. So when my girlfriend dumps me and I get fired on the same day, I do what I always do when I have a problem to solve.

I make a plan and list its component parts.

Actually, I make three separate lists.

The first is a list of references to use while I hunt for a new job. The second is a list of possible clients I could approach if I decide to start my own accounting firm. The third is a list of my expected expenses over the next six months, which I use to project my necessary timelines in either direction.

While the potential upside is higher if I start my own firm, I'll also face more risk and a longer timeline, meaning I'd need to tamp down in an aggressive way on my expenditures.

"What on earth are you doing?" Bea—short for Beatrice—has stopped behind me, and she's peering over my shoulder.

My sister's an unabashed snoop.

I set my pencil down and pivot in my chair. "That's really rude, you know."

"What is?" Bea frowns. "Asking people you love why they're doing stupid things? Or reading over your shoulder?" She arches one eyebrow. "Because I'm doing you a favor, to be honest. Who else is going to point out your idiocy?"

I lift my chin a little, fighting the urge to stand up so I can tower over her. I don't need the benefit of height. I already command the high ground. "There's nothing stupid in my behavior for you to point out."

"Oh, ho, I beg to differ." She drops one hand to her hip. "First, your girlfriend dumps you because you're not from a rich enough family and she's afraid to tell her daddy she's dating you. Then, on the same day, your alleged supervisor throws *you* under the bus for *his* error, and you just roll over and let him. You refuse to accept that those are tied in any way." She shakes her head. "You got the royal shaft, and didn't fight it because you'd lost the will to live. Now, instead of buying a loudspeaker and shouting about the injustice outside your old office or getting drunk and sleeping all day, you're. . ." She frowns and squints. "What *are* you doing?"

I slide all the papers into a stack and fold them in half. This time, I do stand. "Neither sleeping in nor blasting my grievances with a loudspeaker would fix the problem."

Bea tilts her head. "Before you *solve the problem*, Emerson, it's okay to mourn a little."

I roll my eyes.

"I'm not kidding." Her voice is quiet, and it's not replete with her typical know-it-all, lecturing tone. "There's a reason there are stages of grief."

"No one died, Bea. I don't need to work through stages." It hits me then—the time. The sun's barely been up for an hour. She's usually not awake for several hours yet. "Shouldn't *you* be sleeping in?"

She groans. "Mom and Dad called last night, and I told them about how you got fired."

I throw the papers down on the table. "Why did you tell them? I said I didn't want—"

"I knew you wouldn't, and they deserve to know." Bea drops into a kitchen chair with a beleaguered sigh. "You know they do."

I may have a tendency to handle things myself, and sometimes people I care about don't feel included. "I would've told them in a week or two, when I've finalized my plan. I don't even know whether I'm starting my own business or finding a new job."

"You're such an idiot. That doesn't matter. Your family doesn't care if you have your plan worked out. They care that you're hurting." Bea flops her arms across the table, propping her chin on her elbow. "Plus, if you start your own firm, they'll be your best line to new clients—"

I head for my room, shaking my head almost involuntarily. "No way. I'm not asking them for help."

"It's what parents do." Her voice is quiet, but

crystal clear.

I pause, but I don't turn. "Well, they aren't really my parents, just like they aren't yours."

She's utterly silent, which is strange for Bea. She always has something to say.

I finally turn around, bracing for the tongue-lashing.

"You never let them adopt you, but they always wanted to, and you know that." Her tone's full of reproach this time. "Some of us think you're an idiot for it."

"I need to do this alone," I say. "I can't go running to them my entire life every time there's a problem."

"This is a pretty big problem." Her brow's furrowed, her eyes intent.

"And I'll deal with it myself. Like I said."

"Well." She flops down on the table, her arms limp, her chin mushed against the table. "I'm going back to bed. But I got up because I thought you might want to take a temp job."

"A what?"

"The hotel's looking for some help, and because it's last minute, the pay is decent. They have a lot of events booked today, and they need waiters to carry hors d'oeuvres around and stuff."

After lending a hand with Mom and Dad's inn for years, Beatrice graduated to being the head waitress at the nicest hotel in Scarsdale, the Opus Westchester. It's five hundred bucks a night to sleep there, and the hotel restaurant's correspondingly fancy.

"I've never waited tables, except at Mom and Dad's, and—"

"I told them that, and they said that's more experience than the last four people they used."

"What does it pay?"

"Thirty bucks an hour," she says. "It's not insane, but it's probably the best you'll find for this kind of thing."

A few shifts like that would go a long way toward keeping me from dipping into my meager savings while I try to find a new job or start my own firm. "When do I need to be there?"

"Thirty-nine minutes from now." She smiles. "And it's a twenty-minute drive."

People think she's nice, but in her heart of hearts, Bea's sadistic.

Eighteen minutes later, I'm turning the key in my ignition, dressed like a constipated penguin, ready for my first temp job at a hotel. I hate that, with a college degree, I'm still reduced to walking around a room full of snobs and offering them tiny chunks of who-knows-what. But sometimes trains go off the rails. Until you can get the dumb little cars back on the track, you do what has to be done. I know that better than anyone.

Bea did *not* warn me that the catering supervisor is horrible.

The first fifteen minutes of my six-hour job—they have two events back-to-back, apparently—is spent being lectured on the importance of averting my eyes from all the guests, elegantly staying out of the way, and never letting my platter become empty. She may have a British accent, but that doesn't make her preten-tious list of dos and don'ts less obnoxious.

"But at some point, it's going to be empty, right?" I can't help pointing out the obvious. "It's not the 'magical loaves and fishes' platter."

The stout woman scowls, her face flushing. "I hate new people."

My feelings for her are equally strong, but I manage not to share that sentiment.

She inhales and exhales a time or two, and then she launches. "First, it's not a *platter*. You're not serving pigs at a trough."

I'm pretty sure they fill the pigs' trough with a bucket, but again, I keep that to myself.

"Your serving *tray* will never become empty, because as soon as you realize your assigned appetizer is two-thirds of the way gone, you'll reconnoiter and move back toward the kitchen."

"But—"

She sniffs and throws her chin up, managing to look down on me from a foot below my eye level. It's impressive, to be honest. "Look, Everett—"

"Emerson."

"Whatever." She rolls her eyes. "When wealthy people see hors d'oeuvres coming their direction on a serving tray, they realize they're hungry—if they are— and if they're disappointed because the promise of food turns out to be an empty one, they become crabby. Quickly. It's our job to make sure that they don't. Do you understand?"

I blink.

"Because when the people who come to this hotel get crabby, people like you get sacked. Am I clear?"

I don't mention that being sacked isn't much of a threat, seeing as I don't have a permanent job, nor do I want one. I had to sign a half-inch stack of papers making it clear that this is a temporary position, and that the Opus Westchester isn't liable for anything I do or anything that happens to me while I haul buckets of slop around for these rich pigs.

"Everett, was I clear?"

"Crystal." This may not be worth the thirty dollars an hour.

"You appear to be doing this as a stopover on your

way to something better. This job may even seem trivial to you," the woman says, "but while you're out there, you're the front of our hotel, and we want to make sure—"

"That I'm a suitably invisible frontman," I say. "I get it. I'm actually pretty good at being invisible."

"If you can do this adequately, there will be other jobs like this one, and if you do them well, which I'm not holding my breath about, there are permanent positions for competent staff that pay far better than thirty an hour." She purses her lips before continuing. "Oh, and the very best thing about rich people?"

Oh. That's a question. She wants an answer. "They're. . .rich?"

Her laugh actually doesn't sound forced. "I was going to say that they pay well. That's why we put up with all this. Now go out there and disappear."

Maybe the woman's not such a terrible manager at all. She had me nervous enough that I listened, and at the end, she lightened up so I saw her as a person. It was a little heavy handed, but it's not a terrible strategy with people you don't know at all. I grab my platter—I now insist on thinking of it as a platter—look over the cheese puffs placed carefully on it, noting that there are thirty-seven of them, so one third would be right around twelve, and head out into the great wide ballroom.

Bizarrely, these people are wearing flouncy frocks and suits at ten in the morning. What on earth are they thinking? The banner in the corner reads "Seven Oaks Charity Brunch and Auction."

But they aren't eating brunch.

We're carrying a variety of things out on trays, and they're milling around, bidding on things. Most of the items they're pledging money for aren't even present.

There are photos, and there are even small mock-ups. For a split second, I consider setting my tray down and bidding on a vacation to a house in the Hamptons. Mom and Dad would love it. It might be worth the risk of being fired, especially if it's a good deal for a charitable cause.

But when I scan the sheet, the current bid's eleven *thousand* dollars.

The people here clearly have more money than sense. There's no way any rental is worth that much for a five-day stay.

"It's owned by Elon Musk." The other server's smiling. "That's why they're paying that much."

We both scurry back before anyone can notice we've been looking at auction items, but I can't believe anyone would pay that much just to tweet that they're staying at his house.

But whenever I get really frustrated or tired, I remember that I'm being paid thirty bucks an hour to pass out frou-frou snacks, and it's more than worth the sore shoulders. Two of the people who knock back more than their fair share of mimosas tip me, which turns $180 into more than two hundred.

Who tips a waiter for passing around fruit tarts?

Probably the same people who pay more than I paid for a car to spend a weekend in Elon Musk's house. It's a whole different world. Luckily, we have a half an hour break between the first event and the second. I get to go pee, windmill my shoulders, and I still have time to sit down for twenty minutes.

That's when Lisa calls me back.

I force myself to wait until the phone has rung at least twice before swiping to answer. "Hello?" That didn't sound pathetic, but it wasn't quite breezy either.

"Emerson?" She pauses. "Where are you?"

Where am I? I've called her twenty times since they wrongly fired me and she refused to do a thing about it, and now, three days later, she calls me back and asks me where I am? "I'm working." There. Let her stew about where I may have found a job this fast.

"You're *working*? Where?"

"Not everyone automatically believed Patrick's lies, you know."

"I didn't believe him," she says. "But he's been Dad's friend for two decades."

It stings a little that my own girlfriend thought it would be easier to dump me than stand up for me. I have to remind myself, again, that it's how she was raised. She didn't go through all the drama I did. She was in a safe, solid home with two parents her entire life. Of course she shies away from complicated, drama-fraught situations.

Once I start my own firm or find an excellent job, I'll convince her to date me again, and then she'll introduce me to her dad, the owner of the firm that fired me. That part of the plan will have to wait, because it's almost time to head over to the next event. I can hear the clacking of my boss's chunky black heels coming down the hall.

"It's not a good time. Maybe you want to get dinner later?"

"I have your stuff," she says.

"My what?"

"I'm outside your apartment with a box of your stuff. I wanted to drop it off, but—"

"My stuff? What stuff?"

"The books you loaned me on accounting principles."

"I don't need them. I aced that class."

"The blanket you always used when you came over

to my place."

"That was a gift." Is she kidding?

"The blue shirt I borrowed."

I have no idea what to say. She used to sleep in that shirt, and now she wants to dump it on my doorstep? I thought it was good that she called, but this. . .

"Emerson," my boss says.

"Right." I clear my throat. "I have to go. Just dump it on the mat. I'll text Bea and tell her to grab it later."

"Emerson, it's just that—"

"Yeah. Whatever." I hang up before I embarrass myself by saying something really stupid. Talking to her has me both flustered and now, borderline late. I'm grabbing my tray just as the clock rolls over to one p.m. Apparently for this event, we'll be serving as much alcohol as we serve food.

"I hate carrying champagne flutes," the other server's saying. "Thanks for doing those."

I suppose that's his way of asking.

Thanks to my tardiness, I can't even complain. Thanks a lot, Lisa. I'm holding the platter covered with champagne flutes as carefully as I can when someone practically flies past me, and I stumble. The flutes all shudder and my heart stops beating. For a split second, I think I'm going to drop the whole platter, but my years of helping out at the inn serve me well. I manage to keep all the flutes upright, and very little champagne spills.

I can't help glaring back at the woman who nearly wrecked my afternoon, and I notice she's really, really pretty.

In an I'm-snobbier-than-Paris-Hilton kind of way.

Her long, dark hair's tied back into a high ponytail, and she's wearing a fitted black dress and dramatic heels. Her ensemble probably cost the same thing as my college degree. The diamond solitaire pendant she's wearing is huge—it would probably pay for a nice sportscar. Her eyes flash and her hands wave wildly as she argues with someone around the corner.

Before I can wonder what has her in such a tizzy, I start to attract notice, or rather, my tray does. I dole out the champagne carefully, and more than one person has a look of desperation as they dive for a flute. I hope their liquid courage helps them survive the next two hours, because as I'm headed back to the kitchen, I realize I'm serving at a funeral.

At the first event, I returned each time with a mostly empty tray. I hate to say it, but returning when I have a third left was genius. By the time I reached the kitchen exit, I'd usually have a handful of snacks left. But this time, just as many people grab me and plonk empty flutes back on my tray, so I'm carrying nearly as much crystal on my return as I left with. I thought my shoulders were sore before, but that was nothing.

"I'm sorry about this, but I already told you why." Someone's talking in a very hushed voice in the small side room near our staging area. I pull up short so I can follow the prime directive—staying invisible.

"We can't pass up this offer."

"But you said I could use it for at least another year."

The woman who almost flattened me earlier, the one with the huge diamond, is frowning. It's not even a fake frown. She looks truly upset. "Let me buy it, then."

The person she's talking to laughs. "Where would you get the money? The whole reason we're selling it is—"

"I know," she says. "But I'll think of something."

She inhales. "I can get a loan." The other person must be shaking their head, because her whole face falls. "Just think about what will happen when—"

Out of the corner of my eye, I notice that my boss is glaring. I shoot past the open doorway, the people not even noticing that I'm walking past them. The second I reappear, the food prep staff hand me a new platter.

As I pick it up and arrange my hands underneath to brace against the weight, I can't stop thinking about the argument I overheard. I had no idea that rich people argued about money just as forcefully as the rest of us do. I'm still distracted when I walk back out, and that's probably why I don't notice the younger woman in the black dress coming through the same doorway. Her shoulder clips the edge of my tray, sending it sideways.

If time slowed down, like in the movies, maybe I could catch all the champagne flutes that cant sideways, but nothing slows. If anything, it feels like time speeds up. The champagne flies out sideways and absolutely *soaks* the distraught woman. The crystal flutes keep going, bouncing off her and flying past her so fast that I can barely follow. The glasses shatter in all directions as they strike the floor.

Yep, I'm pretty sure I'm going to get fired.

After a solid three-second glare, the woman straightens and storms off, veering around the corner toward the bathroom, presumably. My boss isn't pleased, but she has them give me another tray and sends me back out, because they're short staffed, and at least I'm wearing the right clothing.

She does promise me something as I go back out.

Something depressing.

"I'm taking the cost of those crystal flutes out of

your pay."

I wonder whether I'll owe them money after she does that. Maybe hotels like this buy crystal glasses in bulk. Maybe it won't be so bad. I'm distracted again, thinking about how much the twenty or so glasses I just broke will cost when I hand a glass of champagne to a very tall man and come face-to-face with a life-size portrait of a man who looks exactly like me.

"Who is that man?" I ask without thinking. "Is that the deceased?"

The tall man sips his champagne and turns. As his eyes take in my face, they widen. "Well, I'll be." He swears then, and turns back toward the portrait slowly. "You look just like Alistair, don't you? Back when he was young."

The man in the portrait, aside from his terrible butt-part hairstyle, could be my twin.

"Who are you?" the man asks.

I shake my head. "Nobody." I'm finally realizing that I've definitely violated the prime directive, in a big, big way.

I turn to go, but before I can disappear, the man raises his voice. "Hey, Catherine."

An older woman, her silver hair cut in a short, sleek bob, wearing a beautifully tailored black suit, turns on her heel and freezes. She's staring right at me. "Alistair?" The single word is whispered. Her eyelids flutter just a bit.

I can't decide whether to acknowledge it. I'm sure it's disturbing to see someone who looks so much like someone you just lost.

"Is that you?" Her brows draw together. "It can't be you." She inhales and her eyes widen. "Who are you, young man?"

"I'm a waiter," I say. "That's all."

"What's your name?"

"Emerson." It's starting to irritate me that I'm being interrogated. It's a little strange that I look like the man who died, but it's hardly my fault. In fact, I've been working hard. I'm not a criminal.

"What's your full name?" She arches one eyebrow. "Or did you spring from the womb with just the one name?"

"The womb—" I snort. "My name's Emerson Duplessis, and I can assure you that I have nothing whatsoever to do with the man who died."

Only, the blood drains from the woman's face, leaving her whiter than the linen tablecloths that are crisply spread across all the tables. "Duplessis?" Her hand lifts toward me, but it's shaking. "Was your mother named Nicole?"

That surprises me. "How did you know that?"

She closes her eyes, and for some reason, it makes her look much older. Maybe even close to seventy. When she opens them again, she looks different. Very different. The woman looking at me at first was tired, hollow, and broken. The woman who's looking at me now, although she's wearing the same expensive suit, the same string of creamy pearls, and the same nervous expression looks. . .

Her eyes are almost hopeful.

"When he was a senior in high school, my son had a girlfriend of whom I didn't approve. Her name was Nicole Duplessis." She purses her lips and glances around as if she's worried someone might be listening to our conversation. At first, I don't really understand what she's saying, but then it hits me—that guy in the portrait. . .

This cold rich woman is saying that he's my dad.

And that makes her my grandma.

2

ELIZABETH

I hate money.

I hate the way everything is always about it.

I hate the way people pretend they have it when they don't.

But mostly, I hate that I never seem to have any of it, and that without it, nothing works right. Today, for once, my issues aren't about money. At least, not precisely. They're about space.

"I told you," I say. "I only have room for eight new animals." I look down at my clipboard, as if the numbers at the bottom might change. "We have limited traffic, and—"

"Elizabeth, this little gal is set to be euthanized tomorrow," Kristy says. "I know you don't have room, but you're kind of her only hope."

I clap my hand over my eyes, but it's too late. I saw her sweet little face. She looks as desperate as Kristy makes her sound.

"Kristy!" I shout.

She always does this. Every single time I come, I tell her I won't keep coming back if she ambushes me with an extra pet or two right before I leave. "You knew I had exactly eight spots. I said hit me with the saddest stories up front, and not at the end."

"But she's such a good dog," Kristy says.

I grit my teeth and drop my hand. I can't help taking a good look now, especially with the image in my mind of her big brown eyes. The thing is, in the six years I've been doing this, I've gotten pretty good at identifying what pets I might be able to find homes for. Scarsdale is full of mostly wealthy people, and they're very particular. They don't want just any old animal. I need an angle to find the pets I take a home, and often, when I don't have an idea of what type of person might be looking for a new pet, they languish at my shelter for a long time.

The border collie in front of me has her ears plastered against her head, her big brown eyes trained on my face in the same quiet desperation I saw at a glance. I swear under my breath. "Kristy." She knows I'm already attached to the eight others I chose—three cats and five dogs.

She knows once I've heard this poor thing's story, I won't be able to say no.

"I don't have kennel space for her."

"That's perfect," Kristy says, her eyes bright. "She doesn't do well in kennels. Her owners kept her in a crate all day and all night for months and months, just letting her out for an hour in the evening."

"They did what? To a border collie?" I'm practically shaking.

"They said she chased their cat, so she had to be locked up when the guy wasn't taking her for a walk."

"But a *border collie*? They're like Sonic the Hedgehog in dog form." Sadly, nothing shocks me anymore. "She was kept in a box for. . .how old is she?"

"Nine months, almost. We got her six weeks ago, and you know the drill. It took a month to get her tail wound treated, and now—"

"Wait, what tail wound?"

"Stuck in that crate all the time, she got bored. Or that's what we think. She chewed her own tail clear through." Kristy looks strange, and I realize she's smug. Ridiculously smug. She knows she has me now.

"That's terrible."

"To make matters worse, it got infected. They couldn't afford to pay the vet, so they brought her in."

I can't take her. A nine-month-old border collie who has never really been properly socialized or trained is a full-time job. "That dog is like sticking a tornado in a bottle and shaking it around."

Kristy doesn't argue.

"She's a full-time job." I can't do it. I just can't. Between the shelter, and fundraising—we're already behind—and the upcoming show. "Kristy."

My old friend sighs. "Alright, I get it. I just thought I'd ask." She tilts her head and drops into a crouch to break the news to the poor girl. The poor little dog— rail thin—races in tiny circles in the concrete box of her kennel. Even so, she looks like she's smiling.

Smiling.

That's what does me in. I groan. "Fine. *Fine.*" I sigh. "Just get me the paperwork."

Kristy claps. "I knew you—"

I shake my head and whip my hand through the air. "No. You don't get to gloat and croon, not over this. It's not a triumph. It's a manipulation, and that adorable little nightmare's going to ruin my life." Her border collie coloring is perfect, with a white face, but black ears that wrap around her eyes, except for a little black circle on the top of the white part of her head.

"You're going to save hers." Kristy looks close to tears. Being the director of an open intake shelter that serves the greater New York City region is one of the hardest jobs I could ever imagine. Without a shelter like this, people would simply let their dogs loose. Dump them in bodies of water. Abandon them in the street.

It's absolutely vital.

But it's really, really hard to be the one in charge dealing with of all these innocent animals. There just aren't enough responsible humans to go around. "Alright, girl." Now I'm the one crouching down, and her tail stump is working overtime as she tries to lick me. "What are we going to call you?"

"The owners who dumped her called her Snow," Kristy says.

I arch one eyebrow. "But she's mostly black."

She shrugs.

"How about Lucky?" I ask. "Because you are one *lucky* dog to have a program director who scored you a reprieve."

"I'm not sure she's been very lucky so far," Kristy mutters as she clips a collar and then a leash to the shaggy mess. "The seven regional border collie rescues are all entirely tapped out—not a single foster available. Normally one of them would take her, but as it is. . ."

"Still." I hold out my hand for her leash. "She did meet me."

Kristy smiles. "That's true."

"Plus, I like to channel my hopes for the future. Once we get her cleaned up, I'll try to find some obsessive idiot who likes to run who will take good care of you."

Within five minutes of reaching my shelter, I'm

regretting my moment of pity. Lucky has jumped up on me seventeen *million* times, knocking me into the counter, scratching my arm, and knocking over the dog food I'm measuring into bowls for the newest members of our small shelter family. She's not aggressive or mean, but she's so energetic and so pathetically attention-starved that I might put her down myself if she doesn't quit.

"Lucky." I crouch down and let her lick my face— but after two minutes, she shows no signs of stopping. I finally pull the plug and stand up. "I know you've had things rough." She stares up at me intently, her fluffy ears pressed back against her skull again. I swear, it feels like she's actually listening and understanding me. "But you are making me cuh-ray-zee right now. Later today, we'll do a little behavioral training, and we'll get you a 'place' command started, and we'll head down the path toward making you into a responsible citizen. Until then, I really need you to calm the crap down."

She jumps up again immediately, then starts racing in maniacal circles round and round the food prep counter in our dog kennel center. So much for her understanding me.

Over the next few hours, as I integrate the three cats—two of whom are terrified, and one of whom is actively aggressive—and the five other dogs—most of whom are not at all interested in food, which isn't uncommon in a new place—Lucky acts absolutely tied to my heels. I trip over her at least a dozen times.

The irritation seeps through into my tone. "Lucky." She crouches down low, her entire body pressed against the concrete, her eyes looking up at me in a terribly sad mix of hope, fear, and shame. I exhale gustily and crouch down yet again. "Lucky." This time, I try to infuse her name with more patience, but it mostly comes out exasperated. "We're going to find you a really good home. I hope. Okay?"

At least she's not dead.

Some days, that's about the best thing I can say for myself, too.

Once the rest of my chores are done, I give her a really good, really long bath. I scrub, and I rub, and then when she's done, I dry and I brush, and I comb, and she holds entirely and completely still the entire time. She doesn't bark. She doesn't whine. She doesn't snap. I've never seen a dog hold that still or be that calm during a bath.

As she dries, she looks transformed. I'm impressed, really. "Maybe someone will adopt you after all." I smile, and she jumps up on me. Of course.

I've avoided it as long as possible, but it's finally time. "Listen, I'm going to have to put you in there." I point at the largest kennel we have. It's intended as a quarantine kennel for several dogs, but the others I adopted today are small breeds, so they're making do with three less expansive ones. Once they've been here without any signs of illness for a few days, I can integrate them into the current fabric of the ever-changing society of our rescue. "I know you already love me."

She scootches a few inches closer to me, her eyes never leaving mine, her tail stump thumping back and forth on the ground as if she can't help trying to wag what's already gone.

"But I have other things I have to do. I can't stay here all day."

When I close her into her kennel, she sits still and quiet, not even wagging her bizarrely long stump of a tail, just staring at me with those intense eyes. Lucky's whine is so soft, I almost can't hear it.

It's not like I don't have two dozen dogs every day

who want to come home with me. They all need homes. They're all cute. They're all sad. They're all pathetic. That's the biggest difficulty about what I do. My heart asks for more than my head can manage already. The one promise I made myself when I started all this was that I would *not* add to my little pack. I have to draw the line somewhere, and I already have not one, but *two* other dogs.

Cute dogs.

Dogs I love.

And they're tiny.

I have two special-needs Pomeranians—one's missing a leg and the other's blind in her right eye. Pomeranians almost never come through rescues. When they do, they're an easy dog to place. They're small. They're wicked smart, especially for a toy breed. They're usually well-behaved, even around kids. But any time you take something lovely and break it a little, it's a harder sell.

That's where I come in.

I always fall for the hardest-to-love dogs, and it gets me every time. Ironically, Scarsdale, New York is probably the place in America that has the least tolerance for things that aren't perfectly beautiful, other than Hollywood, maybe.

I'm worried with her exuberance that Lucky will run over my tiny puffs, and I shouldn't risk putting them in harm's way because I've decided to try and spare another damaged pup.

Right?

Right.

I close the door and head for my car.

But Lucky's haunted eyes keep plaguing me. I can't stop thinking about how she was stuffed in a box for, well, basically for her entire life. Even when she made it to the Animal Care Center, they stuck her in another, slightly larger box.

Like I just did.

Border collies aren't like other dogs. They're made to move.

They thrive on work—on helping humans. We bred them that way. It's our fault they have so much energy and drive, and on top of that, she was tormented by a cat that was presumably left free to roam in front of that crate. In spite of the piles of reasons why this is a terrible idea, I find myself walking back into the shelter.

I'm greeted, as always, by the cacophony of three dozen dogs, all of them shocked and elated that I'm already back. It takes me five minutes to calm them all down—and another round of chicken jerky that was *not* in the budget—but then I'm *finally* on my way, with Lucky sitting completely upright in the passenger seat next to me, panting like mad even though it's not hot.

"I'm headed to the barn," I say. "You're lucky the weather's nice, because otherwise, I could not take you with me. I've had this lesson lined up forever, and I have a show coming up. I can't skip it."

Lucky looks over at me, her tongue lolling out, looking for all the world like she's smiling. Of course, the second I make eye contact with her, it's all over. She hops over the divider in my car and tries to crawl inside my skin. It takes me fifteen seconds and a near-collision with the guardrail to get her back into the passenger seat.

"You know, you really are your own worst enemy." I shake my head at the poor, exuberant puppy. "You really need to learn that you can't flip out every time you get the smallest scrap of attention."

Dogs are so much more honest than we are. I've

felt like she feels—actually, more often than not, I feel about like she does. My parents aren't very warm people, and my brother's my only truly kind family. Now that he's not around much, I have two best friends that I try not to maul with my needy affection, and that's about it.

"It took my parents a while, but I've been taught that I can't climb all over people, lick their faces, and pee on the floor when I get excited," I say. "If I do things like that, my friends stop being my friends. Okay?"

I need to find her a decent home, but no one will want her when she's this frustrating.

"How are you with horses?" I ask, knowing she's not going to answer.

But I'm about to find out, because I'm pulling up at the barn.

One of my two best friends and also my trainer, Victoria Perch, is walking by the parking area when I pull up. She slows down, she squints and leans closer, clearly looking through the windshield, and then she arches *the eyebrow*.

That's how I know I'm really in for it.

"Elizabeth. Jane. Moorland." I can hear her through the closed car doors.

I didn't just get the whole first name. I got the slow-talking, punctuated, whole name. "Dang it, Lucky. I knew I should've left you at the shelter," I mutter.

"Did you—no." Victoria shakes her helmeted head, her sky blue eyes flashing. "Do *not* tell me you brought another mongrel with you to my barn."

"Okay," I say in as chipper a tone as I can manage while opening my door, my hand firmly clasped around the end of Lucky's leash. "I won't tell you that I brought a severely traumatized border collie who has been stuck in a box for her entire life along with me because I could not bring myself to abandon her. I also won't tell you that she—" I drop my voice to a whisper. "—was taunted constantly by a cat, and eventually chewed off her own tail *and* got an infection from it, because her entire life was just *so* miserable."

Victoria's shoulders droop just a little, and that's how I know I'm in the clear. She looks fierce, and she sounds absolutely terrifying, but in her heart of hearts, she's a Godiva raspberry ganache truffle.

Sweet as can be.

"She has to stay inside the tack room—I can't have her spooking the horses."

I cross my heart.

"Please tell me she's housebroken."

"I have had her for three hours, and she has only gone pee outside during that time."

Victoria—prim and proper Victoria—swears like a sailor when she gets annoyed. Actually, that might be an insult to sailors. I imagine that even they would be embarrassed by some of the foul things she says. The dumbest stuff sets her off, too, like sweet little dogs in her tack room.

"Oh, stop it. Take one look at this face, and tell me—"

"If that mongrel soils one of my client's ten thousand dollar saddles, who do you think—"

"Vick, they're all up on racks. If Lucky has an accident, I swear I'll clean it up, and you'll never know it even happened. Okay?"

Blessedly, not many people are around at three in the afternoon, so no one will let Lucky out of the tack room. Even so, I tie her collar to an empty saddle rack, because better safe than sorry.

Most of Victoria's clients come for lessons in the

morning—the rich society wives—or in the early evening for the people with jobs and kids getting off school. With just a half dozen kids in her program, she blocks them all in on Tuesday and Thursday. I'm the only one who hits the middle of the day, usually when she's training client horses.

"Get tacked up fast," she finally says. "I'm in a bad mood now, and it's your fault."

By the time I get Lucky calmed down, I'm running late. So when I reach the far pasture and see that my rescued off the track thoroughbred, or OTTB, One Hot Shot, has rolled in mud. . .I don't cry. I'm proud of that. Thirteen minutes later, I'm filthy as a happy pig, but he's sleek, dark, and clean. Even his bright white face blaze and his three white socks are shining when I swing up into the saddle.

"You're late," Victoria says.

I may be her best friend, but in the arena, she's my trainer, and she often acts like she doesn't even like me. "Today, we're doing cavalettis."

Yep, she's mad.

Hottie, our nickname for my horse, loves jumping high. He loves making tight turns. He adores tearing through a complicated jump course. Those are all the reasons I love him so much. But he *hates* working on rhythm, balance, and suppleness. I should've known we'd wind up doing this when I brought Lucky.

The lesson is brutal.

But the best ones always are. Change—real change—is always painful. By the time I get Hottie rinsed down and back to his pasture, I'm running late. Really, really late.

"Are you coming too?" I ask.

Victoria sighs.

That's a yes. Neither of us likes attending all these

social events, but she's as stuck as I am. Her parents co-signed on her mortgage for the barn, and I think they're still subsidizing it. It's only been hers for two years, and new businesses are hard.

"If you'd get a real job, you could stop going," she says, glaring at Lucky.

"But that'll never happen," I say. "I flunked out of college, remember?"

"Do you know how many NYU dropouts are making small fortunes all over the world?" Victoria sighs. "You could find a dozen jobs with one call from your brother. Or just go work for him. Family has to hire you, right?"

I scratch Lucky behind the ears. "Sad, pathetic people have jobs. I have a calling."

She's still laughing as I reach my car. "Too bad callings don't pay your rent!"

Thankfully I don't pay much in rent, at least, not on the shelter. Even without having to pay rent—my parents are letting me use my dad's old warehouse—I have absolutely zero money in the shelter's checking account to pay myself a salary this month. Again. Hopefully there's enough left in my trust fund to cover my apartment rent one more time.

"Maybe I'll meet someone today, and they'll pledge some money."

"If they do, you need to pay yourself and use that to get new boots." She curls her lip at the duct tape I had to wrap around my left riding boot where the zipper finally broke. "Those are a disgrace."

"It's on the list," I say, "but you know what's higher on that list? Food for the dogs. And for the cats."

"I know. Stuff for you is always at the bottom of your dumb list."

She's not wrong about that, and on my drive home,

I can't help thinking about all the things I desperately need in my personal life. My car blinker's held together with baling twine. My boots really need to be replaced. Duct tape is a very short-term solution that I've been using for weeks already. My apartment was furnished with castoffs from Mom and Dad—but that's fine, because no one ever comes here. Plus, I never have to worry about dogs hopping up on the sofa. I haven't been to the dentist in over a year, and my hair needs a cut worse than the high school swim team, but it's all fine.

It can wait. I know, because it always does wait.

And then I'm home, and there are a few chaotic moments as Floof and Boba are barking and jumping, and Lucky is crouching down with her head near the ground. But after a moment, Lucky stands up, and the dogs stop circling her so badly, and they all sniff each other's backsides, and then I move into my room while I get dressed, and they all follow, Lucky letting the little ones take the lead. They all calm down pretty quickly after that, thankfully.

The other two eye Lucky strangely, and she crouches whenever they snap at her, but she doesn't seem to have any desire to argue with them for dominance, which surprises me.

Once I'm dressed, I keep one eye on them, but as I finish getting ready, I can't help thinking about how Lucky looks. She may be damaged, and she may be struggling. She may be missing most of her tail, but when you look at her, she's beautiful. I'm a little like that. My life may be falling apart, but the things in my life that matter, the things people see?

Those all look perfect.

As I clasp the sparkling solitaire pendant around my neck, I don't even regret selling the diamond my grandmother gave me when I turned eighteen to fund the shelter. I replaced it with a fake, so Mom and Dad will never know.

I don't regret buying knock-off designer heels to replace my Christmas and birthday presents I returned for cash—even if they pinch. That money paid for a new washroom. The shelter may always seem to be held together with fishing wire and gorilla glue, like my life, but all the animals I've helped would have been killed if not for me. That's worth an awful lot of faux designer shoes and cubic zirconia pendants.

I work with Lucky while I finish getting ready, and then I take a gamble, and I decide not to lock her up in the laundry room or a crate when I leave. "Please, please, please be good and don't destroy anything. Okay?"

I've sold most of my designer stuff at this point, but I close the door to my bedroom just to be safe. The fluffers aren't delighted, but I leave them in there. They have food and water in my bathroom, and I'm just not ready to trust them alone with Lucky yet.

"I'll be back in an hour or two, and hopefully I'll find some rich person with a big heart and come back with a nice, fat check."

Only, things don't ever work out quite like I plan.

Instead of a check, when I reach the funeral Mom texted to say I had to attend, my parents tell me they're selling my shelter. Apparently some friend needs a new warehouse here, and they're making a killing.

Which is good, because Mom told me last week that Dad was a hop, a skip, and a jump away from bankruptcy. I just wish she didn't intend to sell me down the river to deal with it.

"I'm sorry about this, but I already told you why." Mom's eyes widen. "We can't pass up this offer."

No one can know they're broke. I may be the one selling diamonds and designer heels, but they're the ones who taught me to hide my money issues. The sale of Dad's old warehouse will float them living extravagantly until he can figure something else out. "But you said I could use it for another year."

Mom sighs like she's dying.

"Let me buy it, then."

Dad laughs.

Mom's lips compress. "Where would you get the money? The whole reason we're selling it is—"

"I know," I say. "But I'll think of something." What do normal people do? "I can get a loan."

Now Mom's laughing too, silently, her sides shaking and her face contorting. She thinks it's *funny*? Mom and Dad have never liked pets, and I know this isn't their passion, but do they really not care about the animals at all?

"Just think about what will happen when—"

"That's not our job. It's not even yours. And charity's fine, but when the chips are down, you cut bait and save yourself." She sighs and shakes her head. "Surely we've taught you that at least."

"Oh, you taught me that," I say. "I just didn't want to learn that lesson."

"At some point, Elizabeth, you're going to have to grow up and be an adult. Superheroes aren't real." Mom steps toward me. "Fairy tales don't exist. The real world runs on money, and saving fluffy bunnies isn't viable unless you find someone to bankroll it. I've been telling you that for years."

"I'm not going to marry someone I don't like just to fund the shelter." She may have married Dad to fund her life, even though she doesn't like him and never did, but I'm not doing that. Not even for all the fluffy bunnies in the world.

"Then close the shelter," Mom says. "It's that simple. Everything in life runs on money. Find some, or stop complaining."

And that's it.

They have nothing else to say, and no other options to offer their only daughter.

I realize that I'm about to cry, and that's the worst thing I can do in this moment. A visible display of drama would horrify my mother, so I spin on my heel and head for the door instead. Getting into the main party area will startle my body into sliding back beneath the mask—what Victoria, Rhiannon, and I have always called the way we interact with people at these things.

It's safe.

It's familiar.

It'll keep me from crying.

But instead of sliding into the mask, I crash into a waiter carrying a hundred champagne flutes and collapse, my purse sliding across the floor. The champagne dumps out on me and the crystal shatters all around me like a huge, liquid-filled chandelier. Nothing hurts, so at least none of the shards cut me, but I'm one hundred and ten percent positive my nostrils are flaring as I glare at the stupid waiter who was in exactly the wrong place at exactly the wrong time.

Only, he's way, way hotter than I expect him to be.

His jaw's square.

His eyes are bright—a startling shade of golden brown.

His mouth's sultry, and his hair's shiny, and it falls in

waves around his face. Plus, he's tall, broad, and he has beautifully bronzed skin.

He wrecked an already bad afternoon, and now he's staring at me like it's *my* fault. I can't handle anyone else yelling at me. I'll *definitely* break down and sob, and then Mom will probably kick me out in two days instead of two weeks. I should tell him I'm sorry for causing the crash. Or I could offer to try and clean up or something, but I just can't do it. Mom's right behind me, looking a strange mixture of embarrassed and angry, and I have to escape.

I snatch my purse with one hand, shaking shards of crystal free so I don't cut my hand, and then I run for the bathroom.

I've been hiding for all of two minutes when I realize that my outfit and hair can't be salvaged— maybe for normal life, but not for an event like this. My only play is to run and hide at home.

When I finally get to my own front door, my fake designer heels squelching with sticky champagne with every step, and I unlock it, Lucky doesn't jump up for once. She's too busy sniffing my dress, my knees, and my shoes. Apparently, the little vagabond likes champagne.

I need to go by the bank and talk to someone about a possible loan, but I need to spend a little bit of time with my dogs first to settle my nerves. The last thing I ought to do is show the bank just what a jangly mess my nerves are by forcing my way over there right now. I spend an hour or two working with Lucky and helping her integrate with my tiny dogs. At least that's something I'm good at.

It's the non-four-legged parts of my life that always screw me up.

3

EMERSON

Every foster kid whose parents didn't die worries that they were abandoned because their parents didn't love them. I definitely felt that way, even though Mom said Dad didn't know about me.

Now that I'm meeting my grandma—or my sperm donor's mom, anyway—I realize that for me, that fear might actually be true.

After Catherine, or that's what the guy called her, drags me over to the side of the room, she asks me a few more questions.

"Where have you been living?" She frowns. "And how old are you now?"

"Wait." I have a few questions of my own. "Did you know my mom was pregnant?"

She drops her voice. "I could lie to you. I hope you'll remember that." She stares at me. "Yes, I did. And I paid her quite a lot of money to terminate her pregnancy and disappear from Alistair's life."

Super. She paid my mom to eliminate me.

Catherine tilts her head slightly, still staring at me

like I'm an experiment in a petri dish. "She disappeared shortly after that, but I'm beginning to think she didn't terminate the pregnancy as promised."

"You think?" I ask.

I must have spoken too loudly, because Catherine ushers us into a side room—the same room where I just witnessed another rich parent sharing disappointing news with her child.

Interestingly, all the times I've wondered about my father, I never once considered he might be hugely wealthy, and it never occurred to me that the family that abandoned us might have wanted me *dead*. No matter how well prepared you think you are for something, it can always be worse than you think.

"I'd like to talk to your mother." Mrs. Richmond sits carefully in a chair at the head of the smallish table in the corner of the room. "We have a lot of things to catch up on."

"Sorry to disappoint you," I say, "but she died, kind of a long time ago now." I can't help folding my arms, even though I know it looks a little aggressive. She can hardly blame me, right?

"She—" Mrs. Richmond blinks. "Your mother *died?*"

"I was eleven."

I'm a little surprised when her face falls. "You were eleven." Her brow furrows. "But then, who took care of you?"

"I went to a group home."

When her lips twist, it's satisfying. I want her to feel bad for what she did. But after a single moment, I feel a little guilty. I was in a group home for eighteen months, but then I met Seren and everything changed. "I did eventually find a good foster home placement," I say.

"A *foster* home?" She may as well have said I went to a brothel. Or a landfill. That one actually hits a little close to home.

My foster father Dave's family owns a landfill, and they're some of the best people I've ever met. "Ever heard of Best Trash?" I arch one eyebrow. "The owner's son, Dave, and his wife, Seren, took me in."

Her lip is fully curled. "How lovely."

"Well, while we're judging, for the record, they'd never even consider forcing my girlfriend to abort her child, so. . ."

She stiffens. "I didn't force anyone to—"

"I'm still working right now," I say. "If you don't need anything further?" I glance back at the doorway.

Mrs. Richmond licks her perfectly colored pink lips. "You're a waiter?"

I think about explaining that I'm an accountant, and that I just lost my job, but I can't do it. I don't owe her an explanation, and I refuse to scramble around trying to make her proud of me. She clearly never wanted anything to do with me, so I'll give her what she wants.

I head for the door.

"Wait." The words sound torn from her.

I turn and look at her over my shoulder. "Yeah?"

"You look *just* like him."

"I think that's how genetics work," I say. "But I'm not really sure." I shrug. "You know, being a waiter and all."

"What if—" Her breath hitches.

Now I'm getting annoyed. "What if *what?*"

"I don't have—Alistair was my only child."

Oh, how sad. She lost her only son, and now she's all alone. "I'm very sorry for your loss." My voice is so flat that it's rude, and Seren definitely taught me better. But Alistair's death isn't my loss. She saw to it that I didn't even meet the man.

"But would you—would you like to get to know me better?"

There it is. I was waiting to see if, now that she has no one else, she'd be interested in the child she rejected. "I appreciate the offer, but no." My mom's surely up in heaven, cheering. "You didn't want me before your perfect son was gone. I'm pretty sure you won't like me now that he is."

I'm feeling pretty self-satisfied as I walk through the doorway when I hear her broken plea. "Please —wait."

What now? I sigh as I turn around. "I really do need this job, even if you think it's not a very good one."

"I own this hotel." She stands up. "You won't lose your job."

She *owns* the hotel? I'm trying to adjust to exactly how rich my sperm donor was as she stares at me. Maybe I should tell her I'm just working here as a temp —seems likely she'll find that out herself.

"I'm willing to make you a deal," she says. "I know you don't know me, and clearly we didn't get off to the best start, but I'd like a chance to get to know you, and I'm willing to pay for it."

Rich people think everything's for sale. That's probably the thing I hate the most about them. "I'm sorry," I say. "I don't think that's a good idea."

"I have no one to leave my fortune to," she says. "It's valued around three and a half billion dollars right now, and as things currently stand, my distant cousin and his son are going to inherit it all. If I don't leave it to a charity of some kind."

Three and a half *billion*.

I guess with that kind of money, everything probably *is* for sale to her. And if I were in line to inherit, there's no way that Lisa's dad could disapprove of her dating me. It would be like acquiring a Get Out of Jail Free card. I didn't think those existed in real life, but. .
.

"You said you had a deal to offer me?"

She smiles, finally on solid footing now that she's convinced me to listen. I hate that I'm not just walking away, but I'll swallow my pride if that's what it takes to win Lisa back. "I'll make you my new heir—you can inherit it all. But you have to meet a few requirements first."

"I'm happy to get a DNA test," I say. "If that's what you're worried about."

She sits down at the table again and points at the chair next to her.

I pointedly take the one two chairs down, across from her.

"A DNA test? Sure, but what I'm more concerned about is something no test can tell me. The success of your future."

The future? What's she saying?

"If you want to inherit, you'll have to demonstrate that you're able to speak and act like a Richmond should. Only then will I change your name—"

I shake my head. "I'll never change my name. I'm Emerson Duplessis."

She frowns.

Three and a half *billion*. I know I'm being stupid. I should sign my name in blood on any contract she thrusts at me, but I have too much pride for that.

But after a moment, her frown gives way to a smile. "You really are a Richmond."

I hate her.

"Here are my terms. You'll learn to run the business —at my direction. The training will take as long as it takes. You'll date a woman during that time of whom I approve. And then, when the time is right, you'll marry her and promise to produce an heir within three years."

"An *heir*?"

"In light of recent events, two would be better," she says. "But I'll only require one." She arches one eyebrow. "It's probably not reasonable to demand more of you than I accomplished myself."

Is she kidding? "You think you're the queen of bloody England."

"Not quite, not yet anyway. They're worth almost ten times what we are, but we're a much younger dynasty. We have time."

A younger. . .I can't help spluttering. "You're crazy."

She laughs. "It's good that you already see that. Alistair used to tell me that all the time." She leans toward me, her eyes intent. "I speak and write in four languages fluently. I played piano at Juilliard. Yale awarded my MBA, and I chose them only because I'd already gotten my undergraduate at Harvard, and I couldn't stomach the thought of attending a school as ridiculous as Stanford." She shakes her head. "California's still the worst. Every day I hope the news will report that it has finally slid off into the depths of the ocean where it belongs."

She's like a real, live caricature of a villain.

I stand up, ready to refuse her outright. Again.

But three and a half *billion* dollars. If I refuse her and leave, she might change her mind, or she might go to her grave as doggedly determined not to give me a dime as she was about ridding my father of my mother and me.

I think about Lisa again—she's from a good family.

Her dad owns a top accounting firm. Maybe she'd approve of her right off the bat.

"I have a girlfriend," I say. "Her dad owns Jennings Accounting, which is one of the most robust accounting firms—"

Her nose scrunches. "Jennings?" She shakes her head. "Absolutely not." She leans closer. "Emerson, I know you hate me right now. I know you think I'm disgusting. You might even think I'm everything that's wrong with corporate America and wealthy people or both. But what I'm offering you isn't a trust fund or a big chunk of money. It's not a fresh start. It's much, much more than that. What I'm offering you is *huge*. It will come with a California-sized target on your back, too. The only way you'll survive running Richmond Steel is by having someone who can help you navigate the world I live in—someone who already knows how things work. You need someone who was raised in it." She stands up, pulls something from her purse, and holds it out to me.

It's a business card.

I take it from her and read it. Catherine Richmond, Chairperson of Richmond Steel. "You're not even the CEO?" I look up at her.

She snorts. "That's a good example of something someone in our world would already know. CEOs are paid employees—for them, this would be a *job*. It's not a job for me. I can't be ousted. I own the majority share of Richmond Steel, and I will until the day I die. No one can fire me, and no one can even second-guess me. I'm a *chairperson*, not a chief executive officer. You can't earn my title—you only inherit it."

The more she says, the more this feels like a bad movie.

"Think about it, and call me."

I'm walking out the door, without being stopped this time, when my boss stops me. "Those champagne flutes you broke were disastrous, but now you've missed half an hour of the event." Her face is bright red. "If you think that this is how we—"

"He missed that time at my behest," Mrs. Richmond says. "Do you know who I am?" She tilts her head.

My boss freezes. "Mrs. Richmond." She drops her head into a bow, for all the world acting like she's a serf and this is her master.

"You won't dock his pay a dime, and you won't discipline him for anything to do with his absence or. . ." Catherine frowns. "The incident with the glasses. Am I clear?"

My boss nods without raising her eyes.

Mrs. Richmond walks past us and out the door.

"How do you know her?" My boss's eyes are wide, and she actually looks. . .afraid.

I can't help my smile. "Actually, she's my grandmother."

Her eyes goggle and she bobs around like a fish caught on a hook.

"I'm kidding," I say. "I barely know her, but she had some questions about a friend of mine. It came up while she was grabbing some champagne."

My boss finally drags in a breath. "Thank goodness."

But seeing how people might react to the truth is a revelation. In my entire life, no one has ever cared much what I thought, because I've always been a nobody.

But—plot twist—maybe I'm not.

To change how people react to me, I just have to give up all my free will and basically everything else I care about. Talk about irony. For a split second, I almost pity my spineless, dead father. I wonder what *his* life must have been like?

He did fall for my tempestuous, impetuous mother. Maybe there was a spark in him after all. When I get home, Bea's talking on the phone. I thought she'd be at work, but it must be her day off.

"No, he just walked in the door."

I raise my eyebrows.

"It's Jake," she says. "He's almost done filming."

One of our two foster brothers is making his third movie. I'm not sure you could call him a movie star, but the budgets keep going up, and so do his paychecks. He was obnoxious enough when he was just a model, getting paid for smiling or flexing his abs or whatever. But now? I won't be able to handle him at all.

"Is he coming back soon?"

He and Bea have this strange sort of brother-sister love-hate thing. I'm not crystal clear on all the details, but it started a long time ago. Apparently he was trying to con her when they met, and after his dad went to prison, he came to live with us.

Jake's really easy to love.

Unfortunately, he's even easier to hate.

As a roommate who spends about an equal amount of time in New York shooting commercials and in LA on movie sets, he's not too bad. He always pays his share of the rent, and he's rarely here. But when he is here, and as a brother. . .it's complicated. If one of us is causing Mom to get more grey hairs than anyone else, you'd think it was the teenager who's still at home.

But it's definitely Jake.

"He said he'll be back next week," Bea says. "I think we should celebrate when he gets back."

"Sure, as long as he pays." I only agree because Bea

hates going to parties even more than I do, so I know it'll probably just be the three of us. "Just tell me which night. I don't even have a job to make time around."

Pitiful.

"Hey, Jake, I'll call you back," Bea says. "Looks like Emerson's finally moved on to moping."

"I'm not moping." I kick the leg of the table, because she's being annoying. I don't mope.

"You are." She sets her phone on the table. "What happened?"

"I don't know what you're talking about." I cross the room to the fridge and start putting ice in a glass.

"Mrs. Herbert called, and she said that you broke a bunch of crystal, but for some reason she was told to just expense it, no questions asked."

"I didn't break it," I say. "Some idiot rich lady just crashed into me."

"Yeah, but why did the upper ups write it off?"

I try to act nonchalant. "No idea."

"You're lying."

I spin toward her so fast that I spill the water I just filled up. "Am not."

"Every single time you lie, your right eye twitches, just a little bit."

"No way," I say. "Now you're the one making things ups."

"Ha." She stands and drops her hands on her hips. "You just agreed you were making things up first. But also, that eye thing is true."

"No way you'd ever notice—"

"Jake told me," she says. "And he's never wrong."

Not about stuff like that, anyway. After spending twelve years conning people, he got pretty good at uncovering people's tells. Actually, he says that's what makes him a good actor. He's great at telling people what they want to hear and spotting their lies.

"So, what happened?" She steps toward me, and then points. "Just spill, Emerson, or I'll call Mom and tell her you got dumped."

"You already told."

"Only about the fired part."

"You wouldn't screw me again."

"Try me." She crosses her arms.

Sisters suck. "Fine. Something weird happened." The idea of telling someone. . .but if I'm going to, it may as well be Beatrice. Thanks to her parents, or maybe more specifically, her grandpa, she's surprisingly good with strange things. Way better than I am, anyway. "I met my dad, kind of."

She drops her phone on the floor, and the screen cracks. So much for her being better with weird things.

"I found out because one of the events I was catering was his funeral, so I guess I didn't really meet him, but I found out who he was, and I met my grandma, and I found out that she paid my mom to kill me. So."

She still hasn't even leaned over to pick up her phone.

"Oh, and she offered me a deal. Since my dad died, she'll inherit me or whatever, but only if I agree to be a good little puppy. She said her company's worth, like, a *lot* of money." It doesn't feel like now is the time to disclose exactly how much.

Bea blinks.

"It was a weird day, but as an upshot, she told that Mrs. Hughes lady not to bill me for the champagne flutes that broke, so." I pull $300 out of my pocket. "Between the hourly rate and the tips, it wasn't a bad day."

"Mrs. Herbert," Bea says. She finally picks up her phone. "What does a 'good puppy' mean, exactly?"

I drop onto a kitchen chair. "She said I have to marry someone she approves of and then I have to have a baby. Also, I have to let her teach me to run the family business."

"Does she think it's eighteen-oh-nine?" Bea's look of disgust is pretty impressive.

"Well, she is talking about giving me like three billion dollars or something."

Bea stares at me blankly for a moment, and then she says, "I'll marry anyone she chooses, including an eighty-year-old man. Or, you know what? I'd marry a woman for half that. You should tell her. I'm a bargain." Bea sits next to me and stares straight ahead. "That was a weird day."

"You're telling me."

"Three *billion dollars*, Emerson? It's hard to believe. I'm not sure I can even write that. How many zeroes is it?"

Catherine Richmond didn't look like she was kidding. When I googled Richmond Steel, it looked legit. "What if it's real?"

"I was mostly kidding, but there's not much I wouldn't do for that much money," she says.

"I don't know," I say.

"If you did get it, you'd never have to do what anyone else said ever again."

"Yeah, but she wants veto power on everything that matters until she croaks." I hold up a finger. "Who I marry." I hold up another. "Having a kid." I hold up one more. "My job and work every day." I laugh. "And she said two kids would be better."

Bea doesn't seem nearly as upset as me. "Do you remember the first time I made you eat kimchi?"

We sure are changing gears fast. "Um, yeah."

"What did you say about it?"

I shrug. "I didn't like it."

"You told me it tasted like carbonated socks."

I can't help snorting a little. "It did, kind of."

"But now?"

"I love it, especially with bulgogi or ramen."

"That's called an acquired taste," she says. "And don't take this the wrong way, Em, but you're an acquired taste yourself."

I'd like to argue with being compared to kimchi, but she might be right. "I do talk about numbers too much for most people."

"And you argue with people sometimes just to annoy them."

"Hardly ever," I say.

She pulls a face. "My point is, let your grandmother get to know you a little. She might change her mind about dictating everything to you."

"But—"

"She just lost her son," Bea says. "And she doesn't sound like the most easy-going person, or maybe even the nicest, but you might find that she's an acquired taste too."

"Are you suggesting that I become friends with the woman who paid my mom to prevent me from being born?"

"She didn't know you," Bea says. "And sometimes people can do things to someone they don't know that they'd never be able to do when they know them. Think about internet trolls and the horrible things they say. Most of them would never dare in real life."

"You're saying that I should take the deal, get to know her, and try to convince her to let me have the money *and* live my life however I want?"

Bea shrugs. "I'm saying that for three billion dollars, it's worth a little effort to try."

I think about it for a moment and decide to give it a chance. I call my grandma, expecting to get an assistant or something, but to my shock, she picks up.

"Hello?"

"Um, this is Emerson."

"Oh."

No 'nice to hear from you?' No 'I'm so happy you called?' Okay. Fine. "I've been thinking about the offer you made."

"And?"

"I'll give it a try."

"Oh, good. You can come over tonight or tomorrow. Which would you prefer?"

"Come over?"

"Obviously you'll need to live with me," she says. "In the Richmond mansion."

I blink.

Bea nods and waves her hand in a little circle, encouraging me to actually say something.

"Oh. Uh, well, I guess I can pack tonight and come in the morning."

"Please don't," she says.

"Don't. . .come tomorrow?"

"Don't pack anything. We'll buy you a whole new wardrobe, as well as anything else you may need."

"But—"

"Trust me on this," she says. "It's the beginning of a whole new life for you."

"Other than a few small things, I really like my current life," I say.

"That's because you don't know any better."

I don't argue with her. It would be a waste of breath. "I'll see you in the morning."

"Eight a.m. Don't be late." She rattles off an address and hangs up.

I scrabble to write it down before I mix anything up. "Well, that didn't give me warm fuzzies."

"I think we should have bulgogi and kimchi for dinner," Bea says. "Looks like it'll be your last relaxing meal for a while."

"Or, you know, forever." I shake my head.

"And you know, she is your grandma. Your real, live grandma that you didn't know you had. You may wind up loving her, Emerson. This could be really, really good."

"I'm just hoping neither of us kills the other—at least, not before she writes me into that will."

❧ 4 ❧

ELIZABETH

ven though my heels today aren't squishing with champagne, even though I put on my nicest lipstick and my last actual designer sheath dress, the lady at the bank looks at me in disgust and says, "There's no way we could approve you for a real estate loan."

Thanks for sugar coating it, lady. "No way?" I ask.

"You don't even have a job." She thinks I'm an idiot for asking.

"What if I did have a job?"

"Wait, do you?" She looks at the form. "This is blank."

"Well, I like to think that running my charity almost full time each week is a job," I say. "But I could probably get another one if it would help."

"One that pays?" She arches one eyebrow. "It says here that you've only received a paycheck in your capacity as director of Posh Pets. . ." She glances at the paperwork, including my bank statement and that of the 501c3 and crinkles her nose. "Seven times in the past eighteen months."

47

Seven times? That's better than I thought it would be. "But surely the bank can see that—"

"You received a trust fund with several hundred thousand dollars in it when you turned eighteen, nearly a decade ago," she says. "But that's now down to a balance of eleven thousand and four hundred dollars."

"Eleven thousand, four hundred *and twenty-three* dollars," I say.

She frowns. "You've spent all of that money in the past eight and a half years, and now you want us to loan you more?"

"Most of that money was spent on the charity—it's not like I was out taking a vacation or shopping with it." Or, not with most of it, anyway.

"Is your grandmother likely to leave you more money?" the woman asks.

"She died five years ago and my parents took the rest," I say. "So, probably not."

The bank woman flattens her hands against the desk. "I don't like giving people bad news," she says. "But unless you earn quite a large sum of money—loans from friends and family are specifically disallowed— and you found some kind of steady employment, there's no way you're going to be able to secure a note of. . .how much did you say?"

"Four hundred thousand would be enough to buy a functional shelter, I think." I can't help cringing a little. "How much would I need for the down payment?"

"At least a hundred thousand for a non-residence note if you want a loan of three hundred."

How depressing.

As I'm trudging my way out to my car, I can't help dragging my feet a bit. Maybe I could find some new donors—to lots of my friends, this isn't an insane amount of money—but to find them before the sale goes through? Mom intentionally waited to tell me until I had almost no time, I'm sure of it.

If my back wasn't up against a wall, I'd never even consider this, but. . .I whip out my phone before I can second-guess the impulse and call Easton.

"Hello!" He always sounds so darn chipper.

"Hey," I say. "Did Mom tell you they're selling my shelter?"

"Wait, people buy shelters?" he asks. "That surprises me."

"No," I say. "They're selling the building. She didn't even bother evicting me. She just told me I have two weeks to be out."

"That's not very long," he says. "So what will you do?"

"It's no time at all," I say. "Even if I push hard, there's no way I can find all the animals homes by then, and I'm scrambling around now trying to figure out how to buy it myself."

"Wait, would they sell it to you instead?"

"I don't know," I wail. "I mean, I want them to. I spent years getting it all set up as a shelter, and now I'll have to find a new place, where I have to either buy it or pay rent, and I'll be starting all over."

"Then what's the plan?"

I love Easton. He gets me. "Okay, so I talked to the bank."

"About what?"

"A loan," I say. "It didn't go well."

He's laughing, the jerk.

"But they said if I had a job, and if I had a down-payment, then—"

"And if the sky was orange, and if the wind blew from underground. . ."

"You suck."

"You know I'd help, but all my money's tied up in my startup," he says. "Which is going really well, by the way."

"Ooh," I say. "Then maybe—"

"Sadly, I won't have anything on your timeline," he says. "I'm flat broke until the IPO. But have you tried to delay the sale? That might buy you some more time."

Delay the sale. "You're a genius."

"So they tell me," he says. "Who's the buyer?"

"They didn't tell me anything." When did I get so whiny? "Do you think you can find out? Mom won't even answer the phone when I call."

"Of course she won't. She's hiding for sure. Dad's business must be on the verge of collapse again or they wouldn't be selling."

"But to either buy this place or find a new place, I need to find a job and come up with money for the downpayment. Which is why I'm calling you."

"How much do you have now?"

"Personally?" I ask. "Or the charity?"

"The fact that you're asking me that question pains me," he says. "But either, I guess." I can hear him cringing.

"Personally, I have more than eleven thousand dollars."

He groans. "Elizabeth."

"Look, if you saw these little animals, you'd be in the same boat."

"Your boat has a cracked hull. What were you thinking, shoveling all your trust money into it?"

"The same thing you were thinking when you dumped yours into your startup."

"I really doubt that you were thinking you'd wind up rich as Croesus by betting on yourself."

"Maybe not exactly the same."

"What about the charity?" he asks. "Surely it has some capital it could contribute."

"Posh Pets has about three hundred and eighty-one dollars in the account."

"*About* three hundred and eighty-*one*?" He sighs heavily.

"Because I bought some food yesterday that hasn't gone through yet, and I can't remember what it cost."

"Elizabeth." He doesn't sound impressed. I shouldn't have called him, clearly.

"I know."

"You're a mess."

"I'm a delight," I say. "And I save a lot of animals."

"Notwithstanding those things, you're a *mess*."

"Can you get me a job?"

"Did I mention the IPO?" he asks. "I could get you a great job in a few months, but not right this minute." He exhales. "But."

"But what?"

"I heard Ace is looking for an assistant."

"He's horrible."

"You wanted me to find you a job," he says. "And you're qualified for nothing."

"I can cure bumble foot in a chicken," I say. "I can treat really irritable dogs, and I can bathe horrible cats. I can do most anything at all with a horse—worked as a vet tech for years. Oh, and I'm great at giving cats their meds."

"As I said, you're qualified for nothing."

"Rude."

"Just let me call Ace. He might be willing to give you a trial."

I'm supposed to pin my hopes on being an assistant

to Easton's oldest friend, who's a notorious playboy? Pass. "I'll figure something else out."

"I'll talk to him anyway, just in case."

I make vomiting sounds as I hang up the phone.

My phone rings again immediately, and I pick up. "Dude, I'm being serious. I'd rather die than work for Ace."

"Miss Moorland?"

Whoops. Not my brother calling me back. "Uh huh."

"We found two credit cards with your name on them in the corner while cleaning a room at the Opus Westminster yesterday, and we have your name on file from a prior reservation."

I swear under my breath. "I'm so sorry. I had a collision with a drink tray," I say.

"We'll have them at the front desk, but you'll need to bring an ID with you. You can pick them up any time."

"Thanks."

I don't really have time to drive over there, but I kind of need my credit cards. I text Victoria to see whether I can bump my lesson back and train the horses she wanted me to train a little later. She, thankfully, agrees.

I hop in the car and head for the hotel.

When I get there, the front desk does *not* have my credit cards. "They left a note, though," the concierge says. "Because of the sensitive nature of credit cards, the manager thought it best if they were kept back in the staff offices." He points.

And now I'm hiking, in my stupid heels, to the back of the hotel, still trying to recover the credit cards I lost after I was broadsided with Mom's news and then a tray of champagne.

I finally reach the offices, and the helpful lady at the front desk points me even further back to event services. When I get there, the woman who seems to be in charge is already talking to someone else—someone I know. Someone scary. Someone whose conversation I definitely don't want to interrupt.

It's Catherine Richmond, chairman of Richmond Steel.

The richest woman in Scarsdale New York, who also owns this hotel.

"I know it's sensitive information, but surely I can still get a copy of it."

"I suppose." The woman with the British accent frowns. "Do you know the boy? Is that why you need it?"

"Do you dislike your job? Is that why you keep asking me questions instead of doing as I asked?"

The poor employee ducks her head and shoots past the doorway, not even noticing I'm here. I look around for somewhere to hide, but there's nowhere. Catherine's sure to see me when she comes barreling out, and I always try to avoid any run-ins with the great Catherine Richmond. Anyone smart avoids them, because she's terrifying.

Only, instead of leaving, she answers her phone. "Hello?"

And now I'm officially eavesdropping on her.

But I have no idea where else to go. I need my credit cards, and no one's here to give them to me.

"No, I said I want the document to say that I will acknowledge Emerson Duplessis as Emerson Richmond and as my sole heir if and only if he marries a woman of whom I approve, *and* if they produce an heir within two years of their marriage. The rest of the stipulations looked fine."

She grunts.

"I don't care whether it's legally enforceable. He won't know that it's not. Of course he's my blood—he looks exactly like Alistair. But sure, a DNA test for the file is fine. They can come to the office to do it. He'll be working with me every day, but I won't change my will until the terms have been met. Having an heir who's a disgrace is worse than having no one at all. Am I clear?"

She snaps the phone shut, and I nearly jump out of my skin. What exactly did I just overhear? Her son had a secret child?

Of course the Brit chooses that very moment to rush back. "Who are you?" she asks.

I want to sink through the floor and die. "I'm Elizabeth Moorland," I whisper. "I left my credit cards here yesterday at Alistair's funeral."

I wait for the jaws of Catherine to snap, breaking me in two, but they never do. I glance sideways and realize she's on the phone again, and blessedly, she's not paying me any attention. The woman hands me my cards, and I practically sprint out of the hotel and back to my car. My heart's still racing when I pull into the barn and change clothes, getting a late start on my riding. I'm so late, in fact, that I miss half my lesson.

It's a real bummer, but I do training rides on the lower level jumpers and lesson horses for Victoria to pay for Hottie's board and my own lessons, so I have to do the training before I can focus on myself. Even so, the lesson goes alright, and at the end, we do a mock run of twelve jumps that look really high. One of them's a triple combination, and one's a pretty mean looking oxer. I'm actually a little nervous as Hottie sails over it.

In the three years I've been working with him since

he left the track, he's always been forward, but we've really fixed his mouth and his propulsion. It's been a joy to fine-tune him lately. I had no idea he'd have so much scope when I rescued him.

"That was the best I've ever seen him look," Victoria says. "I think you should try the Grand Prix next month."

"You're kidding," I say.

She shakes her head slowly. "No, I'm not. You both looked really, really good."

I've been show jumping for a long time, but I've never jumped at Grand Prix level—over five feet for the tallest jumps, with as many as sixteen obstacles, and spreads of up to more than six feet. We've cleared five-foot obstacles in lessons, obviously, but never in a show, and never when I was racing against time faults. "Do you think you should show him first?" I ask. "Just to make sure he can do it?"

Victoria's smile is kind. "If you're nervous, I can. But I think you could do it yourself. He adores you—he tries harder with you than he does with anyone else."

"Because he knows her," a woman says from the risers next to the arena. "If he got to know someone else, he'd probably love them, too. He has that kind of face." She's probably right, but it's a little rude to say that. With the backlight, it's hard to make out the speaker's face, but when I do, I understand.

Henrietta Watkins is an excellent show jumper. Actually, excellent might not be high enough praise. She's qualified a dozen times for the World Equestrian Games, and she made it to the Olympics twice. She owned this barn before Victoria bought it. "I'd like to buy him, if you're keen to sell."

Of course she would. Henrietta *is* an excellent rider,

but she also has a nearly unlimited bank account, thanks to marrying quite well—three times over. She keeps outliving her spouses, and each time, they leave her a veritable mint. It makes it easier for her to keep qualifying, since she always has the best animals at her disposal.

The fact that she wants my rescue pony is a real compliment.

And. . .it also may be exactly what I need. Sure, I've always dreamed of qualifying for the Grand Prix and riding at that level. But I only started riding because Mom and Dad insisted it was the most socially accept-able way to love animals—for rich people. It was some-thing they understood.

It became my dream. . .but it was my second dream.

My first was always to help as many animals as possible find good homes. It pains me to wonder, but how much would Henrietta pay for my darling Hottie? My beautiful sorrel turns his head back to look at me, as if he knows I'm considering betraying him. His ears swivel toward me, and my heart sinks. I've been with this guy for so long, through so much. And we're close now—right at the finish line.

"She couldn't possibly sell One Hot Shot for less than. . ." Victoria pauses, looking my way. "Seventy-five thousand." Shoot—Victoria didn't just aim high. She shot right out of the park with that one. For a rescued OTTB? Has she lost her mind?

"I could do that," Henrietta says. "Think about it and call me." She nods once, her eyes still on Hottie, and pivots on her heel, hopping off the bottom of the stand to disappear.

Victoria's eyes widen. "For a rescue horse," she mouths.

Seventy-five thousand would go a long way toward getting me the hundred grand I need as a downpayment. But as I tack down, brushing Hottie as he nuzzles me with his nose, my heart sinks. Do I really have to sell my baby to fund my dream? Is that how the world works?

Sadly, that's how it's always worked for me.

❧ 5 ❧

EMERSON

I should be packing.

No matter what that crazy lady says, I'm not going to show up at her house with a laptop bag and nothing else tomorrow. I should be making lists of things I might need so I'm not stuck driving back to the apartment every day after my temporary relocation.

Instead, I find myself getting in the car and driving home with Bea in tow.

I still get a tiny twinge when I think of the word *home*. I spent a very long time not having a home, so knowing that I have one now is always a bit awe-inspiring. And what a home it is. In the center of bustling Scarsdale, the Colburn Mansion—now Serendipity Inn—is a secluded haven from the rest of the world.

When it's not absolutely teeming with guests, that is. When I pull through the side gate, I can't help glancing at the main house, bracing myself for a lot of foot traffic. But it's a Tuesday night. I should've known it wouldn't be too bad.

Mom's car, and Dad's, are parked to the side of the

carriage house—our house. When they turned the old mansion into an inn, they remodeled the carriage house. They've added on to it twice in the intervening years, as they brought in more wounded birds like me, growing the nest as necessary.

Thanks to Mom, it's still tasteful.

Thanks to Dad, it was done as inexpensively as possible. And of course, he made all of us help with everything we could. The feeling of safety and peace still washes over me the second I walk through the front door. I love having my own place with Bea, but it's not quite the same.

And as if she knew I was coming, Mom's been baking.

For most kids, their mother's cookies bring back fond memories, but for me? They're epic.

Mom's a professional pastry chef, but from the day she took me in, she never worked outside of the inn. The guests all enjoyed her muffins, cookies, pies, and cakes, but no one appreciated it more than we did.

"What are you making?" Bea asks.

I wanted to come over alone, but Bea's worse than a toddler who's been promised ice cream. When I said I was going home—she sold her car last month—she saw the opportunity for a ride and took it.

"Apple turnovers," Mom says. "I didn't know you two were coming over. I'd have made more."

"It's fine," I say. "We can eat Killian's."

"Hey!" A shout from the back room, followed by three loud crashes, tells me that our younger brother's definitely home. A moment later, he comes shooting out the door, yanking a white wife-beater over his head as he stumbles toward us. "Hands off."

"There are plenty," Mom says with a smile. "I was

kidding about making more. I just won't have any left-overs to freeze."

"Is Ardath home?" Bea asks.

Mom shakes her head. "She's studying—been at the library every single night lately."

"What's new?" Killian asks. "She's always studying every night."

Ardath joined our family almost ten years ago, and I can attest that Killian's right. She's literally *always* studying. People hassled me for my love of numbers and lists. . .until she showed up. "She makes me look *chill*," I say.

Killian snorts.

"Maybe not chill, but at least normal," I say.

"You're all exceptional," Mom says. "Who wants normal?"

Dad opens the back door and wipes his boots on the mat. It's not exactly spring anymore, but summer hasn't really set in yet. "The bushes are trimmed, and that birdfeeder that fell down is officially rehung."

He still hates the garden, but he loves Mom enough to do anything she wants, including gardening tasks.

"Wait, which bushes did you trim?" Mom arches one eyebrow, her hands freezing mid-apple-filling-and-tucking.

"I didn't cut the butterfly bushes, if that's your question. Just the roses, as instructed."

She sighs. "Thank goodness. I was worried you'd killed them last year."

"If I had, you certainly know where to buy more." His smirk is a kind one. Mom doesn't handle anything dying very well, not even things that are easily replaced. She has the softest heart of anyone I've ever met, and it has been bruised plenty already.

Her delicate light in spite of it all is why we all love her the most.

"Why are you two here?" Dad frowns. "Need money?" Now he's smirking. "Because I have some lawn that needs to be aerated, and there's a pile of—"

"Emerson did get fired," Bea says. "And he ticked off the head caterer when I got him a temp job."

I can't help glaring at her.

"What?" She shrugs. "You did."

"Did she at least tell you that it was wrongful? The guy I was working for did some things he shouldn't have, and someone had to get blamed."

"You should stand up for yourself more," Dad says. "We could write a letter, or I can call someone."

I shake my head. "It's fine. I have a plan."

"I knew you would," Mom says. "You always do."

"He's filling the landfills with lists," Bea mutters. "You should have Grandpa talk to him about that again."

"Grandpa never talked to me about my lists," I say.

Dad's father has officially retired now—all the way this time—but he used to own the biggest trash collection company this side of the City, and he's passionate about it. Getting stuck talking to him about the garbage business is. . .not always fun. "And I'm not filling any landfills," I say. "Everything's under control."

"His girlfriend dumped him the same day he got fired," Bea mutters. "He's not fine."

"Wait, Lisa did?" Mom actually drops the turnover she's holding onto another one, smooshing both.

The oven beeps to tell her it's ready.

She looks more flustered than I've ever seen her. She always has the first pan ready to go when the oven hits full heat. It's kind of her thing. Effortlessly perfect timing.

"It's fine," I say. "My plan addresses that, too. Lisa's always been worried about what her dad would think about me—he's particular—but getting fired. . ." I sigh. "I think it pushed her over the edge. Once I get my career back online, we'll get back together. Trust me."

"I don't like that she dumped you when things were down." Mom's frowns deepens. "That's not the kind of person—"

"She had other stuff going on too," I say.

"Like what?" Mom asks. "Because that's the point of having a family and loving someone. Being there for them when things are hard."

"Trust me, Mom. Lisa's a good person, and we'll be fine."

After studying my face for a moment, she nods. Then she picks up the turnover, finishes it, performs a little remedial work on the other one, and pops the first pan in the oven.

Whether they're pristine or not, my mouth's already salivating.

"You two are like vultures," Killian says. "Did someone tell you it was turnover night?"

"There's almost always something baking here," I say. "It's all good."

Dad pats his belly, which isn't big, but it's bigger than it was. "Sadly, that's very, very true."

"Did you want me to stop?" Mom arches an eyebrow. That's never good.

Dad crosses the room in four big steps and wraps an arm around her waist. "Not as long as *you* don't want to stop me from eating it. You're the one suffering from your own success."

She laughs, and I notice the tiny lines she didn't have the first day we met at the sides of her eyes. I'm not sure she ever would have had those lines, if not for

Dad. Mom was like me when we met—she didn't smile much.

I think Mom's smile lines and Dad's small gut are both signs that they're doing pretty well. That's when I realize why I came home. Tomorrow, I'm going to the Richmond mansion, and I have no idea what to expect. My grandmother might be distant and cold, or she might be aggressive and overbearing. No matter how she acts, I can pretty much guarantee it won't be at all like this.

But I have a family—a family that's more real than blood. A family that cares about me. As I sit at our big table, eating my second apple turnover, my slightly fractured heart heals just a little bit. It's been a rough week and a half, but I do have a plan, and I have a home. No matter what happens, my real home's still here.

I don't tell Mom and Dad about the funeral, and neither does Bea. She's annoying, and she's a little in-your-face sometimes for an extrovert who's always hiding from the world, but she knows where the line is, and she never crosses it. I think telling them about the job and the girlfriend was her way of making sure she kept the bigger secret until I'm ready to share it myself.

The next morning, I surprise myself by only throwing toiletries, two pairs of pajamas, and a few pairs of pants and button-down shirts—with a weeks' worth of ties—in a suitcase, and heading out to my car. Bea comes tearing after me, hopping on one foot as she slides her second shoe on. "Wait. I'm coming!"

"What do you mean? You can't live there, and trust me, you really don't want to."

"I need a ride to work—isn't it kind of on the way?"

The Opus is exactly the wrong direction, but I just

roll my eyes and drive her anyway. I'm leaving with loads of time to spare, because I hate being late. Also, driving calms my nerves, usually.

Today, after dropping off Bea, a semitruck moves over while I'm in his blind spot, forcing me onto the shoulder, and while my heart's still racing from that near miss, some idiot on her phone practically plows into me—merging across a solid lane line.

I slam on my brakes and barely avoid hitting the car to my left as I slide out of her way. By the time I finally turn down the street where the directions say the Richmond mansion is, my nerves are shot. But then, I see it, behind an imposing iron fence, and set back on a lush green lawn. It's a pretty standard red brick colonial. Three stories tall, which is impressive I guess, with wings on either side that are a mere two stories apiece. But what stands out isn't the size.

No, it's that it's in the very center of Old Scarsdale, where the richest families in town live, and it's on the very biggest lot. It must be at least six acres, right in the center of town. Judging from the outbuildings, which were all tastefully designed to match, there's a gardener, a cleaning crew, and likely staff. I wouldn't be able to spot any of that, except Mom told me about the much simpler but somewhat similar setup at the Colburn mansion before it was turned into an inn.

Sure enough, when I reach the front gate, an attendant meets me with a knowing glance. "Mr. Duplessis."

I nod.

He waves me past, the gate closing as soon as I've driven clear. I pull up to the front of the house and the massive door opens, an honest-to-goodness butler standing in the entry when I walk up the steps.

"My name's Stanley," he says.

"Uh, I'm Emerson," I say.

"I know." He gestures. "Mrs. Richmond is in the library."

The *library*. How pretentious.

But as I follow him into the room to the right of the foyer, I realize that it couldn't really be called anything else. There are not two, but three floors of books along all four walls, with a massive desk in the center, flanked by huge chairs on either side. There's also a generous sitting area with more heavy leather chairs framing up a matching leather sofa.

At least there aren't any glassy-eyed animal heads or terrifying old portraits that glare through time.

"Emerson." My grandmother stands, and I realize she was in one of the leather chairs.

"I expected a larger house," I say, hoping maybe she'll laugh.

She frowns. "It's eighteen thousand square feet. Anything more would be excessive."

Anything more would be *excessive?* I manage to stifle my laugh, and say, "I was only kidding."

"Ah. Well, I'll have Stanley show you to your room, and we have a shopper from Saks stopping by in two hours."

"A shopper from what?"

"Saks Fifth Avenue?" She raises her eyebrows. "Would you prefer Bergdorf? Or someplace else?"

"I usually shop at Macy's," I say. "When they have a decent sale."

She swallows in a rather pained manner. "And I see you did bring a bag. How lovely."

Of course, the way she said it, it sounds like she's saying, *How terribly disappointing.*

"I figured I should bring the essentials, at least," I say. "It's not like my pajamas matter, for instance."

She looks like she swallowed the rind of a lemon. "I'm hosting a welcome party for you tonight at seven."

"Where are you supposedly welcoming me *from*?" This should be interesting. There's no way I'm about to tell everyone I've been in Africa or Europe or something ridiculous.

"You wanted to learn how normal people live, obviously, and now that your father has passed, you're finally being forced to step into the role that was always waiting for you."

"Normal people?" I can't help it. I laugh. "You didn't want to tell everyone I've been studying abroad?"

Her cheeks flush a dark wine color. "Would you be able to maintain that lie? I thought something very close to the truth would be best."

She's apparently not keen on telling everyone that I was an accident that she failed to erase. That's not a surprise, but the welcome party still stings a little.

"Well, I can't wait. I just love a good party. Especially when I'm not the waiter passing drinks around."

"Mrs. Herbert told me that was a temporary position." She frowns. "I'm aware that you're an accountant who was recently fired by Jennings."

"You should also know that it wasn't at all my fault. The person whose fault the mistake was is still there." And I'm clearly angrier than I realized.

"In any case, I've had my lawyer draw up some preliminary documents. The drafts are in your room for your review, but you can also forward them to a lawyer of your choosing. I'll be happy to pay their bill, of course."

"Documents?" What's she saying?

"They establish the rules of our little gambit," she says. "I like things to be crystal clear."

"Like, how I have to marry to someone you choose?" I ask.

She sighs. "Not someone I select, but someone of whom I approve."

Right. Not much difference, I suppose, but it's something.

"And I have to produce two children within three years?"

"Just the one," she says, "though there's an early success bonus for having a second."

She's insane.

I should leave now, while I still think this is all utter nonsense. I'm worried that being here might warp my brain.

But then I think about Mom, Dad, Bea, and Jack. Even book-obsessed Ardath and youngest-child Killian could probably help. I'm surrounded by people who will help remind me if I go nuts. And Bea's right. I should at least look into something this wild before I turn it down.

Maybe, after she meets Lisa, my grandmother might decide that she approves. It strikes me as ironic, in that moment, that Lisa broke up with me for fear her dad would never approve, and now my grandmother's already decided that the same girl's not good enough for me.

People are remarkably stupid, deciding who others can love.

Stanley takes me up to my room, which is more like its own apartment. It has a large sitting area as an antechamber, with a sofa and chairs, a television, and a large desk under a huge bay window with a walk out balcony.

"Mrs. Richmond doesn't like direct light," Stanley says.

My bedroom is even bigger than that area, with yet another desk, bookcases already full of leather-bound books, and a large settee. There's not a second television, but otherwise, it looks like what I'd imagine the nicest hotel might have, including a small kitchenette. The bathroom that opens off the bedroom has a huge jacuzzi tub, a tremendously large walk-through shower with three heads, and an adjoining closet that would fit a small elementary school class.

Once I've finally found my way back to the sitting room, I see them. The massive stack of papers. They say just what Grandmother said they would, but in a more irritating way.

And she wasn't kidding about the personal shopper coming later, either. A tall and commanding woman shows up almost exactly as I finish reading the preliminary handcuffs, and she orders me to put on at least three dozen different ensembles—her word—one after another. She clucks after each one, like I'm some kind of living doll who isn't performing up to standards. After half a dozen more, my grandmother's summoned for her opinion.

This is even worse than I thought it would be.

When I slink out in my third 'ensemble,' I ask, "Is this really necessary?"

My grandmother scowls. "I'm about to introduce my twenty-seven-year-old grandson to hundreds of people who have never met him as though it's natural. As though it's perfectly normal." She narrows her eyes. "We need to make you feel as familiar to these people as we can. What you wear, what you say—it's all important. Tonight will set the tone for all the relationships that are about to be most valuable in your life going forward."

She's clearly nuts.

"I have parents, you know," I say.

"Your name is Duplessis." She frowns. "You said your mother died."

"I was fostered by—"

She waves her hand through the air. "Fostered." She rolls her eyes. "We'll line you up to attend Columbia for your MBA this fall."

"What?" Now I'm rolling my eyes. "What if I don't want an MBA?"

She shrugs. "You can take a few classes, and they'll award you the degree, if you really don't want to learn there."

"I'm pretty sure that's not how it works."

Her half smile's condescending in the extreme. "Oh, you're cute. With the amount of money we've donated, they'd give you any degree you want."

It's like everything she says is worse than the last. Can that possibly be true?

"He'll wear the blue sweater over the white shirt with the khakis. Luckily the weather cooled down this weekend enough to make that viable. I want a subtle country club vibe."

Subtle? "It looks like a country club puked on me," I say. "Maybe we should lose the sweater."

She doesn't even bother saying that I don't get an opinion. She just stares at me for a moment and pivots to leave. "We'll have to fix your hair later."

"Wait, what's wrong with my hair?" I hate that I'm shouting at her retreating frame, like my audience with the queen has ended, and I'm not ready for that yet.

My closet's now full of a bunch more things that look just as bad as the one she wants me to wear tonight. If that's not bad enough, when I check the tags on the clothing, all of it brand new, I practically choke. One sweater would have paid my college tuition for a year—Tom Ford and Brunello Cucinelli must really be proud of their sweaters.

When it's five minutes until I'm supposed to be heading downstairs, I decide that I'm not a paper doll for her to play with. I toss the clothes she picked on the floor and pull on a pair of jeans instead. The denim's still two thousand dollars, thanks Prada, but I pair it with the ugliest shirt I've ever seen.

It's louder than Bea throwing a tantrum.

It's more like grotesque, really. Yellow and black, and it's patterned so heavily that I have no idea where to look. I should look as ridiculous as I feel, right? She can't get too upset. Her shopper picked it for me. But when I try to walk out the door, I just can't. I'd start laughing or crying the second someone really looked at me. I toss it on the floor, or at least, I try. The price tag says it was eleven hundred dollars and change, so I hang it up, inside out—take that, Grandmother—and put on another, slightly less exaggerated monstrosity. I also hang up the country club trash at the same time.

I mean, there are other ways to rebel, right? I don't have to leave thousands of dollars in a pile on the floor. What does that prove?

The shirt I choose actually says the words "Dior Tears," on the front of the shirt, but you almost can't read them, because the company blobbed the words over a bunch of Hawaiian looking flowers. I swear, the people like this shopper who are buying this junk must be blind. Either that, or they're bored. The emperor pretending to wear clothes was smarter—at least he hadn't paid a mint for them.

As I walk down the stairs, Grandmother arches one eyebrow, but she doesn't say anything. I should've just worn the sweater—if I want to convince her to approve of Lisa, I shouldn't irritate her over and over with dumb stuff—but I always seem to do this. I have trouble when someone tells me I have to do something. I had a vague concern that people would already be here, and that she'd be introducing me like some kind of debutante. Thankfully, they appear to just be arriving now.

Grandmother sticks to my side like we're partners working a beat until a man close to her age shows up and starts asking questions about some kind of development. After introducing him as her CEO, she finally walks off, thankfully, grilling him about something or other.

"You've been freed," a tall guy in the exact blue sweater I was supposed to wear hisses. "Make a break for it." He looks like he walked right off the cover of *Horse and Hound.* Or *Golf Pro Today*, if that's a real magazine. Shaggy dark blonde hair. Five o'clock shadow. Piercing blue eyes.

"My grandma wanted me to wear that exact sweater." I shake my head. "We could've been twins."

He laughs. "I doubt I'd have noticed." He looks around and drops his voice to a whisper. "Everyone here looks the same, and I doubt any of them bought their own clothes."

"I certainly didn't buy this," I say. "What a stupid shirt."

"You wore it to send her a message?" The guy whistles softly. "You're a braver man than I am. Your grandmother's absolutely terrifying."

"I can't disagree with that," I say. "That's why I've been hiding all this time, pretending to be a normal guy."

"Ace Devonshire." He holds out his hand.

"I suppose you already know who I am."

"The long-lost grandson—Emerson Richmond."

"My mom wanted to spare me exactly the life you see." I shrug.

"She's a smart lady," Ace says. "Is she around here somewhere? I bet she's irritated."

"She passed away," I say.

Ace winces. "I'm sorry, man. I tend to do that—say just the wrong thing. And your dad just died, too."

I don't tell him that I never met the guy. I'm not sure Grandmother wants that getting out. "It's fine. You didn't know."

"Here." Ace flags down a waiter, which could have been me a few days ago, and grabs a drink. "Take this. Drink enough and they'll make this whole thing more bearable."

"Trust Ace to be passing out the booze," another guy says, stepping toward us. He reaches for a glass for himself.

"Oh, you can have mine." I offer him the short, squatty glass.

"You don't drink?" The other guy has nearly black hair and even lighter blue eyes than Ace. "That's a mistake in this crowd."

"Especially today." Ace takes a sip and closes his eyes. "Your grandmother must be happy you're here, because she broke out the McAllister."

"The 2001?" The dark-haired guy smiles. "You should make an exception."

I shrug. "My mom never drinks—neither do I."

Ace nods slowly, accepting my somewhat cryptic response without pushing. "Well, we'll drink yours for you then."

"You're still not drinking?" A familiar voice behind me has me turning. Before I even see him, Uncle Bentley drops a hand on my shoulder.

"Uncle Bentley," I say. "I didn't know you were coming."

"Wait, Bentley's your uncle?" Ace's brow furrows. "He's, like, what? Forty?"

Bentley laughs, the same lines Mom has crinkling just a bit by his eyes. "Close. Emerson's not really my nephew, but I'm close with his family, so he's always called me that."

I have no idea what to say. I didn't tell Mom and Dad. It didn't even occur to me that he might be here. "I thought you were in Europe."

"Just got back."

His half smile's the only familiar thing in this room, and I cling to him like a life preserver.

"I could work hundred-hour weeks in Europe forever and never run out of business. They have no idea how to fire people over there, even when they're clearly dead weight. The only reason their bloated corporations haven't all gone belly up is American consulting firms."

I just nod like I understand.

"I missed cheeseburgers so much that I finally came back, and it's a good thing. I would've hated to miss this—pretty big day for you." He lifts both eyebrows.

"Sure," I say.

"Who are you, exactly?" the dark-haired guy asks.

"Bentley Harrison."

"Harrison Consulting?" The dark-haired guy's eyes widen. "I applied to work at your firm, and—"

"I don't make hiring decisions," Bentley says. "And I *never* hire the children of people I know. It's too awkward. You probably never had a chance."

"How many employees are you up to now?" I ask.

Before Bentley can even answer, the guy jumps in

again. "I'm at Sorenson now, but if you're ever looking for someone, I'd love to reapply."

Bentley eyes him and nods. "Let's talk now."

Before I know what's happening, my life preserver's floating away, chatting about a bunch of business things I don't even really understand much about. Margins. Shell companies.

Great.

This is where I drown.

"Why haven't we met before now, even if you were avoiding all the successor drama?" Ace asks. "One of the best things about it—the only way I survived—was making friends who got it."

"We definitely went to very different schools," I say.

"Ooh, did you go overseas? I got my MBA at London School of Economics, but mostly because I love British accents."

"Actually, I went to a local school."

"Cornell?" Ace asks. "NYU? Columbia?"

I laugh. "Not quite."

"Don't tell me you commuted all the way to Yale." He frowns. "Georgetown? No, Dartmouth?" He looks incredulous. "You really don't look like the Brown type."

"I actually think all the Ivy Leagues are terribly overpriced and most of the curriculum they deliver is a study in uselessness."

Ace's jaw dangles open.

"Come again?" A man with greying hair turns around. "What did you say?"

My new pal Ace turns his thumb sideways. "David Oldham. Provost of Columbia, meet Emerson Richmond, rogue heir."

Shoot.

"I can't wait to hear his explanation of why Ivy Leagues aren't worth the price tag." Columbia's provost looks seriously peeved.

"Well, maybe for children with wealthy families it makes more sense, given their ample resources, but consider people from lower income families. If they spend two hundred thousand dollars on a college degree they could obtain for twenty to thirty thousand elsewhere—often while working part time—it will take them years and years to ever repay the price tag for Harvard. The statistics show that those people don't make commensurately more money in their chosen careers, on average, to offset that expenditure. Most people from a modest background who attended an Ivy League in the hopes of changing their lives, when polled, said they wished they hadn't spent so much on a meaningless piece of paper, and that doesn't even get into the frivolousness of the curriculums compared to the more practical classes offered at state and trade schools."

"Frivolous? A piece of paper?" the man next to the Provost is sputtering.

"Who's that?" I whisper.

Ace winces a little. "Joseph Lundgate, one of the overseers at Harvard."

That's what I get for running my mouth.

"The one thing that never changes about good old Emerson is that he's always riling people up, just for effect." A woman I do not know walks toward me, shaking her head. "Don't mind him. He partied a little too much in college, like me, and he flunked out. Had to go to a city school after refusing to pull the family card, and he's been sore ever since."

"No kidding," Ace says. "Smart to do it then—you'll never get away with partying now."

"Right?" the woman smiles. "Don't let him rile you up, though. He's always making straw man arguments. His grandmother's the funniest to watch when he does it, but I'm not as brave as he is." She drops her voice. "Caroline scares the pants off me."

Apparently she scared them too, because David and Joseph, whom I will always mentally call Columbia and Harvard, both nod and back away slowly.

"Elizabeth Moorland, coming in clutch with the de-escalation." Ace shakes his head. "When your brother called me today and said you'd be a good assistant, I think I laughed for an hour. But maybe he's right."

"Your assistant?" She rolls her eyes. "As if."

"Easton said you're desperate." Ace looks pretty confident.

"Well, I do sort of need a job, but working for you?" She cringes. "Will I ever really be that desperate?"

"Hey, now." Ace is smiling broadly now. "I'm not that bad."

"The ditch incident." She holds up one finger. "The blueberry ice cream." She holds up another. "And the kite." She shakes her head. "Just. . .no."

"Hey, I was—that was a long time ago."

"The ice cream was last year." She shakes her head.

"This is different. It's not fun—it's work."

"And you're a good boss?"

I'm impressed. This girl turned Ace around from possibly considering her to actually working hard to try and win her into taking the job.

"Look, I may not be voted boss of the year, but I'm also not the worst, and my company's doing great."

"I might consider the position, but I'd have rules." She folds her arms.

"Like what?" He's frowning. "Usually as soon as I hear about a rule, I'm jonesing to break it."

Elizabeth rolls her eyes. "Yeah, that's what I thought. I'm passing. Thanks anyway."

"Oh, c'mon. Just tell me what they are."

I can't help watching this interaction in awe. She's herding him around like some kind of working dog.

"I won't schedule dates of any kind for you as part of my job."

"Jealous?" Ace's smile deepens.

"Hardly," she says. "Disgusted is more like it." She shakes her head. "I won't send flowers or gifts, and if some woman comes after you with a gun or something, I'm ducking. Don't expect me to defend you."

"I can handle that." He laughs. "Wow, how badly do you need a job to work for someone you clearly detest like that?"

"Easton says you're not that bad." She doesn't look very reassured.

"I hope he's wrong," Ace says. "I kind of like the idea of being the absolute worst."

She looks pretty unimpressed. "Send me an email or something. I can start next week on, like, a trial basis."

"Great," he says.

"But you?" She turns to face me. "I need to talk to you right now."

Oh, no. Now the shepherd's coming for me—but where's she planning to herd me? That's the question. "Do you even know who I am?"

Her smile's wry. "More than you realize."

Ace swears. "Well, now I feel left out. You better be ready. I'm going to try and figure out what this is about on Monday."

"Not a chance." Elizabeth points at the coat closet. "I just need a moment alone."

Ace is whistling again as we walk away, but he looks as lost as I feel.

❧ 6 ☙

ELIZABETH

aking it to the Grand Prix level—winning —requires three things. A horse with plenty of scope, a rider who's talented and has put in the work, and a whole lot of luck combined with perfect timing.

Your horse can colic or get an abscess the night before the competition and you're done. You can get the flu, and it's over. If you happen to sprain your ankle, or if your horse throws a shoe, you'll miss your window.

It's really that simple.

Change one or two small things, and your win is just another loss. By the time we were teenagers, I already knew the key difference between Victoria and me—other than money. Victoria has always had a burning desire to excel at showjumping. More than anything else, she wants to win. So whichever horse is looking great right before the show, she wants to be on it.

Whereas, I fall in love with my horses.

That's it.

It's what has always kept me amateur instead of pro. If you told me I had to choose—ride three top level horses every single day, or ride only the horse I love—I'd choose the horse I love every single time and twice on Sunday. That's just not what makes a Grand Prix rider. I mean sure, if my timing is good, I might get to compete one day. We might even win the show we enter.

But it's not about to become my career.

That's not who I am, and I made peace with that a long time ago. I can't afford a life of Grand Prix level riding, either. My family does really well. . .sometimes. Other times, it just *looks* like we're doing well, because no one can fake it like they've made it like my parents.

That means I've gotten really, really good at reading rooms and knowing just what to say to keep people from sniffing out the truth about my family. I've gotten great at polishing up my bargain bin horse so he can trot alongside the six-figure warmbloods. I've become an expert at fobbing a wardrobe full of fakes off by throwing in one or two authentic items.

I'm basically a professional fraud.

That just so happens to be exactly what Emerson needs in this moment, because a bigger phony I have never seen.

"I have a proposition for you," I say.

His eyes widen. "I'm not sure what you're thinking, but I have a girlfriend, and I care about her."

That stops me short. "Wait, you do?"

"Well, not exactly." He squirms like a worm faced with a really big hook. "But I did until just recently, and I mean to win her back."

"Does Catherine Richmond know about that?" I can't help thinking about all her *produce an heir* talk.

The blood drains from his face, and he looks

around frantically, as if he's wanting to be sure no one else can hear us.

"This is a safe place to talk," I say, which is more than his grandmother verified earlier today. "But listen, I overheard your grandmother, who clearly wasn't as careful as you, and I'm here because clearly you need someone to guide you." If he has a girl he likes, and what's more, it's a girl Catherine doesn't approve of, this is an even better offer. "If you help me out, I'll pose as your girlfriend, and you don't have to feel bad about using me at all."

"But—"

"I can help you navigate all this—just like I did with that Ivy League faux pas."

"But I don't—"

"You can dump me whenever you want, and—"

He grabs my hand. "What do *you* want from me in return?"

"I run a charity," I say. "It's about to be sold out from under me, or at least, the facility is. I need a downpayment to pay for that building myself instead. Almost every person in that room out there could donate enough for me to buy it, but it's hard to just go ask. Rich people can hear the ask a mile away, so you have to approach them carefully."

"I'm not sure what you're thinking, but I can't—"

"You're not going to be able to get me the money," I say. "You can't just start this thing by asking Grandma for a fistful of cash. But you can work with me to bring up the need. Unlike me, since you're not asking for yourself and it's clear you have money, you'll even be able to suggest that people you meet donate. Trust me, one good wingman can make a huge difference. And if Catherine Richmond's grandson says he wants people to support me. . ." I don't say that people will leap to get a write-off that buys them goodwill with Richmond Steel, but I hope he's smart enough that I don't have to.

He narrows his eyes at me. "It's an attractive offer. I won't lie. But it's too complicated, with too many possibilities of going wrong."

"How so?"

He shakes his head. "Thank you, but I'm going to pass." Without another word, he brushes past me and back into the main room.

It's really a pity.

He needs me, and I need him. He was my best hope, and I blew it somehow. I'm just not sure quite how. I guess my timing was off—or maybe luck wasn't with me. I can't help feeling a little dejected as I wander around the party. I do manage to pull a few donations of people's literal pocket change—I promise to email them receipts—but it's nothing great. I've lowered myself to casually begging, and it's only gotten me enough to finance another week or two of basic supplies. Honestly, that would be fine. I don't care a lot about my pride, as long as I don't sink low enough to stop being invited to things like this.

Except that I need a hundred grand in the next ten days to have a *prayer* of pulling this off. Every time I think about surrendering all those animals. . .and not even having a place to bring new ones going forward.

I want to crawl into my bed at home and cry.

But then I think about my only other alternative, and that almost feels worse.

I keep thinking about Hottie today, his ears pricked forward, his nostrils rippling as he calls for me from the field. My heart hurts for just *thinking* about selling him, but so many other tiny faces clamor for my attention. Selling my one sweet horse could fund countless other adoptions.

I'd be the most selfish creature in New York to keep him when his sale could do so much more good. Even Hottie would probably understand. After all, he's a rescue himself, slated for the kill pen when his career as a racer ended.

I'm dragging my feet on the way home, but when I reach my apartment, my tiny fluffs are all giddy I'm back. They don't care that I totally bombed out tonight. Lucky looks even more delighted than they are, but she hangs back a little until the tinies have bounced and licked and bounced against my legs. Once I call her, she practically knocks me over with all her jumping, but at least I don't have to wonder whether she's happy to see me.

When I check the back patio Astroturf, it's. . . Just eww. I got the small dog door installed to lead out to my second floor patio. My tiny dogs often shoot through and bark at nearby walkers or other residents. They also go potty when I'm not home to walk them. I guess Lucky was also able to squeeze through thanks to how emaciated she is, and let's just say that her deposits are *far* more significant than Floof and Boba's. I gag a few times cleaning it up, but then I'm really ready to get out with the babies for a walk.

Of course, my poms run out of energy after I circle the building just one time, and I'm practically dragging them by the time we get back to the apartment. I decide to leave them there for a bit and head back down with Lucky. She pulls ridiculously, and I decide to do a little work on it now. I'm doing my third lap when my phone starts ringing. "Hello?"

Lucky chooses that moment to spot a squirrel and take off after it—spinning me around like some kind of demented ice skater. I nearly drop my phone, catching it with my fingertips just as I get hold of Lucky again.

I have no idea what the caller just heard, but they probably think I'm insane.

Thankfully, it's Easton. My brother's used to this kind of nonsense.

"Hey," he says. "You alright? Sounds like World War Three just started in Scarsdale."

"I'm currently fostering a border collie," I say.

"Oh, no. It's finally happened."

"Hey," I say. "Don't be rude." I can tell he's about to ignore me.

"You've finally lost the very last of your mind."

"If you'd seen her, you'd understand."

"But you subject yourself to all these miseries by actually going to shelters and seeking them out."

"If I don't, then—"

"Don't say it," Easton says. "I know they'll die. Everyone knows that. But you can't save the whole world."

"I can do my best to try."

"But aren't the border collies those black and white ones that never stop moving?"

"They come in brown and multicolor as well," I say.

"Yes, that makes it better."

"Actually, she's also a puppy." I can't help groaning a little, and that makes Lucky's ears come forward. She looks so lovely when she's paying attention and not mauling me with her overflowing and uncontrollable love.

"You're a masochist."

"I think you mean sado-maso—"

"Speaking of that," Easton says. "Ace called."

"Oh, geez."

"He said you took the job."

"He's worse than I remember," I say.

"He said you were hotter than he remembered."

"How are you still friends with him?" I think about texting Ace to back out of it, but I really do need steady income. Even if I wind up not being able to buy the shelter from Mom and Dad, I'll need someplace new, and the bank's not going to budge on my reliability and steady income or whatever. Or if I decide to rent another place, they'll want me to show that I'm making money as well.

"Most of his outrageous stuff is just a show, like there's some kind of weird role he started when he's around groups of people, and now he can't seem to stop playing it."

"It's tiring," I say.

"If you hate the job, you can quit. Plus, we're good enough friends that I'm pretty sure he won't say anything about you to anyone."

As if I'd care about that.

"But listen, the real reason I'm calling is that I finally got an answer out of Dad."

"About?"

"The buyers on the shelter," he says. "Didn't you say you wanted to know who it was?"

My heart lurches. "Yes. Who is it?" Please, please let it be someone I know, or more importantly, someone who can be reasoned with.

"Apparently there's this big company that's buying all the buildings in that area to make an inland warehouse. It took them a good six months to convince everyone who owns buildings near the shelter, so I'm not sure how easy it'll be to change their plans."

My poor excited heart sinks. "Really?"

He grunts. "I think you may know the name—Mom used to go to a lot of parties at her house. Catherine

Richmond's running things again right now, because apparently her son who was in the process of taking over just died. The company leveling all the buildings over there is Richmond Steel."

My shelter's right on the corner—perfect frontage to the road they'd be using to come and go. How exactly did I go wrong with that Emerson guy? He was so cute that I got distracted, and now my hasty blunder may cost me the shelter. How perfect would it have been if he agreed. Talk about the inside track.

What a missed opportunity.

Unless. . .his grandmother seemed keen to keep their deal a secret. Maybe I could blackmail her with telling. . .no. That would be too awful, even for me. Right?

"Elizabeth?"

"Yeah," I say. "I'm here. Sorry. I've got to get some things done, though, so I better. . ."

"Right. Look, if you need anything else, let me know. I hear Mrs. Richmond's pretty preoccupied, because apparently she's had to drag a grandson who didn't want much to do with the family back in to run things."

"I may have heard that too," I say.

"I'm not sure whether that makes it more likely or less that she might reconfigure, but I hear the grandson's about your age. Maybe you could get to know him or even befriend him. If I had to guess, I'd say he'll feel a little like an outsider right about now. Plus, I have it on pretty good authority that the Richmond family has a foundation that donates like twenty billion dollars a year. A tiny chunk of that would go a long way for all your mangy dogs and screechy cats."

"None of my dogs have mange," I say almost reflexively. Not much to say in defense of the cats. They do screech a lot.

"Thank goodness for small blessings," Easton says. "But I really think you should see what you can do about meeting that Emerson kid. And when you do? Definitely bring your A game."

I don't tell him that we've met twice now, once when I crashed into him and I mistook him for a waiter and stormed off, and a second time when he was wearing one of the tackiest thousand dollar t-shirts I've ever seen and talking to Ace, who was at his most obnoxious.

I do start making plans to meet him a third time. This time, I'm determined not to crash and burn.

When I was little, we couldn't afford much in the way of entertainment. At one point, one of the few things we had were old videos of the Muppets someone had left in the apartment we moved into. I watched them over and over and over.

And I always felt a little sorry for Kermit the Frog.

I mean, he was funny, sensible, and a very nice shade of green. What did he do to deserve being stuck with the obnoxious, loud, and very pushy Miss Piggy? If I were him, I'd do what frogs do best and hop right out of there.

In this moment, I'm really *really* wishing I could hop. Sadly, I'm pretty sure I'm stuck here until I can pay the check for this train wreck of a meal.

"How old is your grandma, anyway?"

"How old?" I shrug. "She didn't tell me."

"But you can't take over until she dies, right? Or does she want to step down now?"

Is she actually trying to make macabre small talk about when Catherine Richmond will die? Or is she pressing in order to find out when I might be running the whole company? Either way, ew.

"Because my parents had *three* kids, so I knew from the start that I'd never be in charge of anything, really. I mean, I'm the second child, but my older brother is a disgusting little kiss-up."

"I was told that you run publicity and marketing for the company."

She rolls her eyes. "That's just what they tell people."

"It's what *who* tells people?"

She frowns. "You didn't say before—where did you go to school?"

"Let's see," I say, wondering whether this might be enough to dislodge her perfectly manicured talons from my back. "I started at Bronx Community College, and then I transferred to Brooklyn College for my four-year degree. I saved a bundle of money doing it that way, so if you haven't actually graduated yet, I'd be happy to send you some info."

"On Bronx Community College?" She looks like she can't tell whether I'm kidding.

"Or Brooklyn College. Either one could work, really." I force a smile.

Her lip is curled, and I bet she doesn't even know it. "I already graduated. Thanks."

"Oh, good for you." I nod as if I'm actually surprised. As if I couldn't tell that she thought my educational path was a dark alley leading to nowhere good. "So where did you go?"

"Oh, you're kidding." Her forced laugh sounds like a car that won't quite turn over. "You're so funny."

"Wait. What did I say that's funny?" I ask. "Unless you think my very respectable accounting degree is some kind of joke."

Now she looks unsteady, like she's trying rollerblades for the first time, and she's worried she'll fall and wreck her nose job. "Your grandmother said you have a different sense of humor."

"She did, did she?"

The Princeton Barbie in front of me laughs this time, but it's not as forced, thankfully. "She also said you don't date much."

"Probably because when I do, it tends to upset my girlfriend." I probably shouldn't have said that, but this is getting irritating.

When Princeton Barbie's eyes widen and her hands clutch at the napkin she was using to wipe her fingers —salad dressing is messy stuff, apparently—I realize she's actually upset. "Your grandmother didn't say a word about that. I wouldn't have come if I knew you had a girlfriend."

"Ah, well. Granny's not a big fan of my girlfriend," I say. "Not yet, anyway."

"Still, she shouldn't be setting you up with other people if you're just going to make ridiculous jokes and blow them off."

"You did get a free salad out of it," I say.

Princeton Barbie pops to her feet. "As if I care about that."

"So, you're leaving?"

She drops back into the seat with a flounce and a pout. "You're supposed to stop me."

"Why?" I'm so lost.

"Emerson." She sticks out her lower lip like she's a toddler. "Look, I didn't want to have to bring this up, but I made a composite of what our kids would look like. They're really cute, both of them. Look."

What on earth? "You did. . .what?"

"If you put in two photos, there's this website that

will show you what your kids would look like. It's important for people like us to know that right away."

I'm beginning to think that she needs to be evaluated and put on some kind of medicine. She's not very level. Two seconds ago, she was curling her lip about Brooklyn College. "But that's hardly—"

"Emerson?"

I can't help it. I turn toward the voice with a completely unfounded and yet desperate hope that it might be someone on a balloon-strung house that can carry me away from here. Ideally, not to the middle of some talking-dog-infested forest, but I'm not that picky. I'd go most anywhere at all.

"Yes?"

It's the girl from last night—Elizabeth something or other. And like a lightbulb has gone off in my head, her face jostles another memory loose and I realize this is actually our *third* meeting. She's the same girl who crashed into me at the funeral, shattering all that crystal. Is that when she heard who I am and what Grandma was offering? She looked amazing before I doused her in champagne that day—she looked pretty good last night as well.

But today?

Her hair's in a messy topknot, wisps fluffing out on all sides, big knot bobbing back and forth as she wrestles with a lunging black and white dog. "What are you doing here?"

"He's on a date," Princeton Barbie says.

"Nonni?" Elizabeth asks.

"Do you know each other?" I ask.

"It's a very small world," Elizabeth says. "Sometimes it's a real drag that everyone knows everyone else." She looks like she means it.

"Don't call me Nonni," Princeton Barbie hisses.

"She prefers to be called Princeton Barbie," I say.

Both of their heads whip in my direction.

"Excuse me?" Princeton Barbie says.

I lift my hand and catch the waiter's eye. "Can I get the check?"

He nods and grabs a black book out of his apron—bless him. I have a black American Express with no limit thanks to Grandmother, but I'm not going to be here long enough to wait for him to run that. I plonk down my own cash for this overpriced meal, like a coyote chewing its leg off. "You're on a walk?"

Elizabeth nods woodenly.

"Great. I've been meaning to start doing that."

"Walking?" Elizabeth looks amused.

"Yes." I nod. "Exactly."

"It's her." Princeton Barbie shoots to her feet and chucks her napkin at the table. "You're already dating Elizabeth, aren't you? There's no way you'd actually pick this terrible little diner in this horrible neighborhood otherwise. You must have planned that she'd be walking by."

"Actually," I say, "this is my favorite diner in the area. Their egg salad is amazing, and since I don't eat meat, I'm always looking for a good protein source."

"Aren't eggs meat?" Elizabeth asks.

I shrug. "It's a grey area, especially if the chickens are free range and happy."

She blinks.

"You clearly haven't been dating long." Princeton Barbie stomps her foot. "You should at least give me another chance. I'm way better in the sack—"

I throw up my hands to stop her. "Trust me. Any more meals would be a huge waste of both our time."

"Why?" She frowns.

I reach out and take Elizabeth's free hand. The dog

leaps up to lick our joined hands. "Because as I already told you, I adore my girlfriend."

"But you said your grandmother—"

"I'm confident she'll come around."

When Princeton Barbie storms off, Elizabeth turns to me and drops her eyes to our hands. In that moment, a tiny thrill runs up my arm and I drop her hand like it's a burning ember. "Sorry."

"It's been a long few days for me, but I really thought you turned me down when I suggested that we fake-date?" Her mouth turns up on the corner.

"I don't like the idea of trying to pump people for money," I say. "But I did have an idea of how I might help you." I pick up my phone and dial Bentley.

He picks up on the first ring. "I wondered when you'd call. This is actually a lot later than I expected."

"Mom and Dad don't know," I say. "I just found out. I'm trying to wrap—"

"I won't tell them," Bentley says. "This is your thing."

"Thanks," I say. "But I'm actually calling to ask a favor."

"What?" Bentley chuckles. "Don't tell me you finally want a job."

"You said you never give jobs to kids of your friends."

"You're different. Dave's not a contact—he's my best friend. And you're smart, a hard worker, and a good kid. I've offered you a job at least three times."

"Good to know I'm an exception, but I'm spending all my time learning about Richmond Steel right now. What I need is something else."

"Shoot. This should be interesting."

"So, my new girlfriend Elizabeth runs an animal shelter, but they're a little tight on funds. Don't you have some money earmarked for charities? Maybe a little that you haven't assigned yet?"

"Really? In fourteen years, you never once asked me for money, but two minutes after you find out you're worth far more than I am, you call me up and start begging?"

"It's not that—"

His laughter booms so loud that it makes the speaker on my phone sound tinny. "I'm kidding. Geez, relax, kid."

"Until my grandmother decides I'm worth keeping around, I doubt I can get any money for the shelter from her."

"We usually have it all locked down by January for the year, but sometimes I keep a little bit in miscellaneous for things that come up. Let me ask you this. If I decide I want a dog, would I get first dibs if we donate?"

"Do you want a dog?" I can hardly believe what I'm hearing. Uncle Bentley's always traveling. What kind of life would that be for a dog? "So you can board it all the time?"

"Actually, I'm sick of always being on planes. I'm assigning people to do the overseas cases. I think it's time for me to stick around a little more. But yes, the answer is, I'll see what I can do. I should be able to get at least ten grand or so. Would that be of any help?"

"Of course," I say. "Thanks." I hang up.

"You're a natural," Elizabeth says. "By the time I'm done with you, you'll be a regular Patrick Rothfuss."

"Who's that?" I ask.

"If you search his name online, you'll quickly learn that he's a fantasy author that people love in spite of the fact that he can't seem to finish his series." She smiles. "But he's raised also like six million and change for Heifer International—a charity trying to end world hunger."

"Puppies are cuter," I say. "Do you have any of those? I think we could do a lot with some good photos."

"I can always find cute animals," she says.

"And now I have a goal. Let's raise more than six million."

"I like your initiative," she says. "But why did you change your mind? I thought you said no."

"Did you meet Princeton Barbie just now?"

She's smiling again. "You really shouldn't call Naomi Princeton Barbie. Her dad's pretty influential."

"Sure, sure," I say. "But trust me. Calling her that was way better than any of the other exit strategies I came up with."

"Like what?" Her lip's twitching.

"I had three options," I say. "First, I could have pretended that I couldn't hear her and run off without paying, leaving her with the check."

She nods. "Not a terrible plan, or at least, not the worst I've ever heard, but how would you explain to your grandmother that you went temporarily deaf?"

"That's why my second idea was to accidentally spill water all over her head."

"That I'd have liked to see, but. . ." Now her eyes are dancing. "How would you get anyone to believe that you *accidentally* dumped it on her head? You'd have to aim lower, and spilling something on her feet or lap is so pedestrian."

"Sure, sure. I thought so too, which is why I was considering holding her down and force-feeding her the hamburger from the next table over."

"Except you're a vegetarian. Doesn't shoving meat into someone else's mouth, no matter how anorexic they are, constitute a violation of your code or something?"

"Probably."

"Still. People would've paid to see that, and we could've used that money for the shelter." All the humor melts off her face. "But seriously, why did she leave?"

"I told her I had a girlfriend," I say. "And then before I could explain who it was, you showed up, and you knew her, and I realized that your idea was better than I realized."

"You just got lucky when I showed up."

This is clearly my opening. "I guess I did, but you should know that I *do* have a girlfriend," I say.

"Oh." She nods her head slowly. "So that's why it's complicated."

I can't help cringing a little. "It's actually more complicated than that, really. I had a girlfriend, but she dumped me, and now I'm trying to win her back. So having a fake girlfriend gets really complicated."

I expect her to reassure me that she's fine with telling Lisa that it's all fake.

But she doesn't say that. Instead she drops into a crouch and rubs the dog's head. "That may be a deal-breaker, because I have a major stipulation for the deal. I do need money to save the shelter, and I'll need to convince the buyers not to go through with the deal so I have time to come up with my downpayment. But the only way this will work is if *no one* knows we're faking." She points between herself and me.

"Why?"

"Have you ever told just one person a secret?" One eyebrow arches. "It's never ever ever, not in the history of the world, gone well."

"But—"

"You may not know your grandmother very well yet, but she's scary, and she's powerful, and the only way this works, the only way I'll do it, is if literally only you and I know the truth."

Well, shoot.

"But you can break up with me at literally any time, and I promise to provide whatever level of drama you want. None? Fine. Lots? Also okay."

"The thing is, Lisa's a very low drama person, just like me."

Elizabeth curls her lip and says, "How fun."

Ah, sarcasm. The lowest level of humor. "She's exactly what I want."

"Duly noted, but trust me when I tell you that dating me won't hurt your chances. Girls' brains are quite strange. If you broke up, finding someone else who's pretty and socially comfortable will only help you win her back."

"You think?" I'm not at all sure that she's right. Lisa and Elizabeth couldn't be more different. What Elizabeth likes would probably royally tick off Lisa.

"Wait, you didn't break up over infidelity on your part, right?"

"Of course not," I say.

"And she dumped you?"

"How did you know that?"

"Emerson, one hundred percent of women like a guy more if someone else who is objectively desirable also wants him."

"Statistically, that impossible."

"And yet it's true," she says. "I swear, I'm not wrong about this, no matter what personality type Lisa is. I need your help right now, but I'm attractive, and I'm well-spoken, and I come from a family that people think is great. Trust me. If Lisa does find out we're dating, it won't ruin your chances of getting back together. It'll improve them."

She is attractive, in a 'please park my Porsche while I play a round of golf' kind of way. Since she was at both the funeral and the party yesterday, I'm guessing that my grandmother would approve of her. If I have to help her save her shelter so she can keep rescuing unloved cats and dogs, well, I've done worse things.

I hate even thinking about the time I helped someone try to rob a home improvement store just so I could buy a marker for my mom's grave. Ugh. "We should make sure we're clear on all the rules."

She looks at the table I just left, which hasn't even been bussed yet. "Do you have a minute?"

"Are you hungry?"

She shrugs. "I could eat, but I bet Lucky's thirsty, and if we're doing this, we may as well hammer things out now."

"Uh, okay." I sit down and wave the waiter back over. "I'll have another lemonade."

"A second date?" The waiter bobs his head. "Nice, man."

"More like his actual girlfriend caught him." She fakes a scowl.

The waiter looks genuinely concerned for me.

"Okay, I'll have. . ." She squints at the menu. "Can you come back in a minute? I haven't even looked at this yet."

"I hear the burgers are good, and people seem to eat their wraps a lot, too."

"Ooh, they have a turkey club. I'll have that, with extra french fries, and a side of a plain hamburger patty."

I must be making a face.

Because she slouches in her chair and pats Lucky's head. "What? I like to eat, and so does my dog."

"I just wouldn't have pegged you for a border collie owner." But then I think about how she crashed into me because she was racing without looking, and I look at the dog's face, which is objectively quite beautiful, just like hers, and I shrug. "Or maybe not. Maybe you're a perfect fit."

"Actually, she's a shelter dog who was kept in a box for her entire life. Now she can't bear to be stuck in a kennel, so I'm keeping her with me until we can find her a perfect home."

"Running an animal shelter must be really tiring."

She rubs Lucky's head until the dog tries to climb into her lap. Then she shoves her off and glares. "Actually, saving animals has always been the only thing I wanted to do. I started when I was supposed to be in college."

"Supposed to be?"

"I spent my first semester's textbook money on a racehorse I saved right off the track."

"You did?"

"I bought him for five hundred bucks, but later I found out you can often get them for free. I'd train them for a few months, and then I'd sell them to someone who needed a reasonably priced horse who could do a normal horse kind of job. Some became therapy horses. Some became jumpers. Some of them just started doing trail rides or joined lesson programs for kids."

"Thoroughbreds did? Really?"

"They get a bad rap," she says, "but only because they don't take the time to properly train them. All they want is one that can run. If you had a terrible diet and bad hoof care and people only cared about making sure you ran fast so you never learned basic manners, you'd be flighty and fractious and rude, too. But if someone took the time to teach you how to use your hind end the right way, and they taught you how to hold the bit properly, and they didn't tear at your face, you might completely change how you behaved and what you were suited to do."

Clearly she's passionate about this, and it's actually kind of fun watching how her face transforms when she's talking about the horses changing. But. . .she said she runs a shelter. Not a barn. "I might have missed something, but what does saving horses have to do with the shelter?"

"Right. Sorry. Yeah, so I sold four different horses in my first year of school, one every other month or something, and I then had this little pile of money, and I got all excited about what I could do with it."

"And?"

"I met Floof."

"You met. . .what?"

"She was this tiny little dog who was blind in one eye, and she was super growly and scared because of it. But she never felt safe. The woman who owned her was on her way to dump her at the county when I ran into her, and adopting her changed everything for me. I decided to take that money and try and save more little dogs like her. It grew with time, but later that year, after I failed out of school, I managed to convince my parents to let me use one of their underutilized buildings. I turned the rooms into kennels, and later I added a wash rack, and I've been saving animals that were on a kill order from the New York State system ever since."

"That's. . ." I can't help staring at her. I would never have guessed that she dropped out of school so she could spend all her time trying to help neglected and abandoned animals. "It's impressive, really. What's the shelter called? I want to look it up."

"At first I was going to name it something to do with death row, but people didn't really get it. They all kept saying it was depressing. So instead I called it Posh Pets, because that's who we cater to—people who have money and want a unique animal with a story they can tell."

"You only focus on adopting dogs to rich people?"

She laughs. "Not hardly, but quite a few of my pets need surgeries or special care. They've lived hard lives. I often match them with people who can afford that, and in this area. . ." She shrugs. "It's rich people more often than not."

"How do you find the homes for the pets?"

"We're staffed by a lot of part-time volunteers, many of whom found a dog or cat with us. We're open for people to come adopt every day from eight until noon, but we actually find most of our adoption place-ments through social media. I have a friend who donates her time to photograph each new pet, and then I post on our page and ask people to share and comment to help find the pet a new home."

"That's actually pretty nice," I admit. "I don't hate the idea of helping you."

"My big problem right now is that my parents are selling my building," she says. "This big company's buying it so they can build a huge storage warehouse for things they need most in their supply chain."

"I kind of overheard part of that," I admit. "On the day you crashed into me."

"Sorry about that." She bites her lip. "I might not have been very polite. I was pretty stressed, and I also thought you were a waiter, for some reason."

"And you don't need to be nice to waiters?" I can't help being annoyed by that, even though I'm sure they all feel that way.

"No, it's not that. I just figured. . ." She frowns. "Well, I guess since it's part of their job, yeah. I didn't think I needed to worry if you had to clean it up."

I shrug. "That's about what I expect from rich people."

"Says the man whose grandmother is richer than the Hiltons."

"That's my grandmother, though," I say. "Not me, and I was a waiter that day."

She blinks. "You—what?"

"I'm kidding," I say.

"Oh." She still looks confused. "Well, don't worry. I plan to help you get your name officially changed to Richmond. Soon, it'll be you who's rich, too."

"I sure hope so." But as I say it, I realize that it may not be true.

⚛ 8 ⚛

ELIZABETH

Most of the animals we adopt are strange in a notable and significant way. My own little Boba has the world's sweetest face, but only three legs. Floof was poked in the eye by a small child with a stick. Her eye isn't even there anymore, and she's been totally blind on her right side for years.

Lucky chewed through her own tail because she was so miserable in the tiny box where she spent nine months. None of these three are really notable in the grand scheme of pet adoption. Every pet we take in has a sad story. When we go to spay them, they're often pregnant, even though they were starving. When we check their teeth, it's not uncommon to find that several are either broken or injured in some way. We take in stray cats that have been fed nothing but rice, because it's all the person who found them had, and now the poor thing's both malnourished and wormy.

I'm not sure what exactly happened to Emerson, but I can recognize broken better than most people.

And he is.

Like the adorable critters with paws I work to save all day, he's absolutely lovely, but there's some real damage underneath. I know to tread lightly. Instead of telling him that I want him to torpedo the sale from his end, I don't mention the warehouse is being built by his grandmother. Yet.

And instead of pushing for more time today, I set up an appointment to go on our first official date tomorrow—I don't even warn him about what we'll be doing. He may think it's a given that his grandmother will like me, since I was at her party and the funeral, but I'll have to win her over like any woman in our circle would. Some guys don't like being made over, but my most important selling point will be showing her that I can improve him—that he listens to my guidance, and that my advice is good.

After he pays for my meal and Lucky's burger patty, we head our separate ways. "Wait." I spin around so fast that Lucky's eyes widen, and she starts looking around for a threat.

She barks three times before I calm her down.

"Sorry," I say. "But I didn't get your phone number."

"Oh." He nods and rattles the numbers off.

I save it as Boyfriend with a heart, and then I tell him mine. "But make sure you put me in there as something cute."

"Your name's already cute." He looks uncomfortable.

"Elizabeth Moorland is *not* cute." I swivel my phone around and show him. "See? If you want to convince people that we're actually dating, you're going to have to work a little harder."

He sighs mightily, but he shows me that he's saved my phone number under "Honey." I didn't take him for a 'honey' guy, but it's better than my full name, I guess.

This whole thing may be a sequence of baby steps, like when I was getting Boba fitted for his false leg. It actually ends in a tiny wheel. We only mess with it when we're going out for a walk, usually, but it took weeks to get him used to using it.

I'm assuming Emerson will adjust faster, since he's a human and can talk, but you never know.

I spend the rest of the day running shelter errands, but I make it to the barn near the end of the day. I flat two horses, one of whom has an atrocious mouth, and the other who barely reacts to my leg cues for the first ten minutes, but by the time I'm done, I feel way better. Helping fix problems is therapeutic, especially for horses whose fault it's *not* that they're having trouble to begin with. I do warn Victoria that whoever was riding that poor lesson horse is not using their legs, but it's on her to fix the cause of the problem.

I save my ride on Hottie for last, because I know it's going to be hard.

He's an angel, as always these days.

I've always wanted to ride Grand Prix, but I'm not like Victoria. I haven't been able to separate my love for horses from my love for one single horse. Riding Hottie, progressing with him, it's the thing I love most about riding. The idea of selling him—I know I should do it. I just told Emerson that selling retrained thoroughbreds is how I funded the start of Posh Pets.

If I do it again, it'll breathe new life into my original goal. It's my whole *thing*. I find broken horses, repurpose them, and send them off into the world to do great things.

But I've never loved any horse quite like I love Hottie. When we finish our ride, I take an extra long time brushing him, and then I hang out with him in the pasture for a bit. A lot of horses would wander off once they're released. Not him. He stands next to me, happy just to be near me. He likes when I scratch his rear, but he doesn't demand it. He likes to rest his enormous head on my shoulder, but he asks first, tapping me with his velvety nose, and then lightly dropping his chin on my shoulder.

When I don't object or move away, he sighs and drops the full weight of his stupidly big head on top of me. It's the closest thing to a real hug from a horse I've ever had. He's not the only horse who's ever done this, but he's the only one who healed my heart by doing it.

"I don't want to sell you," I whisper as tears stream silently down my face. "Does that make me a selfish person?"

I guess it probably does.

I mean, I know it does.

It's not like he'd be going to a bad place. But it feels like selling him might break my heart for real. I'm deep in thought as I leave the barn, and I nearly run Mrs. Watkins over. "Oh, I'm so sorry."

"Thinking something over?" Her eyebrow rises, but she doesn't look angry, even though I had to grab both her shoulders and brace them to keep from knocking her flat on the ground.

"Yeah, sorry."

"Have you been considering my offer?"

I can't help it. My face contorts a bit, and I inhale. At least I don't actively start crying.

"Ah, girl, I'm not trying to wreck you. Just tell me no. He's a beauty, but I'll get over it."

"The thing is, I really should sell him," I say. "I run this charity, you know, and it's in bad shape. The money from his sale could fix, well, not everything, but a lot."

"I wish I was a better person," she says. "If I was, I'd offer to just fund your charity." Her eye twinkles.

"But I do want that gorgeous beast of yours, so I'm going to wait and see what you decide."

"How long do I have?"

"Let's say a week. How's that?" She smiles. "It gives me some time to find another if you turn me down."

I nod.

"But." She leans a little closer. "I hope you don't turn me down."

She's a funny one. "A week is kind. Thanks."

That night, I dream over and over of winning the Grand Prix with Hottie. No matter how many times I win, Henrietta's always waiting at the end to take him away, because I'm just the rider. He's her horse. It's probably not much of a nightmare as nightmares go, but it wasn't my favorite way to spend a night.

I'm almost looking forward to picking Emerson up. He assures me via text that his grandmother's gone, so I pull right up and wave at the guard. "Hey, Harold."

Most people I know don't talk to the support staff. They can't be bothered. But I find that, especially when you come to a place relatively often for events, it's strange not to get to know the people who are letting you in and out, who are cooking, and cleaning, and helping with, well, with everything.

"How's your horse?" Harold asks. "My daughter watches those videos you send over and over." His little girl is here sometimes, so a few years ago I started sending him videos for her after shows.

"I haven't shown much lately, and when I'm just riding my horse, I rarely get any footage, but the next time I do, I'll send you some. Or maybe I can take some videos of my friend Victoria. She's an even better rider than me."

"I don't know about that. My Lonnie says you look like a rainbow, and she likes that she knows you."

"A rainbow?" I can't help laughing. "How so?"

"You're moving through the air like magic, and you make pretty arcs when you do it."

I like that. "Tell Lonnie I appreciate the compliment."

He waves me through, logging my entry in his little notebook like always. He's been here for every single party I've ever attended at Richmond Mansion. Emerson's grandmother may have a notorious reputation as being hard to please, but she rewards loyalty. I've seen Harold's car.

It's much nicer than mine.

Once I reach the house, I start to worry. Will Emerson freak out about my plan today? Will it offend him, what I have in mind? Will he call this off before we've even gotten started? His friend, Bentley Harrison, already began the process of getting me ten thousand dollars—the confirmation of fund allocation email came early this morning.

So far, I'm the real winner in this deal.

I really don't want to tick him off. But when I walk through the front door, chatting with their butler, I cringe internally. Mrs. Richmond is not gone at all. She's standing in the entryway, staring at me. "What on earth are you doing here, child?"

I blink.

"She's here to meet me." Emerson's jogging down the massive curved staircase. For a split second, I worry he'll hop up on the banister and slide down, like the girl in *Little Orphan Annie* or something. Luckily, he keeps on jogging until he reaches the bottom. "My date yesterday was a total flop, but I ran into Elizabeth, and actually, she saved me."

"Elizabeth Moorland." Catherine Richmond narrows her eyes as if I'm clearly not what she had in mind for her precious grandson. I can't really blame her. If she knew more about my parents' ongoing financial woes, she'd really be glaring. Luckily, they've kept that mostly under wraps. "Where did you go to school?"

She didn't ask where I graduated—that's a boon. "Duke."

Her harumph is surprisingly impolite. Usually she's scary, but she's always the soul of propriety. I suppose when her grandson's future is hanging in the balance, she's a little more raw. "Well, what are you two going to do?"

"We'll probably catch a movie and grab something to eat," I say. "But before that, we're going to do a full makeover."

Her lips actually part as she inhales. "You're what?"

"I'm not at all trying to criticize you, but at the party he looked like a popstar wannabe, and yesterday he looked like he was applying to Eton." I can't help scrunching my nose a little. "Neither of those looks work for him, and his *hair*."

To my utter shock, she laughs. "You're not wrong."

"The first time I saw him, I thought, 'hey, this new guy's handsome. He looks a little like Chad Michael Murray, but he needs to fix the haircut ASAP."

"Isn't Chad Michael Murray blond?" Emerson asks.

I smile. "A man who knows his pop references."

"My sister's obsessed with movies, and she and Jake are always talking about actors. I've picked up a thing or two."

"Your *sister*?" Did I hear him right?

"She's not actually my sister," he says, "but I've known her since we were young, and I've always called her that."

Strange, but I don't press for more information

now. Mrs. Richmond looks pained, like her toe just knocked against an aberrant trim mold.

"Alright, well." His hand lifts up and strokes the side of his head. "I don't think my hair is really that bad, but—"

"You're wrong," I say at the exact same time Mrs. Richmond says the same two words.

That's a little scary.

"Let's go," Emerson says.

"Don't rush back," Mrs. Richmond says. "And make sure you buy anything she likes when you go shopping."

I wish my parents had said that to me, just once. We always had *money*, but we never had Richmond money. Then again, who does? We've barely reached my car when he stops. "Whoa."

"What?"

"That's yours?"

My Audi A3 was my dad's before it came to me, but it's dark and mostly nondescript. It's the cheapest luxury car you can buy, probably, and it's almost ten years old, but the body style hasn't changed *dramatically*. Even though most of my friends would never buy an Audi, it was a safe choice, usually saving me from too much scrutiny.

"Is that a 2014?"

I sniff. "A 2015."

He smiles. "We have the same car, but yours is one year newer."

The same car? "How on earth? Your grandmother lets you drive a ten-year-old car around?"

"We have a lot to discuss," he says. "But I want to make sure we're clear on the rules. Everything I say, and everything I do, is strictly confidential. You'll reveal only what I want to reveal, always."

I nod. "Sure, unless it's something illegal."

He rolls his eyes. "You can be sure it won't be."

"Alright, then sure. And likewise, you cannot tell a single soul—not your sister-friend, not your grand-mother, no one, that our relationship is fake."

"You said that already."

"You can't even tell your girlfriend."

That makes him squirm, but eventually he nods.

"Your ex, whatever." I sigh. "And what else?"

"I'll do my best to get you funding any way I can think of, but you can't order me to say or do specific things. I have to feel comfortable with all of it."

Given that he's already managed to get me ten grand, or soon will have, I feel alright with that. "Sure."

"And you will break up with me when and how I ask."

"Yep, I said that already."

"And while we're together, you'll let me decide what we do, and what tone we take."

I shake my head. "No way. If we're together, I have to be myself, and you can make requests, but I will behave authentically. Most of these people have known me for years. They'd immediately know if I started doing weird stuff."

He huffs. "Fine. Well, another rule—while you're dating me, you can't date anyone else. Too much of a chance that someone finds out."

"Same goes for you."

"You're starting a new job, and you run a charity, and you said you ride horses. When will you have time to even date me?"

"I'll figure it out," I say. "The charity and the job are both part time, so it should be fine. I'll still be free most evenings."

He sighs. "I think that's the big stuff."

"What about holding hands?" I ask. "Kissing?"

He swallows, his hands clenching. "I'd feel like I was cheating on Lisa."

"The girl who dumped you."

He scowls.

"If you want to sell this, and I think to keep Grandma happy, you should, you'll need to at least be fine holding my hand." I step a bit closer and drop to a whisper. "I promise not to bite."

He steps away and full-on glares. "Stop that."

I can't help it. I laugh. "You're really cute when you're annoyed. I'll be sure to irritate you often."

"How about this? You make time for me at least three days a week, coming to the house so Grandmother can see you, and I'll try to hold your hand at least once a week."

"I'll counter." I half smile. "For your own good."

"With?"

"I can hold your hand whenever I want, and you have to act like you like it."

"How's that a counter?"

"It's different than what you proposed."

"No, it's exactly what you said at the beginning."

I smile. "You're finally learning a little something about women." I point. "Now get in the car, and I'll teach you lesson number two. It'll help you win Lisa back."

"What?" He's standing outside the car like he's not sure it's safe.

"The more money you're willing to spend on us, the more we'll like you."

"I'm terribly afraid that's not a joke." He finally climbs in, and I notice that Lucky's hair is all over the seat. Thankfully, he doesn't seem too fussy.

We'll be replacing his clothes soon anyway.

"Why do you hope it's a joke? The one thing the Richmonds have always had is loads of money."

"But do you think I want a girl who likes me because I'm rich?" He looks genuinely annoyed.

"I guess not?"

"That's why I'm not sure I want any of this," he says. "Because I grew up without even knowing Alistair Richmond was my father. I actually only realized he was my dad on the day of the funeral—the day I really was working as a waiter."

I'd been going over that in my head—why I mistook him for a waiter. He was wearing a suit, and maybe someone had handed him a tray? Or maybe he was next to a waiter? Somehow, my brain was just positive he was the waiter.

Which was impossible.

Only, it turns out, it's exactly what happened. I really did run over the waiter at Alistair Richmond's funeral, who also happened to be his son.

"But how did you—"

"My beloved grandmother paid my mother to abort me," he says. "Only, my mom didn't listen very well. She kept me and never told anyone. If Mom hadn't died, I might never have found out at all."

I'm not proud of swearing so much in that moment, but I'm not really embarrassed. That's a lot of information to unpack. "Wow." I finally understand why he might not want the Richmond legacy—and why his grandma's so insistent upon making him marry someone she approves.

"She wants your wife to be a guide—or like, a partner—to help you fit in."

He nods.

"So all that stuff about Ivy Leagues being overpriced?"

"I actually think all that," he says.

"Oh, man. We have more to make over than your hair."

But I'm honestly a little excited about the challenge. This is turning out to be even more interesting than I hoped. But one thing bothers me. For a guy I'm helping and have to dump on his command. . .I like Emerson more with each thing I learn.

And that's dangerous for me.

Things I love always seem to disappear.

❦ 9 ❦

EMERSON

My mom gave me the worst haircuts when I was younger. Once, she actually put a bowl on my head and cut around it. Sadly, that was probably the best haircut I ever got—at least it was even on the ends.

The only good thing was that we could never afford the school pictures and she rarely took photos herself, so there's not much documentation of the disaster that was my sandy brown hair. Once I got older, I watched YouTube videos on my friend Tuck's phone and figured out how to cut it myself. It looked pretty good, honestly—way better than when Mom was doing it, even if I did use kids' safety scissors more often than not.

So when Seren took me to Great Clips the first time, I was actually a little overwhelmed. You could *hear* the scissors expertly snicking over and over when you walked through the door. Those ladies could cut most anything into submission. When I walked out the door the first time, I was pretty proud of my haircut.

After I graduated from college, my friend Harry

told me I had to get a 'good haircut' as a professional. He recommended a barber—a guy who charged *forty* dollars for a haircut. I had finally made it, and although I could afford it, I certainly felt that I was paying more than enough for the work.

That's why it takes me off guard when both my grandmother and Elizabeth say that my hair looks bad. But when Elizabeth pulls up in front of a huge brick building and drags me up to the third floor, I'm really nervous. It doesn't help that the receptionist desk looks like it cost more than my car, and that the wall behind it is covered with living ivy. I can't help wondering how long that took to grow. You'd think the place would look dated with that much plant life established, but everything looks sparklingly new, including the water wall on the far right side, and the enormous bay windows that overlook the distant New York Cityscape on the left.

The overhead on this place must be astronomical, and that's not very reassuring. What kind of hair place looks nicer than a posh country club spa?

"They don't even have prices posted," I hiss. "How much is this going to cost?"

Her eyes widen and she shakes her head slowly.

"What?"

She closes her eyes and mouths the word, "Later."

Why we can't talk, in a place of business, about the price of a service they're providing, I do not comprehend, but that seems to be the gist of what she's saying.

"Hello." The most flamboyant man I have ever seen in my life prances around the corner of the receptionist desk. I mean, I wish I could say he was walking or strolling or ambling, but the man is *not* doing any of those things. His hands are floating akimbo, his feet coming up higher and with way too much spring for a normal step, and his lips are pursed while simultaneously smiling. He's saucily prancing—nothing else accurately describes him.

I have no idea how to react right now, so I just say, "Hi."

"You must be Emerson Richmond, heir apparent."

I glare at Elizabeth.

"How do you think I got you in here with one day's notice?" she whispers. "I'm not a magician."

"You were right." The man nods knowingly at Elizabeth. "He is a diamond in the rough."

"What about me is rough?"

They both laugh, like I made a hilarious joke.

"Don't worry. When I'm through, you will—"

I throw both hands out, one with my palm facing Elizabeth and one toward the guy. "Wait. Through with *what*, exactly?"

His high, bubbly giggle is more than I was prepared for, and I really hope I'm not making a strange face. "Let's move back a step, shall we?" The man makes a look I've seen before—when women are trying to look both cute and coy in profile photos. I hate it on them. On this guy, it's actually pretty funny. "I'm Jian. I perform miracles, by the grace of God, and I'm about to perform one today." He frames up my face with his hands. "We'll transform those caterpillars of yours into eyebrows, we'll discover something lovely under that utter mop of hair, and we'll put a peel and a mask on your face that will even out all that blotchy, patchy skin. When I'm done with you, you'll walk into rooms and people will stare."

They certainly stare at him, but I'm pretty sure I'm not interested in his brand of help. "This might be more than—"

Elizabeth shakes her head and points. "No. Go."

It turns out that I'm more afraid of her than I am of being transformed into a beauty pageant contestant, so I march. And two hours later, when I look in the mirror, I have to admit. Jian knows his stuff. I don't look like him.

I look like me.

But a movie star version.

It's startling, honestly.

I was worried he'd pluck me into having girly eyebrows. He didn't. He just cleaned them up so they aren't grandpa-bushy. He took out a lot of nose-hairs too, and I might have screamed once. Or twice. And the haircut—I thought my Great Clips haircut was a transformation, but this is so far beyond that—I'm not even sure how to compare them.

I look like a model.

"I told you he looks like Chad Michael Murray."

"Girl. You have the sight." He high fives her, and I hate it, but I'm actually feeling a little left out. Jian isn't what I'm used to, but he's pretty funny.

And he really does work miracles.

If he also rocks multi-colored highlights, platform shoes, and an orange and brown plaid suit, well. We can't all be the same, can we? I may not be floating on my way out, but I'm in a pretty good mood.

Right up until we pay.

"I'm sorry, but did you say it's fourteen *hundred* dollars?" I blink. "Are you sure you don't mean it's fourteen dollars?"

The receptionist laughs. "You're cute."

My hand's actually shaking as I hand the black credit card that grandmother gave me to her. She has to tug to free it from the pressure of my fingertips.

"He's hilarious, isn't he?" Elizabeth pretends it's a

joke, but then she whips her head around and glares. "It's not even your money."

I pop my elbow on the counter and turn to face Elizabeth, blocking my face a bit with my arm. "You don't think she'll get angry that I spent so much on a haircut?"

Elizabeth's brow furrows. "Oh, Emerson."

"Is that a no? Or a yes?"

"You're cuter than a puppy, and I'm exceedingly qualified to say that."

That irritates me, and the more I think about it, the more upset I become. We're in the elevator on the way down, soothing music playing, and I'm fuming. Right as it stops, I turn on her. "You know, you guys all think I'm a country bumpkin or something for being appalled at spending fourteen hundred dollars on a men's haircut, but that's barely less than my tuition was for an entire semester. The kind of money you people throw around in a single day could completely transform a lot of people's lives."

She looks up at me impassively. "I know that, Emerson, but in order to fit in with *people like me*, you'll have to learn to meet or exceed their expectations. I know this felt like a waste of money to you, but trust me. I don't waste it lightly."

For some reason, she actually seems to mean it.

She's full of a lot of confusing incongruities. She went to Duke. She has rich parents who let her use their building for her charity. She knows the people and wears the right clothes and presumably gets pricey haircuts. But she also offers to make deals with me to raise money for her animal shelter. Why not just dip into her trust fund a little? Or beg her daddy for more help?

I think about the conversation she was having

with her mother. They didn't seem very supportive of her chosen passion. They told her to grow up, in fact, and it almost sounded like they were saying she needed to marry someone rich if she wanted to keep doing good things like saving animals. Maybe she's right.

Maybe I need to spend a little more time watching and learning and a little bit less time judging.

"Sorry," I mutter.

I'm not at all surprised when we walk through the front doors of Saks Fifth Avenue as our next stop. The main differences between this shopping trip and the time the lady brought clothing to me is the sheer volume of options and the fact that Elizabeth asks my opinion.

The first time she does, it surprises me. "Do you care what I think?"

She blinks. "Of course I do. If you hate it, when would you ever wear it?"

Huh. I tell her, "I hate it."

She chats with one of the clerks. "More understated than this, please."

Two hours later, I hand the clerk Grandmother's credit card. I can't bring myself to look at the total amount, but Elizabeth seems so sure that she won't mind. It galvanizes me.

"You'll deliver this to the Richmond residence." It's not a question, I realize.

The woman ringing us up just nods.

I think we're done, but apparently not. "That's not nearly enough," she says. "Next we need shoes and suits from Bergdorf Goodman."

"But why—"

"Their suits are about the same, but they have the best tailors, and. . ." She lowers her voice as if this is a shameful secret. "They're actually doing a once a year sale on shoes."

"Heaven forbid anyone hear that we're shopping a sale," I say.

She laughs. "It's not something people brag about in your grandmother's circles. Trust me."

"Don't you mean your circles?"

"Sure."

By the time we're finally finished, I feel like I could eat an entire cow. Well, if I ate animals, anyway. "Can we get food? Please?"

Elizabeth pats my arm. "You've been a moderately good boy. I suppose that's fine."

"I'm picking the place." I stare at her, daring her to argue with me.

"Sure," she says. "You pick."

But when we reach my pick, she stops and stares. "Lefteris Gyro? Really? A Greek sandwich stand?"

"Their falafels are amazing."

"But they spelled things all wrong." She's looking at the menu like my grandmother looks at me—preparing herself for disappointment.

"Trust me." I grab her wrist and drag her to the counter to order. "I'll have a falafel with stuffed grape leaves on the side, and an order of hummus and chips." I glance at her. "And she wants. . ."

"I'll have the grilled octopus and a philly cheesesteak."

"Did you order the octopus because it's the most expensive thing on the menu?" I hand the guy my card.

"Of course." She laughs. "But also, I'm guessing you've never had it, and you need to start getting used to eating weird things. Rich people love weird stuff, so even if you hate it, learning to choke it down is a skill."

"Choke it down?" The man handing me my credit card looks like he's going to spit in my falafel.

"Did it escape your notice that I won't eat meat? Seafood's included."

She slaps her forehead. "Well. Huh."

"Is it not allowed to be vegetarian?"

"I mean, it is, but very few rich people have that kind of resolve."

"You don't have many vegetarian friends?"

"Including you, I have one." She winks.

"That's not impressive."

"And rich people don't care what you think," she says. "That's what? Your fourth lesson today? I hope you're keeping up."

I fold my arms. "Well, some of these lessons, I plan to ignore."

She smiles. "Nice job. If I do this right, you'll stay you, but you'll be able to blend in when necessary."

"Kindness is the one thing both my moms share."

"Both your moms?" She looks genuinely curious.

I inhale. "My mom died when I was eleven. I spent more than a year in group homes before I met Seren, but when I did, my entire life changed."

"Kind of like the day of the funeral, huh?"

I shrug. "Not really. I mean, I knew I had a dad, and I knew he wasn't a great one, and all that's still true."

"Yeah, but Richmond Steel's worth a *lot*. I think the family has billions."

"I'm not going to lie and say I don't want it, but even if Grandmother writes me into her will like she's offering, it won't really change my life substantially." As I say the words, I realize she's right. "If I hadn't met her, I'd have found a new job, and I'd have worked hard like Mom taught me, and I'd have won Lisa back all the same."

"Which mom works hard?"

I sigh. "I feel a little disloyal saying this. My biological mom wasn't lazy or anything, but she would blow off work any chance she got. She didn't love it. She didn't appreciate it. And I think she felt cheated—like she had to work so hard because life had been unfair to her."

"It sounds like life *had* been unfair to her."

"If you'd ever met Seren, you'd know that was true for her as well, but she never acted like that. She still never does. She's the kind of person who just stands up after a disaster, cleans up the mess even when it's not her fault, and keeps on going. She's quiet about it, but she's probably the hardest worker I know."

"She sounds. . .delightful."

I can't tell whether she means it, but I decide not to pick a fight. "She is, and so is my dad."

"Your real dad?"

I chuckle. "Yes. As far as I'm concerned, Dave and Seren are my real parents. I mean, sometimes I'll say they aren't, but I don't mean it. It's complicated."

"Sounds like it. But are you sad about your dad? You just found out he died."

"I never met Alistair, and I'll probably never really think of him as my dad. I don't care that he died."

"I'd be careful saying that around your grandmother," she says. "I imagine that would upset her."

She's probably right.

"Losing her son was hard, I'm sure, and she lost her husband a few years ago, too. She may be kind of difficult to deal with, but she's probably hurting, just like you."

"I'm not really hurting," I say. "I actually think my life's pretty great."

"Sure." She nods. "You just lost your job, your girlfriend, and your dad in the same week. Sounds like a walk in the park."

Our food comes before I can say much, but once the lady leaves, I feel like I should explain. "The girlfriend and job thing are temporary," I say. "I was a little upset, but I knew I would fix it. It's like when your light goes out on your car. It's a hassle to drive to the car parts place and buy a new headlight, and it's annoying to need to get out the tools to replace it, but you know it'll be fine."

"Sounds like your breakup really wrecked you."

"You're kidding, but it would have—if I thought it was real."

"So you talk to Lisa, still?"

"I'm giving her space," I say. "But trust me. She and I will be back together soon."

"I admire your upbeat spirit."

"And like I said about my dad, when I was a kid, it upset me that I didn't have a dad. I hated that Mom never talked about him, and later I hated that he didn't take care of her and me, but I have a dad now, and he's amazing. I didn't meet Alistair, but I feel confident in saying that Dave was at least as good as he would have been."

"Well, that's good, I guess."

"Emerson?" A voice I'd know anywhere—although it's a bit shrill right now—calls my name.

When I twist around in my seat, there she is. Three tables over, Lisa's sitting down with a co-worker, Celeste.

"Let me guess," Elizabeth says.

"What?" I turn back, still a little distracted. For all

my big talk, I'm actually really nervous right now. I haven't seen Lisa once since she dumped me.

"That's her, no?" Elizabeth asks.

I swallow, but before I've said a word, Lisa's standing by our table. "Emerson." Her eyes dart toward Elizabeth. "What are you doing here?"

"We're eating," Elizabeth says. "I assume that's what you're planning on doing here too. It *is* a restaurant."

When did Elizabeth get so catty? I'm staring at her when Lisa grabs my shoulder.

"Are you on a date?"

"No," I say at the same time Elizabeth says, "Yes."

Lisa's half smile shows me that she's confused, but pleased.

"I guess you're right. Is it really a date, when you're just eating lunch with your boyfriend after a day of shopping?" Elizabeth shrugs. "I guess maybe not. I enjoy it, but for you, shopping probably feels like work."

"What?" Lisa's glaring at Elizabeth now.

"I pretty much wore him out, but you know how it goes. When you find a new one, you make him throw out everything the last girl picked out. I like my guy to look just right." Elizabeth's half-shrug, half-smug-smile combo is practically lethal.

Lisa's nostrils flare and her hand tightens on my shoulder. "Can we talk for a minute?"

"Honey, we're in a bit of a hurry. We have that thing at your grandmother's later. Remember?" Elizabeth's eyes shift to my falafel pointedly.

"Oh." Lisa releases me. "Maybe I'll call you tonight, then?"

"Are you a friend from work?" Elizabeth asks.

"Because if so, maybe don't bother. He's not looking for a job anymore."

"I heard you got a new job," Lisa says, "but I also heard a rumor today, and they may be firing—"

"Trust me," Elizabeth says. "No matter who gets fired, he won't be going back to that horrible place."

I kick her under the table.

Elizabeth looks like a glass-topped lake. Utterly smooth and delightful.

Did I miss and hit the table leg?

"I'll call you." I realize that Lisa has only spoken to me, while Elizabeth has addressed her repeatedly. Elizabeth may sound snippy, but Lisa's been the rude one, honestly.

"Why would you call?" I ask. "As my girlfriend said, I found a new job, and I'm doing great. It doesn't really matter who was fired." That feels really good to say, even if it's not strictly true.

I don't have a new job—not even a trial one. You can't audition for being a grandson, but that's all I'm doing. An audition that comes with a job if all goes well.

"She's really your girlfriend?" Lisa asks.

"I really am." Elizabeth doesn't even look upset.

Even though Lisa continues to ignore her. "But we just broke up."

"Wait." Elizabeth stands up. "This is *Lisa?*" She half-laughs. "But I thought you said she was 'really beautiful.'" Her air quotes are probably too much.

When Lisa balls up her hand at her side, I actually worry that she's going to punch Elizabeth. She doesn't, luckily, but it looks like a near miss. "I'll call you later."

"If he doesn't answer, don't get upset." Elizabeth widens her eyes. "Emerson and I usually stay pretty *busy.*"

Oh my word. She's insinuating. . .

But when Lisa gets back to the table, she grabs her purse and storms off.

"Wait," Celeste says. "Our food." She waves at me a little sheepishly, and then darts off after her friend.

"That went really well." Elizabeth sits down and leans back in her chair with a grin. "Better than I thought it could, actually."

I lean toward her. "Are you kidding right now?"

She smiles. "You were right. You *are* getting back together."

"How on earth did you get that from what just happened?"

"No woman on earth would catfight in a restaurant over a man she doesn't care about." She shrugs. "When she calls later, do not answer. I mean it. You'll undo everything we did today with your pathetic, puppy-dog replies. Girls say they want the sweet guy, but they're lying."

Once we get back to the house, I get stuck spending the afternoon talking to Grandmother's CEO and CFO, learning the basics about what main chan-nels of production Richmond Steel focuses on, and what their plans are for the next year. But when I finally finish the back-to-back meetings, I check my phone.

Lisa called.

Twice.

Bafflingly, it seems like Elizabeth was right.

ELIZABETH

It's strange to be dating someone who has access to so much money that he could literally pave the driveway at his house in gold bricks, because staring at Posh Pet's bank account—the ten grand hasn't hit yet—is depressing. I couldn't even pave a shoe box with regular bricks.

I mean, we're not *really* dating.

But as I watched him drop what some people spend on a downpayment on a house on clothing and a haircut in one day, I could see his frustration. I felt the same way. But walking and talking like a leopard means that you need spots.

And spots around here aren't cheap.

He's clearly still so new to everything. He hasn't noticed that I only said that I *attended* Duke—which is true. I never said I graduated there. Because his grandmother didn't press, I got away with that statement, but most people would have followed up with a question about when I graduated and in what major. Our world is full of carefully phrased explanations, casual name-dropping, and unacknowledged label recognition.

Meanwhile, some of us are faking it, because our family hasn't really made it in a very long time.

As an expert at faking it, I can attest that it's a stupid way to live.

And yet, it's all I know.

Which is why I'm stuck staring in the mirror at my fourth outfit. I haven't had a first day of work in four years, and I'm stupidly nervous. Not because I think Ace will fire me, but because I don't want to give him any cause for it.

Other than dealing with unloved and neglected animals, I really have no experience. I'm not even sure exactly what he wants me to do. I'm about to rip off the boring beige suit I inherited from my mom—she should have known she was never going to get back down to my size when she bought it—when my phone bings.

It's Emerson. GOOD LUCK ON YOUR FIRST DAY OF WORK.

I can't help smiling. He really is a big old golden lab puppy. What was that woman thinking, dumping him? Was it the hair?

Either way, I bet she's regretting it heartily right now.

I HOPE YOU DIDN'T ANSWER WHEN SHE CALLED.

He doesn't reply. That's not promising.

PLEASE TELL ME YOU STAYED STRONG.

Still nothing. I'm about one inch from driving to his house when he finally replies.

I IGNORED HER. BUT I CAN CALL HER TODAY, RIGHT?

NO. BAD EMERSON. NOT UNTIL I GIVE THE ALL CLEAR.

ARE YOU SURE?

VERY.

And now I've got my purse, I'm kissing the dogs and clipping Lucky's leash to her collar so I can drop her off on my way, and then I'm *en route* to the car. I totally forgot that I was going to panic-change clothes again.

That's probably for the best. The suit's fine—like it even matters what I wear. No outfit will improve my basic competency at a desk job for which I'm utterly unqualified.

When I stop at the shelter, Lucky looks at me with wide eyes, her ears all the way back, almost flattened on her head.

"I know," I say. "You don't like to stay here. I've spoiled you. But if you're never here, no one can fall in love with you and adopt you. Maybe your new owner's right around the corner."

She ducks her head.

"I mean it," I say. "Someone who comes in there today might need a high-energy bestie. A runner, or maybe, like, someone who loves frisbees. Ooh! I know. Maybe someone with sheep." Stupid, Elizabeth. Who has sheep around here? I can practically hear Lucky thinking the same thing.

But when I tug on her leash, she vaults over the console in my car and out onto the ground, pressed up tightly against my side, barely pulling as I walk. It's very nearly a miracle, honestly. I've never had a dog pull as persistently and as obnoxiously as Lucky, not in ten years. She's usually just so excited to be moving that she gets pushy. Only, not today. She notably slows as we approach the door, forcing me to almost drag her.

I crouch down. "It's not that bad, girl, I swear."

She licks my face, blanketing me in slobber, and

probably smearing my mascara. One of these days, I'm going to break down and buy waterproof. . .

"Don't make me feel worse, okay?"

When I walk her inside, I'm a little disappointed. Ruth is here, since it's a Monday, and she grimaces. "Sunday didn't go very well."

"But Hannah said she took six to the event at Petco."

Ruth shrugs.

"How many were adopted yesterday?"

"One."

I close my eyes. At the rate things are going, I'm going to be taking dozens of animals right back to the shelter to die if I can't figure out how to keep this place. It's time for me to broach the deal with Emerson.

"After work," I whisper to Lucky.

She still cries when I leave, but I tell myself it's because she doesn't want to go in the kennel and not because she misses me. I'm surrounded by dogs and cats who need homes, and I can't take them all in myself, no matter how much I want to save them all.

On the way to the address of Ace's office, I think about the fact that we've only had four adoptions in the past week. That would always concern me, but it's especially problematic right now. I have a hundred and nineteen animals in my care. Forty-one cats, six birds, and seventy-two dogs. If I show up with all those animals—they'll have to slate them all for elimination almost immediately. They were all set to be killed when I took them, but it still hurts to consider so many of them going on the block.

I feel like I'm entirely to blame for the mass execution now looming, but I can't think what more I can do to prevent it.

When I pull up in front of the building Ace gave me, I'm confused. It doesn't look like an office at all. It looks like a French-inspired brownstone or something. Didn't Easton say he was doing well? When I park around back, I realize there are quite a few cars. There's even another woman walking in at the same time.

"I'm Rebekah." She smiles broadly, and I notice her teeth are lovely. Her hair's very, very processed, and it shows at the ends, but her genuine smile more than makes up for any other deficiencies. "You must be Elizabeth."

I nod.

"Mr. Devonshire told me you were coming, and I have to say, I'm delighted that he hired you."

"What do you do?" I ask.

Rebekah laughs. "I should maybe have led with that. I'm his office manager, but I've been his *de facto* assistant for over two years, and it's high time he found someone to do all the odds and ends that entails. Someone who's not me."

Right. I'm going to be doing odds and ends. That makes sense.

Rebekah unlocks the door—apparently at eight-fifty-one, we're the first ones here. "What did he tell you?"

"Um, not a lot."

"Do you have questions?"

"I might need to know more before I have questions."

"What do you know?"

"Nothing, really," I say. "He didn't even tell me the name of the company."

Rebekah freezes in the doorway, blinking. "Are you serious?"

It feels ridiculous now that I'm saying it. I needed a job, and Easton told me Ace needed someone. Then I saw him at a party, and he said I could start today.

But clearly it's not a normal way to get a job.

Of course his office manager finds it strange.

"Are you friends from school?"

"Not exactly," I say. "But my brother and Ace are good friends."

"Ace?"

I freeze. "Um, Mr. Devonshire."

"You call him *Ace?*"

"You don't?" I'm actually a little embarrassed to realize that I don't know his real name.

"We're pretty relaxed—gaming companies tend to be from what I hear—but I've never heard anyone call him that. You're referring to Austin Devonshire, our president and CEO, right?"

At that exact moment, Ace screams into the tiny parking lot and slams his white 911 into a parking spot. He hops out and closes the door, smiling and waving. "Celly!"

Rebekah blinks. "Didn't you say your name's Elizabeth?"

I swallow. "When I was a kid, I was obsessed with celery and peanut butter. For a while they called me Celery, but that was long. So it became Celly."

"Hey, Ace," I say. "I got here early, and now Rebekah's a little freaked out. Sorry."

Ace barely stops in time to keep from crashing into me and drops an arm around my shoulders. "Wouldn't be doing things right if she wasn't. I poached her from an investment bank, if you can believe it, because I needed someone to bring an air of legitimacy to the place."

"Legitimacy?"

"Dad thought I was wasting my time playing video games all day." He tosses his head to herd us into the building. "He had a point. I kind of was. But what he didn't get is that I was also product testing. I'm crap at designing games, and I can't code to save my life, but I'm amazing at finding redundancies, slow spots, time wastes, and streamlining what people care about in the games. So I bought myself some eggheads and we were making good products. We just didn't know how to keep the business side together."

We're in the center of the brownstone now, and it's more functional for a gaming company than I expected. There's a big kitchen with two large tables, and the rest of the room's just sofas with televisions and gaming consoles. "We do all the product testing here—and we really do test it."

Of course they do. . . Surely they're not just sitting around playing games all day. Why on earth would his dad be skeptical?

"The real magic happens upstairs, but we have to keep the product testers happy, too." His grin's become almost flirty, so I fling his arm away.

"Well, if you'd warned me, I would've called you Austin."

"You didn't even remember my real name, did you?"

"Is that my fault? Did you or Easton ever once use it?"

"Do you know how I got that name?" He smiles. "Your brother was mocking me, because every single time we played Grand Theft Auto, or Mario Kart—you name it. In every car game, he smoked me. He started calling me Ace as a way to rub it in."

"You showed him," I say. "I mean." I gesture at the mooshy looking sofas and the televisions. "Look at all this."

"Hey, now," he says. "My dad bankrolled the startup, yes, but I've been in the black for more than two years."

"Enough in the black to pay for your lifestyle?" I ask.

People are filtering through the back door, some of them climbing stairs, and some of them headed for the televisions in this main room.

"Maybe you should take this into your office," Rebekah whispers.

Ace laughs. "Yeah—see why I hired her?"

"It would be great if you could walk me through why you hired *me* and what exactly you want me to do."

I follow Ace toward what I imagine was the master bedroom at one point. It has it's own *en suite* bathroom, for sure. Once Rebekah has ushered us over, she backs out and pulls the door almost closed. "I'll be going over the expense reports when you're ready."

He groans. "Fine, fine." But once the door's shut, he says, "Listen, I know you and my dad both see me as a screwup, but that's why I did hire you. That kind of contempt makes me work harder."

I don't say a word, but he senses my thoughts.

"And I do work hard," he says. "I cleared a two hundred grand profit last year, after paying everyone and all the costs. And this year, I'm on track to more than double it."

I'm so used to Easton talking about going public that I haven't even thought about having a business that's earning a sustainable long-term profit. "You don't want to sell it?"

He shakes his head. "Never. If I sell it, or if I were ever to go public, I'd have no control over what happens to my people. I have seventeen employees, and I care about them. They're good folks. Right now, they have insurance and a good vacation policy and great retirement benefits. What would happen if Nintendo or PopCap came in here?"

I shrug.

"That's the point. Who knows?"

There are a lot of things I didn't know about Austin Devonshire other than his name, apparently. "Alright, well, I can only stay until one every day, especially right now. I've got a lot of fuzzy animals to save."

"Speaking of, I've been thinking of adopting some cats. They could live here full time. I think most everyone would like that. I asked around and no one's allergic."

I can't help smiling. "Cats need litter boxes to be kept clean, they need annual shots, and they need regular flea treatments."

"You think I'm really dumb." He looks a little sad. "Like, nonfunctional."

"No, but I think a lot of people take on animals without much idea of what their care entails, and the animals are the ones who suffer."

"Dude, I'd take care of them. But if you have a nice one, or like, maybe two so they have a buddy, or three would be alright, can you bring them over?"

He seems to be serious. "We always need good homes." With all the people here, some of the friendlier cats would be in heaven. "But what about weekends?"

"We always have someone here," he says.

"What about holidays?"

"Can you leave them alone for a day or two?" He looks worried. "I thought you could."

"Two days, max," I say. "And you'd need an auto-waterer and feeder."

"Or I could bring them home with me?"

I shrug. "Maybe. Cats can get confused and lost that way."

"Okay, I'll think about it. But I still think we'd do pretty well. Even at Christmas, we never close for more than two days."

That's either a very sad commentary on his role as an employer, or a sign that the people here really love their jobs. The jury's out on which. "But back to what you need me to do?"

He walks me through it, but Rebekah wasn't wrong. Basically, he's here so often that a lot of details fall through the cracks. Personal stuff, business things, and a strange mixture. "Once you get caught up on some of this—" He gestures at a pile of paperwork he wants me to sort through. "Then we can see whether you might have time to help Rebekah out, too."

"Sure." I wind up working on a table in the corner most of the day, but he assures me that he's ordered a desk that will be in soon.

"I didn't think I'd find someone so fast," he says. "So I told the furniture lady that two weeks was fine."

"Well, I do appreciate it," I say.

"Easton says you're having trouble getting a loan?"

"Sort of," I say. "Mom's selling off the building my shelter has been in for years. I've got to find a new place."

"That doesn't sound like the Elizabeth I know." He lifts his eyebrows. "When you were a teenager, you'd have gone after your mom with a paintball gun if you had to."

"I've evolved," I say. "Thankfully."

As soon as the clock hits one, I race back to the shelter and start prepping the new animals for their glamour shots. I'm not quite as good as the lady who usually comes in, but she texted to say she had the flu.

Once I get some good ones, I start posting on our page. It's probably the most tedious thing about what we do, but also maybe the most important. These sweet little pets have no one to advocate for them except for me. Photos are the frontline in most cases.

We do have two late-in-the-day adoptions while I'm working, which is pretty nice. One of them comes from the first post I made today. They rushed over for the very shaky terrier that I hope will relax some once he's in a home without a hundred other critters. Before I've even quite finished, the clock is singing that it's five. I stretch slowly, and then I hop up to get animal food ready and flip the sign over to closed.

While I'm feeding them, I watch the cats pretty closely. We do have a brother and sister—both already spayed and neutered—who are really closely bonded. One is cream, and one is tortoiseshell, and they often sit in a yin and yang position, their tails lashing one another's faces. It's really sweet. I've been worried they'd be separated. . . Maybe they'd be a good fit for Ace's unconventional office.

I try to imagine a bunch of programmers petting them, or a bunch of gamers chatting, while these two rub up against their knees.

I've almost decided to try them out tomorrow morning when there's an awful cacophony from the dog kennels. The very best thing about cats is that they don't bark when people show up. Usually, they hide. I hate having to tell people that we're closed, but when I've let people in after hours before, sometimes I've been stuck here for more than an hour, and I have too many things to do today.

I've been bracing myself all day to tell Emerson that his company's the one buying the shelter. I really do have to ask him to help, but I'm worried he'll be mad I didn't tell him sooner. Or maybe he'll tell me it's my problem. He does barely know me, after all.

When I get to the door—all of the dogs are still losing their ever-loving minds—I'm surprised to see that my visitor is Emerson. When I swing the door open, I discover he's not even alone. His Uncle Bentley's with him.

"Emerson said you might need funds soon, so I thought I'd bring this by." He holds out an envelope that I assume is my check. "He said he wanted to see the shelter and invited me to come. I hope it's okay."

"Oh," I say. "Sure. Thanks so much for this." His check is going to save us this month.

"Sorry it's not more," he says. "That's what we had left over."

Ten grand, just sitting around. Must be nice. "I really appreciate it."

"Then level with me," Bentley says. "You're not really dating, right?"

Emerson freezes.

"I mean, last week, you were with Lisa." Bentley's smile is pretty confident. "This is some scheme to make your grandmother happy?"

"I wasn't with Lisa last week," Emerson says. "She dumped me the week before that, but I just hadn't really accepted it."

"And then in seven days, you just got over her and met someone new?" Bentley's clearly skeptical.

"You've never been in a new place, have you?" I step closer to Emerson and slide my hand down toward his, lacing our fingers together. "A place where you felt out of your element, a place where you didn't fit in?"

Bentley frowns. "Of course I have."

"Then you'll know exactly what drew Emerson and I together."

"You felt out of place?" Bentley snorts. "Nice try."

I squeeze just a little closer, and Emerson loosens up a tiny hair, which is nice. "I have *always* felt out of place at the parties Mom and Dad made me attend. Do you meet a lot of socialites who run animal shelters?"

He frowns again.

"What about socialites who flunk out of school?" It's not helping that Emerson's standing entirely still, saying nothing. I squeeze his hand.

His eyes lift toward Bentley's. "That's what I liked about her."

"That she failed out?" Bentley chuckles. "Nice try. You pushed harder than anyone in school."

"No." He's shaking his head. "That she succeeded at the thing that mattered to her. The second we interacted, which first happened at the funeral." He turns toward me, his eyes meeting mine slowly. "I could tell she wasn't like all those other phonies. She'd argue with her parents about her shelter in the middle of a party. She'd go out in public with her hair in a messy topknot, if that's what a dog needed. And she would jump to my rescue when I was hopelessly sticking my foot in my mouth, just because she could."

"And you just forgot about Lisa?" Bentley still sounds unconvinced. "Because—"

"It's not that I forgot about her." Emerson's talking to Bentley, but he's still looking at me. "It's that I realized I'm a better fit with Elizabeth." When he smiles, it's small, like the beginning of the sunrise in the very early morning.

And his words.

They sure seem authentic. I reach up without thinking, tucking his hair back with my free hand. "And I immediately realized that he was unlike all the other idiots I'd been shoved at my entire life. This guy's the real deal."

Emerson's eyes drop to my mouth, and I realize he's going to kiss me. To convince Bentley, of course, but it would still be our first kiss. *My* first kiss in more than a year. My breathing gets a little choppy, and I'm not sure why I'm so strung out. It's not like I've never kissed anyone. We both want Bentley to buy the story, right? His mouth is just a tiny bit open, and at the thought of him kissing me, I shiver, just a bit.

But when Emerson's other hand grabs my waist, I shift, and my foot bumps the dog food bin. The lid falls to the ground with a clatter, and all the dogs that have slowly calmed down are off again.

"Wow," Emerson says, still looking at me. "That's a lot of dogs barking."

"They're usually louder around dinner time," I say, realizing that we are *not* about to kiss. Hopefully our interaction still calmed Bentley's suspicions a little. "Hey, do you guys want to help? I just finished with the cats, but you can meet some of the dogs."

Judging from the look on Emerson's face, he's not much of a dog person, but Bentley looks excited. "Sure."

"Do you have a dog?" I always ask that—most people say yes. The ones who don't often have a reason.

"Whoa." Bentley holds up his hands. "You're going to start pushing cute little puppies at me now, aren't you?"

The black lab we call Shadow, the German shepherd I named Storm, and the golden retriever who's next to them are barking so loudly that the combination may burst my eardrums. "Guys." I call them to order a few times, and they all sit down. After a few more haphazard yelps, they settle in.

Bentley isn't looking at them, though. He crouches down in front of Lucky. She wasn't barking. She was sitting still, watching me intently. "This one really likes you."

I lift two food bowls. "I bring food. They all like me."

"Hey, that's Lucky." Now Emerson crouches down next to Bentley. "She was stuck in a crate for twenty-three or more hours a day for almost her entire life until a few days ago. She hates being in a kennel so much that Elizabeth's been taking her home with her."

"I was worried about my two Pomeranians," I say, "but she's really careful with them. She'll run a human over in a heartbeat, but around them, she crouches down on the ground and lets them bite and swing over her."

"That's pretty amazing," Emerson says, "that she's careful with small things."

"Border collies are really smart," I say. "But I doubt she's been properly socialized. Time with other dogs is probably exactly what she needed."

"That, and some nice long runs."

"Runs?" Bentley straightens.

"I know—you hate running." Emerson's eyes are dancing, and he looks exactly twenty percent more handsome when he's happy like that.

"Actually, the doc told me I need to be out jogging more." He makes a face. "Apparently my exclusive weight-lifting regimen was fine when I was young, but cardio health requires a little bit of, well, cardiovascular work."

"You don't say," Emerson says.

"I was thinking of getting a running buddy."

"You just said you didn't want a dog," I say. "Now you're just being mean—getting my hopes up."

"Besides," Emerson says. "With all your traveling, you can't have a dog."

"They have places you can leave them," he says. "But I told you—I'm not traveling anymore. Not very often, anyway."

Emerson doesn't look convinced.

"How about I take Lucky home with me tonight?" he asks. "If you're taking her to your place anyway."

"Like, a trial?" I quirk one eyebrow.

He nods slowly. "Maybe."

I'm a little surprised at how disappointed I am. That's dumb. I do not have the bandwidth to manage a border collie. I should be delighted. Though, with what I know about the breed, I doubt she'll even make it the whole night. "She's pretty rambunctious. And if you take her for a jog, just be aware that she still pulls pretty badly."

"I think I can take it."

"It gets annoying fast."

"I hear that about myself a lot," Bentley says.

I laugh. "I doubt that."

"Are you hitting on my uncle right now? In front of me?"

"Who are you?" I wink.

"You're rude," Emerson says.

"Oh! You're that Emerson guy I'm dating. Sorry, I forgot you were here for a moment."

"You said I look like a movie star, but now you've forgotten I exist." He shakes his head.

"You?" Bentley asks. "What movie star could you possibly resemble?"

"I think he looks a lot like Chad Michael Murray," I say. "He was in—"

"I know who he is," Bentley says. "He's filming a movie with Emerson's brother."

"He's done filming now." Emerson huffs. "And it's annoying that she's comparing me to him, right?"

"Wait, do you mean *Jake Priest* is your brother?" I can hardly believe it. "Really?"

Bentley's smiling. "Why am I not surprised that he didn't tell you?"

"That's. . .insane."

"Oh, no." Emerson groans. "Don't tell me you're a fan."

"I was," I say. "Until he beheaded that cow in *Iron Cross*."

"It didn't really die," Emerson says. "It was CGI."

"Still." I fold my arms. "That was it for me."

Emerson laughs. "I'm not sure I've ever been more grateful that Jake's a cow murderer. Can you imagine anything worse than dating someone who has a crush on your brother?"

"Actually, speaking of strange coincidences, my brother called. Guess who my parents are selling this building to?"

Emerson freezes, and his eyes cut sideways. "Bentley?"

Bentley shakes his head. "It's not me."

"Richmond Steel."

Emerson's shoulders slump. "I was afraid you were going to say that. Grandmother was talking about a new warehouse today, and it felt like a weird coincidence."

"Do you think she might reconsider?"

"She said it was a done deal and that the penalty clauses were really steep."

Which means. . .I'm officially screwed.

"I mean, we can talk to her," Emerson says.

"She's not very flexible," Bentley says. "Never has been."

I can't even look at them, not right now. I didn't realize how much hope I was pinning on Emerson asking his grandmother to spare the shelter.

"This may not be what you want to hear right now," Bentley says, "but I have a great realtor friend. Maybe he could help you find a new place."

Sadly, that may be where we are, and even worse, my only hope there is selling Hottie. This day just gets worse and worse.

❧ II ❧

EMERSON

By the time I turned five, Mom told me we'd lived in eleven places. At the time, each new move felt like an adventure. My belongings easily fit into a shark backpack, and I wasn't worried about what it meant that we kept moving.

By the time I started third grade, I was really tired of moving all the time, and I sort of understood that we weren't living in very nice places. None of my friends slept on sleeping bags. They all had beds. But when I asked about why I didn't have one, Mom got sad. I knew not to ask again.

The very last time we went shopping for an apartment is one of the things I actually remember pretty clearly from my time with Mom. The first few places we looked at were really, really bad. After the third apartment, which had so many cockroaches, she found one twiddling its antennae at her from the top of my head, Mom sat down on the very dirty floor and just started to cry.

Our real estate agent was so annoyed that he fired us.

I'm sure that the tiny fee he was getting from whatever junk pile we found wasn't worth the trouble. But the agent who's helping us today, Dad and Bentley's friend Bernie, is really nice. He's already offered to donate half his commission to Elizabeth to help with closing costs, and he's patient.

"Your dad was a disaster when he was shopping for a place," he says. "I was there, in the moment he first saw your mom."

"Wait, he was? You were?"

Bernie chuckles. "We were inseparable in high school, your dad, Bentley, and me. Now you'd think I was the loser of the group, but in high school, it was your dad."

"No way." My dad's really good looking, funny, and smart. Plus, Grandma and Grandpa have plenty of money.

"The trash business isn't exactly glamorous," Bernie says. "Kids kind of picked on Dave."

"Really?" That's hard for me to imagine, but I suppose everyone has their own secret miseries.

"They called him Garbage Guy."

"That's creative," Elizabeth says. "Did they call anyone else Poopy Pants?"

"No, but there was a guy whose mom was an executive with Huggies, and they called him Pull-ups." He shrugs. "It was high school. Being stupid is kind of the thing to do."

Although Bernie's a huge step up from the realtor who abandoned Mom and me, we have about the same luck as we did that day.

"How much did you say this place was?" Elizabeth looks pained.

Bernie glances down at his phone. "Um, it's a little higher than the amount we discussed."

"Was there anything in that lower range?" she asks.

He shakes his head slowly back and forth. "I mean, nothing that you'd want to see."

"And this place falls in the category of a place you think I would want to see?"

He coughs.

And one of the shutters that was dangling from the window outside falls down with a clatter and a crash.

It makes me jump.

"My cough didn't cause that," Bernie says.

"That might actually make it worse." Elizabeth spins around, taking it all in. We're currently looking at an abandoned farmhouse that's been rezoned into a commercial area, now that the entire farm has been sold and it's only resting on a third of an acre. Clearly no one has lived here in quite some time. "I'm embarrassed to say that from the online photos, this place was my top pick."

"I mean, they didn't show the areas with termite damage," Bernie says. "So that was a little misleading."

"Or the opossum family," I say. "Or the leak in the ceiling from that water pipe."

"I think that damage was actually caused by a roof leak," Bernie says.

"No." Elizabeth juts out her bottom lip and shakes her head emphatically. "No, no, no. I can't buy this place."

"Because you can't afford it?" Bernie looks sincere.

That's when Elizabeth starts laughing, but she doesn't look amused. "That's the sad part. This is still a place that I can't afford. I knew my parents were helping me out all these years, but I guess I didn't realize how much." The laughter dies as quickly as it began, and she looks about half a millimeter away from sitting down on the floor and bawling, just like Mom did.

"Hey." I step closer. She's not really my girlfriend, but she clearly needs someone right now, and she's been great for me. Plus, Bernie thinks we're really dating, so I have to make it look authentic, right?

I slide my hand into hers, and she stiffens.

And then she sways toward me.

I catch her before she can slump over, and she turns, burying her head against my chest. My free hand's suddenly patting her back, and I'm saying, "It's fine. New places pop up all the time. We'll find something."

"I need something in less than two weeks." Her whisper turns into a quiet moan about halfway through.

"Actually, I don't think we could even close on this place in two weeks," Bernie says.

Which makes her start to bawl in earnest.

I glare at poor Bernie.

He shrugs.

"Okay, so tonight we're going to have dinner with Grandmother, and if she can't help, we'll make an official plan."

"Maybe we'll find something better," Bernie says. "We have a few more options."

But the next two places we see aren't any better. I can see why that old farmhouse was her most promising prospect. On the drive over to the Richmond Mansion to meet Grandmother, I try to find out a little more about her situation. "Things in Scarsdale are pricey," I say. "I had no idea."

"It's gotten way worse in the past few years," she says.

"How much do you have for a downpayment, exactly?" I don't tell her that running numbers and whatnot is kind of what I do, but. . . "Maybe I can help. Often things aren't as bad as they seem."

"You mean with or without my trust fund money?"

"Oh, without," I say. "You can't use your trust fund money on—"

"Ten thousand."

"Wait, do you mean the ten thousand that Bentley just gave you?"

She sighs.

"And with the trust fund?"

"Twenty-one thousand and forty-nine dollars."

I must look shocked, because she reacts.

"What?"

She drops her head against the window. "Look, the thing is, I can get more money—instead of twenty-one, it could be almost a hundred."

"That would probably be enough," I say. "With that kind of downpayment, I'm sure we can find something. What's your monthly income?"

"It varies."

"What does that mean?"

"It's a charity," she says. "I mean that some months we get more generous donations, like Bentley's, and some months, we don't."

"But surely you have some consistent benefactors."

"Well, every December, Purina donates a whole month's worth of food."

"What?"

"It's this charity grant program they have. They use the photos they take in ads or something."

"Is that it for consistent donors?"

"Mrs. Robinson donates five hundred about twice a year, like clockwork. Well, kind of like clockwork. Sometimes she's a month or two late."

"Elizabeth."

"I've been the only consistent donor, other than Mrs. Robinson and Purina." She drops her face in her hands. "I know I'm bad at this, okay?"

"If you've had such erratic sponsorship, how have you kept the shelter going? How much of your own money was going into this?"

She shrugs.

"How are you surviving?"

"I had a trust fund."

"The one that now has eleven thousand dollars in it?" I can't believe how wrong I was about her. What kind of rich person spends all their money to save dogs? Who takes no salary so that she can adopt more animals? It's irresponsible, but it's pretty big-hearted. "*You* matter more than the animals, you know."

"I'm not sure that's true," she says. "But even if it is, I've had people who take care of me. They don't have anyone."

Oh, geez. She's right, but it's depressing. "You can't save the whole world, Elizabeth."

"Look, this is going to sound stupid, I know, but so far, over the past six years we've been open and operating from that shelter, every time it looks like I can't pay for something, a way has opened up."

"A way that wasn't always just you paying for it?"

"Often, yes," she says. "But look, now I have a job, and Ace is paying me fifty bucks an hour. Twenty hours a week—that's a thousand bucks a week."

"But that's your pay for a job you're doing."

"Right, and I don't need that much. My apartment belongs to a friend of my cousin. They got it for their daughter, but she's doing study abroad, so I get to stay there for just three hundred a month plus utilities."

"But—"

"I know what I have to do now, okay? I didn't want to do it, but I can come up with a downpayment. We just need to find a place that isn't falling apart to buy."

"But first, we have one last Hail Mary." I put the car in park and look at the mansion's porch steps. "Let's see whether someone other than you can save the day for once. Maybe Granny will be feeling generous."

"Do not," Elizabeth says, "under any circumstance, call her Granny."

"She might like that name. When you convinced Uncle Bentley to take Lucky—anything's possible. I've never in my entire life thought that he might be a dog guy."

"And. . . Now I'm worried about Lucky."

"You shouldn't be," I say. "When Uncle Bentley tries something, he gives it everything he's got. I've never seen him fail."

"Yeah, well, this is just a trial."

"When I checked in today, he said they were doing okay. She's eating alright, and she's not bugging him, which is a small miracle, but apparently she's a little too energetic. No surprise there."

"Energetic?" Elizabeth cringes. "That means she's making him nuts. I bet he brings her back by the end of the week."

"Maybe he likes energetic." I climb out and head for the front door, my heart pounding at the thought of asking Grandmother for a favor.

Elizabeth jogs up the steps and grabs my arm. "One more thing," she says. "And believe me, Emerson. This is a cardinal rule."

"What?"

"Do not tell her that I'm in bad shape financially. People like her do not give in to feelings of sympathy. They appreciate strength, organization, and know-how.

If you tell her I'm broke and I've spent my trust fund on this already, she will not be moved by that."

"Duh," I say. "I already knew she was dead inside."

That, at least, makes her laugh.

But her words prove prophetic. The dinner goes remarkably well, with Elizabeth and Grandmother spending the soup course, the salad course, and half of their prime rib course discussing people they both know and how to stay on their good side. Unsurprisingly, Grandmother has a very long list of people who have royally ticked her off. It does surprise me that Elizabeth has had some run-ins with the same people. It really feels like they're bonding.

But then Elizabeth turns toward me with *the eyes*, and I realize it's time.

"Hey, so did you hear that Elizabeth runs a charity?"

Grandmother sets her fork down. "You do? That's impressive. World hunger? Facilitating the distribution of life-saving vaccinations? Providing startup capital for women in third world countries so they can provide for their families?"

Elizabeth clears her throat. "Not exactly. I run a local animal shelter."

"For dirty, diseased dogs?" Grandmother's lip curls. "Please tell me that's a joke."

"Well, when they're dirty, I bathe them," Elizabeth says. "And when they're diseased, I make sure a vet gets involved."

"Pets serve no purpose."

"I disagree," Elizabeth says. "They make the world a brighter place. They provide both service and comfort to a lot of people." She leans forward a hair. "And they're lives already in being. We have a duty to make those lives as clean, safe, and full as possible."

Grandmother grunts.

"Anyway," I say, trying to keep us on track. "She's been running the shelter for six years, all on her own."

"A lot of volunteers do come help," Elizabeth says.

"It baffles me that soup kitchens can't find servers, much less cooks, but people flock to shelters to help mangy animals." Grandmother pushes her plate forward a millimeter, and the waiter in the doorway comes and collects it.

"Maybe that's because animals aren't at fault for their situation and humans often have some culpability. It makes it easier for me to love dogs and cats."

Grandmother looks like she might take a bite out of Elizabeth.

"Supporting one doesn't mean you can't help the other." I force a smile.

"That's exactly what it means," Grandmother says. "Charitable funds are limited, so it's a zero sum game."

"Well, the material point today is that the animal shelter that Elizabeth has been running all on her own for six years is on the corner of where you're building the new warehouse," I say. "Is there any way you could possibly shift the plans a little so her parents wouldn't need to sell?"

"Did someone force your parents to sign that sale contract?" Grandmother arches an eyebrow. "Do they regret making the purchase agreement?"

"They don't know I'm here, and they'd be upset if they did," Elizabeth says. "I haven't even told them that Emerson and I are dating."

Grandmother grunts again, this time even more forcefully. "Well, at least *they* haven't lost their minds."

"I understand if there's nothing you can do to help out," I say. "But it would be awesome if there was."

"Of course I could do something. I own the whole company, and I'm the one who signed the sales documents." Grandmother leans closer to me. "I'm *choosing* not to do anything to disrupt a business deal that benefits both parties. You two look like adults, but you're both acting hopelessly naive. Wants aren't needs, and this is business."

I thought maybe I'd warm up to her, but I despise her more now than the day we met. The day she said she'd paid my mother to abort me.

"I could lie and tell you that my hands were tied. I could have lied and told you that your mother ran away from us. But I never lie about those types of things—let's call them hard truths. People lie to children about Santa and a whole host of other stupid things. It makes children idiots, and I have no use for a dolt. I certainly don't want one running things, destroying my legacy with incompetence or by making sentimental decisions."

"I'm not a child," I say. "And I don't need you to lie to me, either."

"Good, because if I did lie, you might like me more, but you'd miss out on an important lesson. We always have choices in life, and with age and experience comes improved judgment. I won't change my plans last minute because your girlfriend didn't communicate with her parents or take legal steps to protect her shelter. The livelihood of hundreds of humans rests on this deal—on our company staying strong. She's the one in charge of saving her shelter. She should have taken steps to protect what was hers."

Elizabeth doesn't even look upset, and that makes me angrier. "You know, maybe you're the one who needs a lesson. This is the whole point of family. If you really think we need to learn something, then you could teach us while you help us reach our goals."

There are a dozen ways she could offer to help, but instead she just lectures Elizabeth on her failure.

"Firstly, she's not my family," Grandmother says. "And secondly, what I'm doing with that warehouse will save us an approximate eleven million dollars over three years, ensuring the long-term viability and profitability of our company. I'm accountable to our shareholders, and I'm accountable to you for my management. If I were to sacrifice any of that to save a *dog*, what exactly would that accomplish? I'd teach her that there are no consequences for her poor judgment and preparation."

As if we're all happily getting along, the servers step forward and take my plate—my vegetable soup untouched—and what's left of Elizabeth's prime rib. Two seconds later, they're placing strawberry soufflés in front of us.

Grandmother dabs at her mouth. "I doubt you two will enjoy eating this with me sitting here, so I'll take my leave. But, so that you can't say I did nothing, I'll have my legal team earmark ten thousand dollars for your little charity. You can use it to bribe people to work on things faster at your new location, or you can use the funds to facilitate the move." She stands. "Emerson, don't forget that we have a meeting to review the financial reports you were asking about at seven a.m. tomorrow. Have a good night."

In spite of Grandmother's departure, neither of us eats our soufflé. Because one sweet thing after a river of misery is just not enough.

By the time I turned fourteen, I'd been living with Seren and Dave for almost nine months. I was helping with a lot of things around the Inn, and they even paid me for some of it. One of the things I did was help tidy rooms when the cleaning staff called in sick.

I was actually the person who unlocked the room and found Bea hiding in there. She was a year younger than me—thirteen years old. She was also asleep at one in the afternoon.

Seren and Dave had a powwow, and they let me stick around for it. The more we found out about poor little Beatrice, the more they wanted to intercede. But I'll never forget what the caseworker said when Seren asked to foster her.

"With what you know about the complications of this girl's background, why would you want to get involved? She can never be adopted, and she's got major behavioral deficiencies."

Seren's smile was sad, and it took me a moment to realize why. She didn't pity Beatrice. She pitied the social worker for not understanding what Seren thought was one of life's great truths. "I want to be involved precisely because no one else does."

That's family.

Seren didn't even know Bea—certainly she knew her less than my grandmother knows Elizabeth. But when she saw a need and she had the capacity to help, she felt that she needed to do it. That's always been the kind of person she is. Maybe it's because she was so very unlucky for so long. Or maybe she was built with a shocking capacity for love.

Either way, that's how I know my grandmother's wrong.

She wanted to teach me a lesson, but I've already learned plenty of lessons from a much better teacher. You don't help people because you owe them. You don't help people because they're worthy. You do it because you can, and because maybe no one else will.

"Hey, at least she's donating ten grand." Elizabeth pokes at the top of her soufflé and watches it jiggle. "That's better than nothing."

I'm not sure how she's so impassive. "You have to be disappointed."

She shrugs. "I mean, sure. But it was always a Hail Mary. Those almost never work."

"One in twelve," I say. "Or that's what my coach told me in high school."

"You played football?" I hate how shocked she looks.

"For one glorious season," I say. "Then I got sacked, broke my collarbone, and Mom forbade it." I can't help chuckling. "She really tried to support us in anything, but she wasn't built for football. She bit her nails to the quick during those three months."

"I want to meet her," Elizabeth says.

Everyone's better for meeting Seren. "I'd like that." Except, then I remember that we're not really dating. So there's no reason for her to meet either of my parents. Not really. And in fact, meeting Dave and Seren might just lead to more questions. Not only now, but when I get back together with Lisa.

"You would?" She looks excited, which is bad.

I clear my throat and change the subject. "How did you stay so calm? Were you really assuming we'd fail?"

"Do I look calm?" Elizabeth's smile could be on the face of the queen—serene and confident.

"You do."

She sighs. "Years of practice, I suppose. My entire life was a study in disappointment."

Disappointment? I really don't know her at all.

But that makes me think about what she said about coming up with more money. "Where would you get the rest of the money for a downpayment?" I didn't think it would be something bad—she seemed so calm and matter-of-fact about it. But if she always looks that way. . . It makes me nervous.

She spears a bite of her soufflé.

"Elizabeth."

She shrugs. "I'm going to sell my horse."

"You have a horse?"

"I have a show jumper I ride, when I have time," she says.

"Oh." Poor little rich girl. I've been feeling bad for her, spending her trust fund on the animals, but she has a horse who must be worth a *lot* of money, if she can sell him for close to eighty grand. "Well, that's good, I guess."

But this time, her smile looks forced. "Yeah, things always work out."

"Do they?" I stare intently at her face.

She broadens her smile, but her eyes look dead.

"Something's wrong."

She shakes her head. "I knew it might come down to this. If I can sell one animal—to a good home—to save all the others, then I should. It's a no-brainer."

But I imagine she loves him. If her parents bought her the horse, and they want to make her grow up, I doubt they'll buy her a new one. "If you sell this horse, will you have one to ride?"

She inhales slowly. "I can always find another one."

"How did you find this one?"

Her lip trembles. "He was being thrown away." She drags in another breath. "He was a six-year-old who had won quite a bit of money on the track. An iron warrior. But his career was over, and they didn't need him."

"That sounds a little sad."

"When racehorses make it through that long, they really are insanely strong. I knew it the second I saw him."

And there it is. She loves this horse. It's breaking her heart to sell him. Suddenly, I decide that I won't let her. "Let's find another way."

She drops the fork and shoves the plate forward, standing up. "There is no other way, Emerson. But thanks for wishing there was."

"You can't sell him. You clearly love him."

"I do love him, but it's one animal against many." She nods. "Your grandmother was right."

"She wasn't. Love isn't quantitative. It's qualitative. And you love that horse, so you should look for other ways to help the animals you've pledged to save."

"Speaking of," she says. "I need to get home and work on some social media posts to get more people out to the shelter. I have ten days before those animals have to go back to the facility I saved them from.”

“Sometimes you can’t worry about numbers. My grandmother was right about one thing—you matter more than all those animals, because it’s your life. You have done great things for all of them for the past six years, but you can’t save anyone if you’re not okay.”

“I’m fine. Trust me. This setback is nothing.”

I think it may be her burning desire to help that makes me want to help her. It reminds me of Seren, actually. She’s not as solid, not as organized, maybe. But it’s there—the self-sacrifice—and that’s not something I expected to find in a trust fund baby. “I think—”

Before I can convince her to delay selling that horse, my phone rings. We both look down at it.

It’s Lisa.

“You can answer,” she says. “It’s been long enough.”

My hand shakes a little as I pick up the call. “Hello?”

“You finally answered.”

“I’ve been busy,” I say. “I’m sorry. I meant to call you back, but you beat me to it.”

“I want to see you,” Lisa says. “Can we meet?”

I glance at Elizabeth.

She nods.

“Sure,” I say. “Where?”

“Our place.”

“Okay. I’m about twenty minutes away.”

“See you then.”

I can’t believe I’m going to see Lisa. “She wants to get back together, right?”

Elizabeth shrugs. “Probably.”

“Oh, man.”

“Do you want to do that yet?” She glances up the

stairs where my grandmother just disappeared. "I doubt she's ready for it yet."

I sigh. "I'm not sure I care."

"It's only been a few days, but you're already sick of being rich." Her lip's twitching.

"I'm sick of having a miserable, old—"

Elizabeth grabs my arm and drags me out the front door. "Maybe don't insult her in her dining room."

"I'm sure her staff agrees with me."

"I'm not sure they do," she says. "I've known a lot of them for a long time, and one thing I will say for your grandmother. A lot of rich people go through employees like Kleenex, but she doesn't. She's had the same gate guard, the same butler, and the same dining room staff for more than ten years."

That's surprising.

"I'm not her family," Elizabeth says. "She's right about that. She has a lot of money, but if she started giving it to every sad story she met, she'd be poorer than me within a month. Trust me on this one. The number of hands held out, asking for money, would shock you."

"But she won't budge on anything."

"She's old," Elizabeth says, "but that doesn't mean she's wrong. She's seen a lot of things. I think sometimes we get so set in the idea that we're right that we don't even check whether someone else might also be right."

I peer at her. "Are you really Gandhi, reincarnated?"

She laughs. "I'm not, but Emerson. I have a lot to do, and I know we're fake." She sighs. "But we're also very, very new. I'm assuming you wanted me to fake date you to mollify your grandmother long enough that she might change her mind about all the rules. If that's your goal, we aren't there yet. Don't be like me and back yourself into a corner."

I can't help thinking about how we failed to help her shelter. "Do you even want to keep dating me? The shelter's being sold."

"Are you kidding? I'll need your help more than ever. I've got to come up with funds for a new shelter, the move, and turning whatever crap pile I buy into something workable."

"But—"

"The donations from Bentley and your grand-mother weren't what you wanted, maybe, but they're still my two single biggest donations this year."

"You're kidding."

She shrugs. "It's been a rough year. I had no idea how easy I had it the first year or two when it was a new thing to most everyone. Now, six years in, they're kind of tired of me asking, and they usually hide when they see me coming." She's acting like it's humorous, but it's got to sting a little.

"Well, I'm a novelty, so they seem to beeline toward me."

"Another reason I'm not ready to lose my trophy boyfriend yet."

"What if Lisa says she wants me to break up with you or she'll move on?"

She smiles. "She won't. She's decided she shouldn't have dumped you, and you looked happy the last time she saw you. She'll expect it to take a bit to win you back. You have some time."

"How do you know this stuff?"

"Have you ever tried to read something in Russian?"

"Not really."

"They have a different alphabet—it looks like nonsense, unless you've learned how to read it.

That's women, only we're even more complicated. We use a different phonetic system too. Since I am one, I can speak it and read it. Consider me your interpreter."

"Russian. That's funny."

"So Emerson, go see her, but be strong. Tell her you missed her, but you've finally figured out how to be happy. That'll make her push even harder, so you'll have to stand firm and tell her you need more time to think about it."

I nod.

But when I reach the ice cream shop where we had our first date, Lisa's not there. I wait another five minutes, but it's already been thirty. Could something have happened? I text her. WHERE ARE YOU?She calls.

"Hello?"

"I've been waiting here for ten minutes already. I knew that woman would try to stop you."

That woman. Sheesh. It's not like Elizabeth is such a hard name to remember. "No, I'm here." I glance around. Other than two moms with their three kids, no one else is. "The store's empty. Are you in the bathroom?"

"Where are you?" she asks.

"By the front window."

"No, what store, I mean?"

"I'm at the Scoop Shop," I say. "Where are you?"

"I'm at Giannoni's." She huffs. "Why did you think our place was an ice cream shop?"

"We had our first date here. And we came here on our first anniversary. We shared the banana split both times."

"But we ate lunch *here* every Monday for more than a year." She sounds really annoyed.

"I'm sorry," I say. "I thought you—you know what, it's fine. I'll come to you."

"Fine." She hangs up.

As I drive to Giannoni's, I begin to panic a little. She didn't sound like someone who was going to ask me to get back together with her. She sounded annoyed.

I call Elizabeth. "I'm confused. The Russian is making no sense."

"What happened?"

I explain.

She laughs. "Oh, Emerson. That's too funny. She's not mad at you. She's embarrassed, and it serves her right. She said to meet at your place as an emotional manipulation. She wanted you to remember that you two have history—a shared *place*. Only, you clearly don't, because you didn't think of the same place." She's still laughing.

"But that means it's going really badly," I say. "Help."

"You want it to go a little poorly," Elizabeth says. "Trust me on this. The more off balance she feels, the more she'll understand why you want space."

"Okay. Right. Okay." I hang up.

And then I walk into the Italian eatery that's our place, apparently. She's already ordered—and she got one sandwich. The club, which is fine, but it's annoying. For over a year, I picked all the meat off, and she'd add it to her half. She likes double meat, and I'm vegetarian. But then my sandwich tastes like meat, which always makes me vaguely nauseated.

I force a smile, which is silly. I should be truly happy. It's not my original plan, but this one *is* working.

"Hey." She wiggles her fingers in a tiny wave I used to think was cute. Only, now it bugs me.

Why don't I like it? I'm probably just in a funk. It's been a weird day. "Hi." I sit across from her.

She slides my half of the sandwich toward me on the paper—she always keeps the plate for herself. I shake my head. "I'm not hungry."

"Oh?"

"I just ate."

She frowns. "You did?"

"Never mind," I say. "You can have all of it."

"Okay."

Watching as she splits the meat back out and puts it on the half I don't want is a little awkward. She's wiping the mayo off her hands when I say, "What did you want to talk about?"

"Why?" She looks really irritated. "Are we keeping your girlfriend waiting?"

"Elizabeth's working, actually," I say. "She was just leaving when you called, so it was good timing."

"She knows you're here?"

I nod.

"She just *let* you come?" Her brows furrow. "Really?"

"It's not like she owns me."

"Well, here's the thing. At first, after we broke up, I really missed you, but I thought it would get better. Only, it never did." She bites her lip. "I know we were always worried Daddy would find out about us, but I don't care anymore. I want to get back together."

"You think he'll suddenly like me now?"

Her shoulders droop, and she drops the sandwich back onto the plate. "I don't know."

"Probably not, then. I was still fired."

"About that," she says. "The audit team realized it wasn't you who made the mistake. You'll be getting a letter about it."

"They're offering me my job back?"

She grimaces. "Not exactly. They already told the clients it was you, so that would be awkward, but they're formally apologizing, and they're offering to recommend you."

"Oh, well. The whole thing hardly hurt me, then." I wish I didn't sound so bitter.

"But you have a new job, now," she says. "You said."

I hate all the lying. I *have* to lie about Elizabeth, but I'm sick of lying about my job. "Not exactly."

"What?"

"I mean, I am working every day, but it's not a new job precisely."

"What's going on?" She leans closer, her elbow squishing the edge of the sandwich. I shouldn't care, but it bothers me for some reason, her inattention to stuff like that.

Focus, Emerson. "So, the thing is, the other day, I happened upon something strange. You know I never knew my dad."

She frowns. "Your dad and mom run an inn."

"Right, but I mean my birth dad."

"Oh, yeah. I forgot about that."

She *forgot?* "Anyway, the point is that my birth dad died, and I happened to be at his funeral. I met my grandmother, and she's. . ."

"Is she happy to see you?"

"Sort of," I say. "It's a little weird. But basically, she's teaching me about the family business to see if I'd be a good fit to take over now that my dad's dead. She doesn't really have anyone else."

"What's the family business?" She sounds nervous now.

I consider saying that I'm studying to be a plumber. But that's stupid. I don't want to lie to her. I'm trying to be as honest as possible. "It turns out that my grandmother's named Catherine Richmond, and she owns a company called Richmond Steel."

"I've heard of that company," Lisa says. "Wait, do you mean the biggest steel manufacturer in America? Are you serious?"

I nod.

"That's—wow. That feels like something that would only happen in a book written by an epically talented author."

I shrug. "Or maybe a mediocre one. Who knows?"

"It sounds like a fantastic story to me."

"Not if you're the protagonist in it, believe me. My grandmother didn't exactly welcome me into her life. She wants to control me—including who I date."

Lisa leans back, her mouth dropping open, and her eyes closing briefly. "That makes so much more sense. Your grandma's making you date that snobby, rich girl."

"Something like that, though I do really like her," I say.

"You're too genuine to ever fake something that big." Her expression softens. "But you can't care about her that much. It's been, what, a week? And even if you're stuck dating her, we can surely still talk. Right?"

"I really am dating Elizabeth," I say. "And if I make my grandmother angry by ignoring her advice—"

"She cuts you off." Lisa bobs her head. "Say no more. I totally understand."

"So the thing is. . ."

She reaches across the table and rests her hand on mine. "Emerson, I'm here for you. Whatever you need. And I'll wait as long as it takes for you to win your grandmother over with your amazing charm."

Instead of being delighted, for some reason I feel uncomfortable. I tug my hand away and nod. "Okay. Great, I guess."

ELIZABETH

I've spent every day digging through the enormous pile of paperwork that Ace had been neglecting. I've dealt with all sorts of things, from parking tickets to business license paperwork. But no one mentioned that the reason Rebekah's been so slammed was that they have a launch party Thursday evening.

As if I don't have enough other things going on.

"Can you make it?" Ace asks. "I know I said you'd only have to work twenty hours a week, but Rebekah has been loving having you around. She said finding someone competent is hard enough, but finding someone brilliant who understands people like me and works hard is like the holy grail."

"I'm glad she's been happy with my work." Actually, that's an understatement. I'm delighted. It turns out I need this job more than I realized. "But the thing is—"

"You can't come?"

I open my mouth to explain, but he cuts me off again.

"You're mad at me for springing it on you? Or do

you hate it here?" He swallows. "Elizabeth. . .are you quitting?" His eyes widen. "I didn't have you send flowers to anyone, and I haven't even—"

"Ace!" I chuckle. "Calm down."

"I'm sorry." He drops his hands to his sides and backs up, giving me space again. "I'm really stressed out. We've product tested, and we've spent a ridiculous amount on marketing, but this is only our second new series—our first since the company's launch, and I'm worried it's going to flop."

"What do you need me to do?"

He sighs. "Mostly, be a friendly face?"

"Surely Easton—"

"He isn't sure whether he'll be back in time," he says. "And Rebekah's going to be coordinating everything, so I'm probably going to be wandering around alone if you can't make it. Like a loser."

"Wait, are you saying you want me there, or you want me there *as your date?*" Because I cannot handle fake dating two guys at once.

"Tomato, tomahto?"

That makes me laugh for real. "Well, you may think it's not a big deal, but it's probably going to feel different to *my boyfriend.*" I hate how good it feels to say that.

"Wait, you have a boyfriend?" Ace doesn't look upset, but he does look shocked. "Who?"

"Did it occur to you that you may not know him?"

He frowns.

"It's my mechanic."

Now he's the one dying laughing. "Yeah, right."

"Hey, it *could be* my mechanic."

He's laughing so hard that tears are pooling at the corners of his eyes. He slaps his thighs. "Elizabeth

Moorland, dating a mechanic?" He descends into peals of laughter again.

My scowling doesn't help, so I try another angle. "You actually have met him."

He's still laughing, but not as hard.

"It's Emerson Richmond."

The laughing dies. "Wait, the guy who *just* got into town?"

I shrug.

"You're kidding, right? You must be. It seemed like you barely knew him at that party."

"You know how complicated dating is for people like us. We just haven't told my parents yet, so we're keeping things low key. We'd definitely met long before that."

"I guess." He looks up at my face. "So you can come, bring him, and announce it at the party!"

"Why would I announce that we're dating at your launch party?"

"All my investors will be there, so it would be a safe way to do it."

"Wait, who are your investors?"

"Your parents are one of them—they were one of the first, actually. You didn't know?" He's smirking now.

"I can't keep up with what they do."

"Well, anyway, you're coming, right?" At least he's not fixating on how I won't be his date. For a split second, I was worried that maybe he liked me.

I think about what's planned for Thursday. The vet check on Hottie's tomorrow, and we're supposed to sign papers on Thursday. It's sure to be a depressing day. Maybe going to a party's not a terrible idea. It beats watching *Seabiscuit* again and bawling my eyes out alone. Plus, I'd have an excuse to spend more time with

Emerson. Which only matters because maybe he'll help me find some new sponsors.

"Fine," I say. "But I need to check with Emerson, and don't tell anyone about us, okay?"

He beams and then slaps one hand over his mouth. His faux mumbling is ridiculous.

"Yeah, yeah, I get it. You're a vault."

I meet Emerson for ice cream after I finally finish at the shelter. I insist on checking out the place he thought was his and Lisa's place. It's a cute shop.

Which just confirms that she's an idiot for not remembering their first date, et al.

"Want to share a banana split?" he asks.

Is it just me, or does he sound nervous? "Sure, but I want double banana."

"You do?" He perks up. "I love that, too. There's never enough banana to go around."

"Right?"

"And no chocolate."

"You lost me there." I shake my head. "Give me all the chocolate you don't want."

A few minutes later, we're jousting with spoons as he tries to take the last piece of banana. It feels like the right time to ask. "I know you've got to go back now and meet with some people about the trade agreement, but what about tomorrow?"

"It's even worse than today," Emerson says. "I definitely feel better about charging the fourteen hundred dollar haircut. Grandmother's not even paying me for attending all these meetings." His smile slides off his face. "It's not like I'm really adding any value, though. So."

"I'm sure you're learning things quickly," I say. "Didn't you say you have an accounting degree?"

He nods. "A master's. The thing is, I understand the

world through numbers, but a lot of the business people want someone else to crunch those for them. They don't want to look at what I want to look at, and when I ask to look over the underlying figures, everyone gets annoyed."

"You're unique," I say. "Don't be ashamed of that. I can't think of another society guy who has an accounting degree. Just because they don't understand you, that doesn't mean your background isn't an asset."

"I guess." But he looks discouraged, and I hate that. "Hey."

He looks up. "Yeah?"

"You look at those numbers as much as you want. You never know. You might find something everyone else missed."

He snorts. "I doubt it."

"I don't."

"Thanks."

"And on that note, I have something to ask of you."

"What?"

"I'm selling Hottie on Thursday—my horse—and I'm probably going to be a little bummed."

"Are you sure you want to do that?" he asks. "I have some savings, and—"

I don't even let him finish that thought. What kind of person would even consider loaning me their savings —a fake girlfriend? "I've decided that selling him is the smart move. I'll miss him, but Henrietta takes cares of her animals. And that money will let me take care of mine."

"Okay."

"But that night, I have a work party to go to— they're launching a new video game, and Ace really wants me there."

"Ace, like the guy from the party?"

"That's my boss. I didn't tell you that?"

"I figured—you talked about it that day. I just hadn't confirmed." Emerson shrugs. "He's an interesting guy."

"He is," I say. "But he wanted me to be his date, and I told him I had a boyfriend."

"Why?" Emerson asks.

That hurts a little. "You wanted me to go with him?"

His eyes widen. "Oh, no. Right. You meant me."

I know we're fake, but still. "Or maybe I should just go with him?"

"No." Emerson tilts his head. "I'm sorry. I've been really distracted. Some of the numbers I was talking about don't add up, and I want to drop it, but I keep going back to it, and it's making me sound like a halfwit. I was just worried you liked Ace, and that I was getting in the way of your real dating life."

My real dating life. Why does him saying that bother me? "Like I'm blocking Lisa, you mean?"

"I mean, not really," he says. "It's not like Grandmother would let me date her anyway."

"You said you didn't care."

"This is coming out all wrong. Just tell me what happened about the party," Emerson says.

He's right. Why am I getting so irritated? "I told Ace I would go, and I was hoping you'd come with me. But as a warning, my parents will probably be there."

"Is that a problem?" He looks confused.

"No, except they'll be really excited that we're dating. I should apologize for that in advance."

"Oh, that's fine," he says. "That'll be a welcome change from Lisa's dad. We never even told her parents we were dating."

I like hearing about him dating her as a past thing,

and I remind myself that he's going back to her. As soon as we can convince his grandmother to ease up, he'll go back to dating the girl he really likes.

Which is not me.

"Okay, well, as long as we're fine."

"Oh." Emerson smacks his forehead. "Thursday."

"Yeah?"

"My brother's coming home—and I promised to eat dinner with him and my sister Bea. What time's the party?"

"Starts at seven," I say. "You could be late, though."

"Could I bring them?"

"An A-list movie star and his sister? Uh, yeah. I'm sure I can get their names added to the list."

"I'm not sure Jake's A-list," he says.

"Well, he's better than B-list. That's for sure."

He looks annoyed by that, inexplicably.

"I think he's A-list. I mean, he's young, but all his films have done really well—plus, they're snowballing too, right?"

"I guess."

"Either way, I'm sure Ace won't mind, so bring them along. I'd like to meet them, too."

"They'll be shocked that I have a new girlfriend, but be prepared for Bea to be excited. She never liked Lisa much, and now she's a little upset with her for breaking up with me."

Interesting, but I shouldn't be as happy to hear it as I am.

The next day's a long one, and by the time I reach the barn, the vet check's already well under way. I've never met this vet, which is unusual after working with horses in this area for so long. Both of my best friends are there—a show of support, I guess. Or maybe it's just indicative of the fact that they're both always at the barn. Barn rats as kids. A trainer and Grand Prix rider now. They're probably present for most vet checks that happen at the barn, no matter who the owner is.

"It's going fine," Victoria whispers.

"They did find some evidence of arthritis in his hocks and front right fetlock on the x-rays," Rhiannon says.

"Hardly surprising in a nine-year-old jumper," I say.

"Henrietta didn't seem worried," Victoria says.

"She's been watching him for the past few months and she knows he's sound," Rhiannon says. "It's not her first vet check, either."

Pre-purchase exams are a little like a real estate pre-purchase inspection. It's the vet's job to find things that may be wrong with the horse, just like it's the inspector's job to find things that are wrong with the property. At your first vet check, you're absolutely horrified. You think the horse you were so excited to buy is profoundly broken. But by your third or thirtieth, you're really just waiting to see if there's something that can't be managed.

Even kissing spine can be treated, but it would kill a deal for me. Shivers would bother me. Imminent founder. Past or remodeled trauma that might impact long term work. Henrietta knows he's a former track-run thoroughbred—and that he can clearly handle a high level of work with very little pain. Most other things are haggling points.

Usually, I'm nervous at a pre-purchase because I'm worried a sale might fall through. This time is a little different. I do need the money, so I hope he passes. But part of me hopes that Henrietta balks over something small, and then I can keep him without being guilty about it.

"Alright." The vet pulls Henrietta aside to talk, but she gestures me over.

"I'd like Elizabeth to hear. She's pretty honest, and she may have an explanation for some of the findings."

Dr. Stone shrugs. "Your exam." He pulls out a tablet and hands it to her. "You knew he had been on the track for almost four years. Hardly surprising he'd have some evidence of that, and I searched and found a P1 fissure on the front right. Even so, it doesn't appear to have any clinical symptoms. He seems totally sound."

"What would you be most worried about?"

"Honestly?" He shrugs. "Nothing stood out."

My heart sinks a little.

"He's got some maintenance, but no gastric issues, which is almost a miracle, and his feet are really good for an ex-racer."

Henrietta beams. "So you think paying seventy-five for him. . .?"

Dr. Stone shakes his head. "I don't opine on prices, but I've seen plenty of clients pay way more for high end warmbloods that were far less sound."

A sudden surge of emotion overwhelms me, and I have to turn toward Hottie, pretending to rub his nose to get it together. He bumps my face with his nose, and I can't do it.

"Are you sure you want to sell him?" Henrietta looks a lot more understanding than I expect.

I nod. "I need to sell him, but it's still hard. He's a great horse." Before I completely descend into sobbing, I think about the good things. "It helps to know he's going to a great home."

"He's staying here," she says.

"You aren't taking him back to your barn?" That

surprises me. She comes here a few times a month for a lesson from Victoria, but she usually trailers in to it.

"I want him here until our first Grand Prix, at least. He seems to be doing really well with Vickie. I try not to change things a lot right at the start."

I'm not sure whether it'll be good for me to still see him, or if he'll feel betrayed.

"I also thought you might like to do an exercise ride here or there whenever I can't make it," Henrietta says. "He'd clearly love it."

Too late. I'm officially bawling, because the sale feels so terribly real.

But it's fine. Bernie has been sending me more purchase options—we're going to look again on Friday evening—and some of them look like they might not be *so* awful. I really need the income to convince the bank that I can manage one of them. None of them are really what I had in mind, but I'll find something that will work.

Sometimes life is about remembering how it could be way worse.

Even so, signing the papers the next day is *rough*. It's awesome getting the biggest cashier's check I've ever held in my hand, and I have Henrietta make it out as a donation to avoid paying taxes on it, so she adds an extra five grand because she can write it off too, which is pretty nice.

"You okay?" Victoria asks.

I force a shrug, and I manage not to cry. I'm taking that as a win.

"What are you wearing to the party tonight?" Rhiannon asks.

"How do you know about the party?"

"Please," Rhiannon says. "I heard from Christine."

"How did she know?" I ask.

"Ace told her you turned him down when he asked you to be his date. She turned him down too, by the way." Rhiannon's laughing, but she's been his date at least twice.

"I can't believe you thought you could announce to your parents that you have a new boyfriend at a party, and you thought we wouldn't hear about it." Victoria looks annoyed.

"How many people did Ace tell?"

"Probably just Christine," Victoria says. "But everyone knows now, and we weren't even the first."

"Look, you guys have been busy. So have I."

"You didn't have time to text us about your new *boyfriend?*" Rhiannon looks genuinely upset.

Which is kind of silly. She has a new boyfriend every month. As a model, a minor social media influencer, and a Grand Prix rider, her life's as glamorous as a movie star. She does post about most of it on social, but it's not like I get special updates. Or at least, not usually.

Besides. My life's boring by comparison. "It's all really new. I wanted to make sure it wasn't going to crash and burn before I told anyone, but I figured my parents would figure it out sooner rather than later, since it's Catherine Richmond's grandson." Only, as I say the words, I'm reminded that it *is* going to crash and burn. Probably pretty soon.

"Well, I heard he's super hot," Rhiannon says. "I'm not going to lie. I'm a little jealous."

"A little?" Victoria asks. "Well, good for you. I'm a *lot* jealous. That man can fund a *lot* of Grand Prix horses. Or, you know, animal shelters." She shimmies.

"Stop," I say. "Neither of you are jealous. He's not funding anything—he's an accountant, for heaven's sake. I can't think of someone who would be a worse fit for either of you."

"The guys I date are all disasters. Maybe I should be looking for someone steady and normal like an accountant," Rhiannon says.

"A super rich, really handsome, and very connected one," Victoria says. "Sign me up for the next book-keeper you meet." She's smiling, and that means I'm smiling.

I know they're being ridiculous on purpose, to tell me they aren't mad. And maybe also because they're a little jealous. It doesn't really fix the hole in my heart over selling Hottie, since I know it's all fake, but having my friends act jealous of Emerson helps me get it together enough to get ready for the party. Rhiannon even insists on loaning me an amazing dress—the straps are a little confusing, since there are so many of them, but she helps me figure it out.

When we reach the party, I feel as ready as I'm ever going to feel to face my parents. I shouldn't blame them for making me sell my horse—it's not really their fault Dad's business is circling the drain again. I manage to hold my head high, my sparkling, floor-length silver dress barely touching the floor thanks to Victoria's new crystal Louboutins. The front makes the best of my rather modest bosom, and I feel like a million bucks.

Maybe even two million.

Victoria looks even more elegant than I do, as usual, in her simple black sheath dress and magenta heels. Rhiannon looks a little *extra* in her bright red, scoop front gown, but that's typical. With them by my side, at least I know that I won't embarrass myself or Ace.

I text Emerson. I'M HERE—CAME WITH TWO FRIENDS. I'LL SEE YOU INSIDE.

I'M ALREADY HERE, he texts back.

I did not expect him to be early, so I urge the girls forward. But when we walk through the doors to the hotel ballroom, all three of us freeze. The room's absolutely full of sofas and televisions—all of them hooked up to the new game. And. . .everyone is wearing pajamas.

Except Emerson, I suppose. But he's wearing dark, distressed jeans and a t-shirt with a Latin-inspired skull on it. He looks more like a rock star than anything else, whereas Rhiannon, Victoria, and I look like prom-night-rejects. What kind of A-lister party has everyone wearing slouchy pajamas??

Ace waves at me and jogs over. "You made it."

"Dude," I hiss. "Thanks for the heads up on the dress code."

"Oh." His eyes widen like he's only now realizing we're in evening gowns.

"You told me it was at the Four Seasons. Who comes to the Four Seasons in *pajamas*?"

"Losers," Rhiannon says. "That's who."

"Pretty sure losers don't own Balenciaga," he says. "It's a video game launch, though. Who thinks formal wear when they think about video games?"

I might kill Rebekah. She, at least, should have thought to tell me. The waiters are carrying around brunch-themed items on trays as they walk by, and I feel even more idiotic. I cannot eat a tiny breakfast quiche or a mini-pancake wearing *this*.

But Emerson has reached us, and he doesn't seem distressed at all about what anyone's wearing. "It's a fighting game?" He looks surprised.

"What did you think?" Ace asks.

Emerson shrugs. "Role play or maybe a race car game."

"He sucks at racing," my brother Easton says, coming up behind us and shoving me forward. "And you suck at knowing what to wear. What's with the ballgowns?"

I hate my brother. He's wearing flannel pants and a blue t-shirt.

"I'm guessing you got a paper invite," I say.

"Maybe the fact that you didn't get one was your clue not to come." He's smiling.

"That's pretty rude," Emerson says. "The owner of this video game invited her himself. She works for the company, and maybe she decided to look professional as a result. Besides, I think she looks amazing. Unlike you." He's glaring at Easton, and I realize he has no idea he's talking to my brother.

He's defending me.

It's pretty cute, really.

"Easy, tiger. I'm just teasing her." Easton holds out his hand. "Easton Moorland, brother to the impetuous and incomparable but very, very overdressed Elizabeth Moorland."

"He's also my best friend," Ace says. "So don't worry about anything he says. He always means well."

"Oh," Emerson says. "Sorry. I misunderstood."

"A man who apologizes?" Rhiannon practically purrs. "I'm in awe."

Emerson looks like he just stared straight at the sun. I want to snap my fingers in front of his eyes, but I can't really fault him. Rhiannon is a *lot* to handle. She's freakishly tall, and her legs are so long they should be licensed as deadly weapons. She loves wearing miniskirts for exactly that reason, and when her hair and makeup are on point, it's hard to look away.

Even for me, sometimes.

It's no wonder she has trouble making female friends.

"Guys, this is Emerson Richmond, my shiny, new boyfriend." It's not a finger snap, but it regains his attention.

"So nice to meet all of you," he says. "Sorry for being the new guy who really doesn't know anyone yet."

"He's been trying to learn how to live among the socialites of New York," I say, "now that he's in contact with his grandmother again."

"Why weren't you talking before?" Ace asks. "I meant to ask."

More people streaming in the door are going to have to crash into us if we don't move, but before I can usher anyone over and buy Emerson a little bit of time to think about how to answer, he starts talking.

"My mother and my dad's mother didn't see eye-to-eye," Emerson says. "Now that my dad and my mom are both dead, I'm trying to figure out how I feel about all of it."

"That's a lot to unpack," Rhiannon says. "But now you'll have some friends who can help."

"He doesn't need friends," says a new person, who's officially crashing into us. A split second later, my brain processes who just walked in. It's Jake Priest.

Emerson's brother.

"He has family," the girl next to Jake says, "but more friends is always a good thing, Jake." Beatrice is small—barely over five feet—but she's gorgeous. Long, ebony hair. Deep brown eyes. Delicate features that for some reason remind me of a bird. "I'm Beatrice, and Jake and I are Emerson's siblings."

"Foster siblings," Jake clarifies, "in case you're

wondering how Emerson's so ugly while I'm so good-looking."

"Yes, why on earth would he want friends?" Bea rolls her eyes. "They're probably wondering how Emerson's so well-mannered and you're so rude."

That makes me laugh. "Let's head inside," I say. "You can all test the new game, and we won't keep blocking the entry."

"Good idea," Ace says. "But maybe you and Emerson can meander over there."

I follow his eyes to where my parents are staring right at me. Neither of them looks very happy. What reason they could have for being annoyed with me, I don't know, but it's always something.

"Let's get it over with," I mutter.

Emerson grabs my hand and squares his shoulders. "Let's go."

When we reach my parents—who are wearing matching blue pajamas from Nordstrom with little fluffy slippers—they're both staring at our joined hands pointedly, and they look even less pleased than before.

"Hello, Mr. and Mrs. Moorland," Emerson says. "I'm Emerson Richmond, and I'm delighted to meet you. I've been lucky enough to get to know your daughter Elizabeth over the past little while, and I adore her."

"We're dating," I say.

He nods.

Watching my parents' faces is like watching a home renovation project on television but in extreme fast forward. Their scowls deepen at first, and then they transform into beaming smiles. "Richmond, did you say?" Mom asks. "I heard Catherine's grandson. . ." She reaches for Emerson's hand. "We're just thrilled to meet you, young man. And you're so handsome, too."

"You've been keeping this a secret, you little minx," my dad says.

In twenty-eight years, I have never once heard my dad call me a minx. Not one single time. "Uh, yes. You know me. I'm a real. . .*minx*."

Dad glares at me and then goes back to beaming at Emerson so fast that I'm genuinely worried he might suffer from whiplash. Do they think Emerson's an idiot? Ugh. Why do they have to be so sycophantic?

"Will your grandmother be joining us tonight?" Mom asks.

Emerson finally extricates his hand and shakes his head. "Not that I know of."

"Then again, he's not really in charge of her social calendar."

"Although, she certainly thinks she's in charge of mine," he mutters.

"Well, she should be," Dad says. "I'm sure you're such a comfort to her, after losing her son."

"I really doubt it," Emerson says.

Mom and Dad rush to tell him that's not true, but it sounds hollow even to me. I'm wondering how long we'll be stuck here, when there's a giant crash behind us.

Emerson and I both spin around.

"My bad," Jake Priest says from where he's sitting at a table in the corner.

Easton and a chair are on the floor, along with the shattered fragments of a bowl that clearly contained a lot of popcorn.

"Excuse me for a moment," Emerson says.

I've seen my affable fake-boyfriend happy. I've seen him looking determined. I've seen him nervous and even scared. But now, I'm seeing what he looks like when he's angry, and it's kind of hot. His eyes are thunderous, but his movements are still slow and collected.

He strides toward Jake like a heat-seeking torpedo.

I grab his arm before he can explode. "Hey, calm down. I'm sure it's fine."

"I knew I shouldn't let him come. Jake's always drama. So much drama."

"Yeah, but Easton can be a little annoying too," I say. "Maybe it's his fault. Let's just see what they say."

"I told you, though," Jake says as he stands up. "I mean, I was right."

"Right about what?" Emerson's voice is almost scarier for being so quiet and low.

"I told them that no one could beat me at arm-wrestling," Jake says. "For my last movie, I had to do a lot of arm-wrestling scenes, and they hired a few professionals to show me how to do it." He shrugs, his boyish smile out in full force, both dimples showing. "I told him."

"You sure did," Rhiannon says.

Bea's crouched by Easton, saying something I can't hear. He hops up then, shaking her off. "I'm fine." But he's rubbing his arm. I'm guessing it's sore and his ego is in critical condition.

"Look, you don't have to pay me or whatever," Jake says. "I'll let you off this time."

"No." Easton pulls out his wallet and yanks some bills out, throwing them on the ground at Jake's feet. "There's half of it. I'll have to Venmo the rest."

"No rush," Jake says, but his eyes don't leave East-on's, and I see what Emerson's talking about. He looks like he's spoiling for a fight for some reason.

"Alright. We're going to head out," Emerson says. "I'm sorry to leave early." He drops his voice. "I'm doing you a favor though, trust me."

"Maybe we can get dinner now," Beatrice says.

"You and Jake go without me," Emerson says. "I have to meet Uncle Bentley about something."

"Bentley?" Jake asks. "Great. Bring him, too."

"I have to talk to him about some stuff," Emerson says. "We can do dinner later. Saturday. Or Sunday, maybe."

"I'm busy too," Jake says. "You're not the only one with *stuff*."

"He knows that." Bea rolls her eyes.

"Does he?" Jake's still looking for a fight, it seems.

"You need to calm down." Bea reaches for him. "Geez."

Jake shifts back effortlessly, moving like a boxer. "I'm calm. I'm just tired of him acting like he's Superman because his dad was rich."

Aaand people are starting to look at us.

"It was so nice meeting you," I say. "But please don't feel like you need to stick around now that your brother's leaving."

"I'm only leaving to see someone," Emerson says softly. "You're welcome to stay, if you think you can behave yourself. Otherwise, we can go outside and see whether your arm-wrestling skills improved your right hook. I'm thinking not."

"Ah, I get it now," Jake says. "You're meeting with Bentley because now you're one of them. You got a rich girlfriend who says 'get out' so politely that I can't even get mad, and you meet Dad's rich friend for dinner like you're his equal, but I'm still trash." Jake shakes his head. "Whatever."

Jake's pretty easy to read—too much anger and not enough smarts to balance it out—but Emerson actually looks sad when he leaves, and that worries me. I hope

Bentley's someone he can talk to, because my poor boyfriend looks like he needs it.

What bothers me the most is how worried I am about the feelings of my fake boyfriend. I barely survived selling my beloved horse, and I'm worried that when it happens, losing Emerson's going to be even worse.

❧ 14 ❧

EMERSON

Most kids look up to Spiderman. Superman, too. Or they love Antman, or maybe Ironman, if they like comedy. I think I dressed up as each of them one year or another. But if I'd been interested in actually becoming someone else as a teenager, I'd have been Uncle Bentley.

I knew those superheroes were fake. Batman had the most chance of being real—he was just a rich guy with cool toys. But Uncle Bentley really *was* a rich guy, and even if his parents gave him a pretty good start, he earned a lot of his money himself.

That's why, when I notice something strange with Grandmother's accounting, I decide to ask him about it. It feels pretty strange to arrive at Saga, a Michelin star restaurant on the top floor of the 70th Pine Street tower, and tell the hostess I'm meeting Bentley Harrison. "For business," I clarify.

If her smile's a little patronizing, I can't really blame her. I doubt most business people say they're here 'for business.' As she leads me through a beautiful dining room, I can't help noticing the green marble tables and the luxe, peach velvet dining chairs. But not even the decor in the beautifully appointed dining room can compare to the view of downtown New York City.

Uncle Bentley stands and smiles when he sees me coming. "You found it."

"This place is nice," I say.

"I helped Kent restructure," Uncle Bentley says, "as a personal favor. It's the only truly amazing restaurant where I never have to wait to be seated, even on short notice."

"Well, I'm impressed." We both sit.

The hostess hands us menus. "Your server will be here shortly."

"The food's so good that sometimes I forget why I'm even here when I come for business," Uncle Bentley says. "Maybe you better tell me what's wrong now."

"You have to keep it confidential," I say.

Uncle Bentley smiles. "You know what I do, right? My initial consults are always strictly confidential."

"Well, I'm not saying we want to hire you."

He laughs. "I'll still treat this as an official consult, which means it'll be free to you, and it'll remain confidential, whatever you decide to do afterward."

That's a relief. "Okay, so we asked Grandmother to help with Elizabeth's shelter."

"She said no." Uncle Bentley doesn't even look surprised.

I nod. "Even though it's kind of Richmond Steel's fault she's losing it. I mean, I guess technically it's her parents who decided to sell it, but now she's going to have to find a new place. In the interim, she'll have to surrender all the animals she's currently housing to shelters where they will probably kill them. And then she'll have to completely remodel any new place she finds to be a shelter—it's not like there are lots of shelters up for sale. Anyway, Grandmother wouldn't help, which I should've expected, but I was looking into the company's accounting anyway, hoping there might be more charitable funds in some of the subsidiaries."

"She's training you?"

I nod. "I was searching through the different categories, looking for charitable funds allocations, and I noticed something else that seemed quite high in various places."

"Okay."

I pull out some papers I printed off and splay them on the table. Of course, that's when the waiter comes to take our order. Once we've gotten that out of the way, Uncle Bentley dives right back in. "Okay, what did you find?"

"It's standard practice for large companies, when they're expanding, to rent equipment, right?"

Uncle Bentley shrugs.

"But it looks like no one's even checking what has been rented from one department to the next. I noticed that there was a forklift, for example, that was rented for the build out of a shipping office eight years ago."

"Okay." He clearly wasn't expecting to be discussing a forklift.

"I selected a few examples of the rentals I happened to find and track down."

Uncle Bentley looks confused.

"I'm going somewhere with this. Bear with me."

"Okay."

"After the construction was complete, the forklift was taken from the shipping office in Rochester and moved to another location—a manufacturing branch in Buffalo—eighty miles away."

Uncle Bentley blinks.

"The shipping office is still paying rent on it—in Rochester. And the rent's not insubstantial. It started out as just under three grand a month, but instead of being depreciated, the rate has gone up. Now it's $4200 a month. They've been paying rent on that fork-lift for over eight years, and they haven't even had it at their location for at least four according to the assistant manager I spoke to."

"Okay." Uncle Bentley looks more interested.

"Meanwhile, the manufacturing branch is happy. They have a forklift that retails for $45,000 new—and they didn't have to spend a dime for it. Their assistant manager proudly told me that they've been maintaining it perfectly. And get this—he thinks it's owned by Richmond Steel. They did confirm there's a rental sticker on the back, but they never noticed it. That's what the manager said. He'd never even noticed it."

And Uncle Bentley looks bored again.

"Okay, this matters, because they've had this fork-lift for 100 months now, and it was a year old when they got it. So really, it would have retailed for some-where around $37,000. And the company has spent over four hundred and twenty thousand dollars on it. And counting."

Uncle Bentley freezes. "You're kidding."

I shake my head. "And in about three more hours of research, I found four and a half dozen more rentals *just like this.* Excavators. Dump trucks. Skids. Boom lifts. Saws. You name it, we've been renting it, long term, and if we'd just bought the equipment, we'd have paid ten times less. On the other hand, I also identified some machines that were purchased and are just sitting, entirely unused. For most of the rentals, they aren't in the same location as before, so no one even knows *how* to return them, and they just keep paying the rental cost to the rental company—it presumably gets approved simply because it was a line item on the budget in the prior year so it's not questioned."

Uncle Bentley whistles. "If you extrapolate your sample so that it's a company wide figure?"

"Yep." I hand him a paper. He got there faster than I thought. "That's what this document shows. Hiring a single person to manage the rentals and heavy equipment used company wide, assuming they're competent and can run basic numbers, would save Richmond ninety-six and a half million dollars *a year* on rentals alone. That doesn't even get into whether they should sell used equipment and whatnot."

Uncle Bentley swears loudly, right as our food's arriving.

The waiter looks shocked.

"Sorry, Harry," Uncle Bentley says. "Just got some news."

"Nothing to do with the food." Harry sets our plates down and sighs dramatically. "Good news, I hope," the waiter says.

"Oh, yes," Uncle Bentley says. "I think our little boy wonder here will delight his grandmother when he tells her what he just told me."

The waiter beams. "Then maybe he should pay for dinner, no?"

"Nah," Uncle Bentley says. "I'll still pay. No reason to break your bank before your grandmother's showering you with praise."

"Can you look over the numbers I ran to make sure I didn't miss anything?"

We spend the appetizer, the soup, and the main

meal confirming the steps I took. Bentley finds two small errors, but it doesn't change much. Eighty-eight million and change in savings instead of ninety-six. Still a pretty big catch.

"How's it going with Elizabeth?" Uncle Bentley asks.

I want to tell him the truth—that I'm not really dating her. I think that he, of all people, would understand why I need a cover to keep Grandmother happy, but I can't do it. I swore I'd keep the fake dating a secret from everyone. "I like Elizabeth well enough, in spite of the fact that she's one of the rich women Grandmother wanted me to date, but my ex-girlfriend reached out to me, and she wants to get back together, and now I'm conflicted." I'm surprised at how true that feels.

Uncle Bentley arches one eyebrow. "Because she found out you're rich now?"

I shake my head. "No, Lisa didn't know. I had to tell her—and she knows it's not a sure thing. I told Lisa that Grandmother hasn't decided whether to write me into her will and bring me into her life or keep going on as she was before." I sigh. "To be honest, I'm not even sure *I* want to be part of her life."

"Is that why you haven't told your parents?" Uncle Bentley's frown looks a little disapproving.

I can't really blame him. "They barely found out I got fired," I say. "And I wouldn't have told them that Lisa dumped me, but Bea blurted it out."

"When did you stop talking to them about things?" Bentley sets his fork down. "They have pretty good advice—better than mine in a lot of areas."

"I know."

"But?"

"But. . . You didn't see their faces when I said I

didn't want to be adopted. I'm worried that when I tell them my grandmother's alive—"

"They'll be happy for you, like they always have been."

"You sound pretty sure," I say. "But they might be hurt, too."

"If they are, they are," Bentley says. "But hiding it from them will definitely hurt them."

I think about that for the rest of dinner, and on my way home, I text Elizabeth. WHAT TIME IS THE REAL ESTATE AGENT TOMORROW?

FOUR LISTINGS—4, 4:45, 5:20, AND 6 PM. ARE YOU PLANNING TO COME?

I THOUGHT YOU WANTED ME? Although, now I feel kind of dumb. It's not like she needs input from her fake boyfriend. Was I just looking for reasons to see her?

OF COURSE I DO. GLAD YOU CAN MAKE IT.

I like her text message, and then quickly, before I can chicken out, I pull up another message and text Mom and Dad. DINNER TOMORROW? 7?

Mom replies immediately. WE'D LOVE TO SEE YOU! WHAT DO YOU WANT TO EAT?

ANYTHING, I text back.

STEAK IT IS. After fourteen years, Dad still hasn't gone vegetarian, and Mom still seems not to mind. He makes a lot of jokes, but he grills a mean veggie burger. His portobello mushrooms are edible too, usually.

Now I just have to prepare myself to tell them. Tomorrow morning, I'll tell Grandmother what I found in the numbers, and tomorrow night, I'll tell Mom and Dad that I discovered a grandmother I didn't realize I had.

I'm not sure why both things feel like such big

deals. I'm sure Bentley's right. Grandmother will be happy to save money, and Mom and Dad will be pleased for me.

Right?

Right.

Only, I decide to go by my apartment before heading back to Grandmother's. If I show up at Mom and Dad's house in these ridiculous clothes tomorrow —designer labels hanging off everything—they'll start interrogating me immediately. When I unlock the front door of my apartment, I walk right into a kicked hornets' nest.

"—was your fault for being such a jerk," Bea says. "Easton was being nice. If you hadn't challenged him to arm wrestle you and acted like you had no idea what you were doing—"

"I *said* I was good at it."

"In that sheepish, gosh-shucks, I'm a country kid way that you do."

"I said what I said, and if he couldn't see that—"

"Online, they have this thing. They call it 'Who's the Jerk.' And Jake? Tonight, you were the jerk, and I was embarrassed to be there with you. I'm sure Emerson was embarrassed too."

"That entire party was full of a bunch of jerks and chumps, and he fit right in. I told you he wasn't like us."

I close the door quietly, but my foot hits the creaky tile.

Jake turns around slowly.

"I'm not like you?"

Of all the kids Mom and Dad have fostered, the one who causes the most problems has always been Jake, hands down. He picks fights. He lies to people. He fleeces them out of their money. And now he's the richest one of all. He's had not one, but two really big movies that opened to a top box-office slot.

But he's still a complete jack-hole.

"You *think* you're better than us. You always have." Jake grabs a kitchen chair, flips it around backward, and straddles it, his eyes daring me to argue.

"I just came to grab some clothes," I say. "I don't have the energy to fight."

"I thought you wanted to get Lisa back," Bea blurts, "but you have a new girlfriend?" Her eyes are shuttered —which means she's hurt.

"I am going to get Lisa back," I say. "But—" I can't tell her the truth either, not without invalidating my deal with Elizabeth. Only, if I don't explain, I sound like a jerk. "Or, maybe I will. She did tell me yesterday that she wants to get back together."

"Wait, so now you're dating *two* girls?" Bea looks sick, stepping away from me to lean against the wall. "Really, Emerson?"

"Maybe we're more alike than I realized." Jake's eyes glint. "Bravo, brother. Didn't think you had it in you."

"I'm not dating two women," I say. "I—I thought —my grandmother wanted me to at least go out with a few people she knew, and Elizabeth was one of them."

"And now you can't decide?" Bea asks. But it *sounds* like she's saying, "And now you're a terrible person?"

I groan. "It's not that I can't decide. It's compli-cated. Elizabeth's losing her animal shelter right now, and it's kind of our fault."

"Our fault?" Bea asks.

"Not our as in the Fansee family," I say. "Our as in Richmond Steel. They're buying the building—"

"You're trying to get your grandmother to save the

shelter by telling her it's your girlfriend's?" Bea's eyes light up.

"I already tried that," I say. "It didn't work. Grandmother turned us down flat."

"Oh." Her shoulders slump again.

"But I'm going to help Elizabeth look at new places tomorrow, and I just couldn't dump her the second Lisa showed up." I shrug. "I'm—I guess I'm confused."

As I say the words, I realize they're true.

"Lisa wants to get back together *now*?" Jake asks. "Now that you're rich, you mean." The same thing Bentley says.

"It's not like that," I say.

But a tiny part of me wonders whether it *is* like that. She got interested when she saw me wearing nice clothes, with an expensive haircut, and dating a gorgeous and well-put-together woman. It might not have been because of Richmond Steel, but it feels like it was thanks to the glow-up Elizabeth gave me.

A week or two ago, I wouldn't have cared *why* Lisa wanted me back. But now. . . I'm wondering whether my original plan was really the key to happiness in my future. I mean, plans are great, but when big things change, sometimes the plan needs to be adjusted too, right?

"Well, we'd hate to keep you here too long." Beatrice crosses her arms and frowns. "I'm sure you have way more important things to do and way more critical places to be."

It's nearly eleven, and I have a meeting with Grandmother at seven a.m. I yawn involuntarily and shake my head. "It's not that. It's just that I've been meeting with people and going over numbers all day lately, and then—"

"I'm sorry, Cinderella. Are you tired from attending

so many balls? Or are the glass slippers hurting your feet?" Jake arches one eyebrow. "Because you're not the only one with stuff to do. I have two zoom meetings with producers tomorrow. And Bea—"

She waves him off. "Stop, Jake."

Jake scowls.

"Really," Bea says. "We're both really happy for you. We just miss seeing you regularly. I hope eventually you can move back into the apartment."

"Yeah," Jake says. "That's what I wanted to say. I just *miss* you so much." His lip's twisted, and he's clearly mocking me.

But I think that maybe, *maybe* he's mocking me to cover the truth. "I've missed both of you." I mean it unironically.

I also hate lying to them. I hate living with Grandmother instead of them, and I really don't like that Mom and Dad don't even know about it yet. "I'm having dinner at home tomorrow to tell them about all this craziness. Can you just keep quiet about it a little bit longer?"

Bea nods.

"Quiet?" Jake grimaces. "Dude, I already texted them some pics from the party, asking them if they like their Richmond Steel son or their movie star son better." He holds up a peace sign and fake-smiles.

"He didn't," Bea says. "Ignore him."

"I usually do," I say.

But one thing Jake got right—I think one of the reasons I haven't told Mom and Dad is that I don't want to stress them out. . .but I also want them to like me the most. Jake's always been the problem child, and I don't want to take his place now that I've found some living family that's difficult to deal with.

Jake has always seemed like the most obtuse

person I know, but now I'm wondering how much truth there is to his outrageous words, and how much insight he masks with them. When I get back to the mansion, to my shock, Grandmother's still awake. In fact, when I walk through the door, she's pacing back and forth in her library, which opens right off the entryway.

"You're finally here." She's frowning mightily.

"I'm sorry."

Her butler bows stiffly and locks the front door after me.

"You should message us to let us know if you'll be late."

"I—I'm sorry," I say. "I didn't realize. . ." I don't quite have the guts to tell her that I didn't realize she expected a full-grown adult to check in with her about my arrival and departure times. "I'll definitely be ready for the seven a.m. meeting tomorrow."

"You'll be ready—I'll be exhausted."

Before I've thought of a way to defend myself, Grandmother eyes my briefcase and shoulder bag.

"What's all that?"

"It's—I'm going to meet my parents for dinner tomorrow night, and—"

"Your *foster* parents, you mean?"

I sigh. "Yes, that's what I mean."

She huffs. "I'll add it to the calendar."

"I'm sorry you'll be tired tomorrow," I say. "But you don't need to wait up for me in the future. I'm perfectly capable of managing my own life. I've done it for twenty-seven years now, all before meeting you."

Her face flushes like I slapped her. "You're living in my house. Here, we don't go to sleep until everyone's home safe."

"Maybe I should live back at my old apartment," I

say. "My brother and sister were just complaining that they never see me."

"Were they? Your *brother* and your *sister*?"

Everything's making her mad right now. "Let's talk in the morning. I've wrecked enough of your sleep already."

"Once you've told me what's in those." She's still eyeing my bags.

"It's just clothing for my dinner tomorrow. Mom and Dad would find my new wardrobe. . .ostentatious."

She shakes her head.

"And the briefcase—I have some papers to show you in the morning. I think you'll be pleased."

"Show me now." She circles the room and sits down at her desk.

The butler bows and disappears.

"Show you. . .now?" I follow her farther into the library and walk toward the desk. "But it's late. I can just go over it tomorrow."

She points at her desk. "Now."

"Um, okay." I'm not sure why I'm so flustered. I was going to remove the errors Uncle Bentley pointed out, but it's fine. I pull out the papers. "So while I was—" I clear my throat. I can't really tell her I was digging through the files to try and figure out how much charitable giving they do. I certainly can't explain that I was hoping to convince them to reallocate it to Elizabeth's shelter. "I was learning about things, I happened to pull a file or two—"

"You should not be inspecting random files," she says. "When we explained how the system worked, it wasn't so you could go poking around."

"I didn't—"

"One single keystroke, and you could destroy the organization method. An errant save, and you could jumble things around, costing employees hours of lost time."

"Right, but I'm an accountant," I say. "I know how to use business programs, and I'm hardly going to start deleting files or saving them to the wrong pathways. But look, I think you'll want to see what I found."

She compresses her lips into a very thin line, but she's not fussing more, at least.

"Okay, so this is just an example, but about eight years ago, the Rochester shipping office rented a forklift for the build out of the expansion. And then when the build out ended, a few months behind schedule, they didn't return the forklift."

Grandmother's scowl has deepened.

"But what's more interesting is that the manufacturing office in—"

"Stop," she says.

"Why?"

She sighs dramatically. "This company is massive," she says. "I've been trying to show you the scope, but I think I may have failed."

"No, it's not that," I say. "Look—"

"Emerson, the last thing in the world I care about is a forklift in Roanoke."

"But the forklift's not *in* Rochester," I say, "or Roanoke either. It was moved to Buffalo, eighty miles away, and it's not even on their reports or budgets, because the Rochester branch is still paying for the rental."

Grandmother looks like she may be about to spit on me.

"I'll cut to the chase." I pull out my proposal—in the same format I had to make them at my old job—and slide it toward her. "Some of these calculations have shifted a bit, and I was going to clean them up.

But the main point is still good—if we were to hire one single person to manage the rental equipment across all of Richmond Steel, which doesn't even include Barrios Steel, which we acquired but haven't integrated accounting for yet, we could save—"

"Emerson Duplessis." She doesn't call me Richmond like she usually does. She said Duplessis. Does she mean it as an insult? But why?

"Yes?"

"Who are these markings from?" She's glaring at the top page of my proposal, where Uncle Bentley wrote down the two errors and we ran through the calculation to see the change. "It's not your handwriting."

"I think you know Bentley Harrison. He's an old family friend, and I wanted to run this past someone before I brought it to you—"

"Because you're a twenty-year-old accountant and you rightfully had no faith in your own abilities?"

I'm not sure what to say to that.

"Emerson." She flattens her palms against the desk, letting the proposal flip back over until it just looks like a plain manila folder. "I know you're eager to show me that you're as good as your father was. I know you're a bright boy. I can tell that much. But you're very young, you went to an inferior school and earned a very inferior degree, and you're way, way behind. Instead of desperately trying to sprint your way forward, please learn to take my advice and do what I ask, nothing more."

"But if you would—"

"What I will do is forget that you made the grievous mistake of disclosing our confidential financial information to an outsider without my permission. I'll forget that you breached your fiduciary duty as a temporary board member, and I'll forget how enraged I am that you did it all after you signed a non-disclosure document."

"But it was a confidential evaluation," I say.

"Which you had no right to even undertake, since you're not an agent of Richmond Steel." Grandmother sighs. "I have competent people, and I'm a very, very good manager of this company. There's a reason why we haven't had a single unprofitable year in more than forty years running."

"I'm not saying you're doing a poor job," I say.

Grandmother stares at me for a moment, and then she taps her fingers on the top of the file folder she's probably going to throw in the trash. "I should probably revoke your access to the company files and remove you from the board tomorrow, but let's just call this a warning. Don't ever tell me that I'm not generous. Alright?"

There are many things I could accuse my grandmother of being, but ungenerous isn't one of them. "I would never think that."

If only *generous* was enough.

ELIZABETH

Our family has always hovered right on the edge of being wealthy. I often thought that, had Mom and Dad chosen to live somewhere else—anywhere else—we might have been much happier. For instance, if we lived in Yonkers, where the average income is around seventy grand a year, we'd have been the wealthy people around.

But Dad always ascribed to the idea that proximity to greatness made it more likely for him. As a bizarre type of sado-masochistic optimist, Dad always felt like rubbing shoulders with the very wealthy would help him find more opportunities. I'm not at all sure that ever worked. In fact, I'm pretty sure it made Mom miserable, seeing things that her friends had that she couldn't quite afford. It also always inspired Mom to spend just over her means.

We were always chasing ballooning debt payments, which eliminated any windfalls from Dad's spurts of erratic luck.

I'm very familiar with the misery that comes from seeing things you can't *really* afford. . .so when Bernie sends me the listing for the large, spacious old inn that sits on nearly a full acre on the edge of town, just past where my parents and nearly all my friends live, I tell him I don't even want to see it. Sure, it looks like *exactly* what I want, but it's also nearly twice what I calculated I can probably afford.

What I didn't count on was that the saddest property on the list would be right next door to the quaint inn.

"Why are we even looking at this place?" Emerson whispers. "It looks like it should be condemned."

"I think that's why." Bernie squints.

"Uncle Bernie," Emerson says. "Just get reading glasses."

He waves at Emerson absently. "No, no. They say that once you start wearing them, your eyes give out completely."

Emerson frowns, and even frowning, he's so stinking cute. "Who says that?"

"Everyone." Bernie waves his hand. "Everyone does."

"Hand me the iPad," Emerson says.

"Stop." Bernie slaps at his hand. "Listen, this place is actually *below* the price point Elizabeth gave me by fifteen thousand dollars, and I know they're negotiable. Think about how much room that would give her to—"

"But she wouldn't have much extra cash," Emerson says. "She'd still need most of the downpayment, so she couldn't remodel it properly. She'd just have a very cheap pile of rubbish."

I can't help my snort.

Or my wistful glance at the inn next door. "Is it just me, or is that one actually glowing?"

Emerson sidesteps in front of me and grabs my hand. "No. You're both a mess right now. We said *that one's* too expensive. Let's focus on what's in the price range."

He's right. I turn away from the beautiful, glowing navy inn with white shutters and a large, fenced, inviting yard that would be easy to partition into cute little runs, and I focus on the hovel.

"You mean this about-to-be-condemned neighbor?"

My adorable boyfriend clears his throat. "It's not so bad, when you close one eye and squint." Emerson doesn't lie well at all. "I mean, if we painted it, maybe."

"We?" I can't help arching my right eyebrow. "The closest my parents have ever come to a paintbrush is hiring someone who can use one. Are you saying you know how to paint?"

"We had to paint rooms in the Inn at home all the time," he says. "And one summer, I saved for school by helping a contractor I met at the Inn—I painted close to twenty houses that summer."

"A man of so many talents," Bernie says. "He keeps you depressingly on budget, and he offers to help paint turds."

But as we walk up the steps to the front door, Emerson's foot punches through one of the boards.

"Oh, no." I reach for his arm, as if I could somehow lift him up.

It takes him a full minute for us to extricate his foot, and when we finally do, his ankle's bleeding.

"I hope you're up to date on your tetanus," Bernie says.

"It's not a rusty nail," Emerson says. "I'm fine."

"Tetanus can be in dust, dirt, and grime." Bernie shrugs. "Just like, well, every part of this place." He grimaces.

"Did you add this to the list because it's close to that one?" Emerson glances sideways toward the inn.

Bernie splutters. "How could you possibly insinuate—"

"Alright, then. Everyone watch their steps." Emerson's remarkably upbeat for someone who was just injured. And if he's limping a little, well. He did just gash his ankle open.

"What's that?" I point as we walk through the front entry.

Emerson squints and tilts his head. "I think it's just a loose light fixture, but why it's loose. . ."

And that's when a rat drops through the hole next to the dangling light and onto the center of the floor in front of us. In the rat's defense, we startled him too. I think he shrieks almost as loudly as Bernie.

"Dude, chill," Emerson says. "It's just a rat."

Bernie has backed all the way into the wall behind us.

Something about Bernie's reaction makes Emerson laugh. Actually, *roar* might be a better word.

"What?" Bernie asks, a little defensive.

"I think you backed into the rat's nest." He points.

I assumed he was kidding, but Bernie spins around so fast that he nearly breaks the window behind him with his elbow. The swear words he uses are pretty inventive. Unfortunately, when he heads the other direction, he must run right into a massive spiderweb, because he starts pinwheeling his arms and shaking like he's been possessed.

"Here's a question," Emerson says, looking entirely and completely calm.

It's especially impressive since I've leapt up into his arms, and my legs are now dangling several feet off the ground.

"What?" I swallow. "Is it 'how fast can we get out of here?'"

He laughs again. "No." He shakes his head. "How does a grown man—and a real estate agent—scare so easily? It's not like this place is haunted or something. It's just rats and spiders and they always move in when humans move out. Sometimes they move in before the humans move out." Emerson looks legitimately amused, and I can tell.

My face is only a few inches away from his.

I'd have said yesterday—actually, earlier today— that rats and spiders were the anti-hot. But being held by a man who's *not* afraid of them, while he mocks an even older man for being afraid. . .Emerson has never looked hotter to me.

In fact, as Emerson turns around, I can see that Bernie's already entirely outside, narrowly missing the hole in the porch as he sprints out of the small front yard and into the street.

"It can't be the first time one of the houses he looked at had rats or spiders."

"Well." I'm so close, I can see how few pores Emerson has. I can see every single micro expression on his really handsome, really manly face. "I'd have to admit that I'm also not a fan."

"But think about it," Emerson says. "The rats and spiders would be gone within days once you bring in your army of cats."

Now I'm the one laughing. "I suppose that's true."

"Look, I'm not saying this place is an amazing deal, but you liked the spot next door. With a truckload of new wood to replace the rotten stuff, and a little bit of pest control, we could probably turn this rotting pile into what you need."

He sets me down, now that I've calmed down a bit, and I hate how bereft I feel.

"You can't be that scared of rats. You take in dogs and cats constantly."

"They're domesticated," I say.

He shrugs. "Still." He walks into the kitchen, keeping his eye out for more vermin, and he reaches for the counter. The countertops are so filthy that I'm not even sure what they're made of. Maybe formica? He reaches for the knob and turns on the water.

And the knob snaps off, the water still running.

He fiddles with it for a minute, but when he can't figure out how to turn it off, he shrugs. "I'd look for the water main, but I'm worried that it'll burst wide open if I touch it." He sets the knob on the counter and points at the door, his lip twitching a little. "Maybe Bernie's right. This place needs a gallon of gasoline and a match."

We're both laughing as we walk out the door, but Emerson's the one who tells Bernie that he's got to call and break it to the owners that the water's stuck running.

Bernie looks like he wants to cry, but he nods. "Can we at least see the nice place while we're here?"

Seeing the nice place is the story of my life. From the time we walk through those doors, nothing else will ever be good enough. I shake my head. "I think that's a bad plan."

In fact, it occurs to me that walking into that place is probably a lot like fake-dating Emerson. Once you see the best that's out there, you don't want mediocre anymore.

"Are you sure?" Bernie's eyes cut to the side. "It has two bathrooms downstairs, one with a large walk-in shower with a detachable showerhead, and one with a clawfoot tub. Both would be perfect pet bathing stations."

I remain firm. "I saw the photos online. That was hard enough. It's just *way* more expense than I'm able to afford."

"What if we found more sponsors?" Emerson asks.

"We'd have to find a *lot* more," I say. "And so far, the only really consistent sponsor I've found is myself." I try to chuckle as I say it, but it comes out more as a whine. "And after I buy something, I'll officially be flat broke. It would be a real shame if I lost it right after buying it."

"Okay," Bernie says. "The last thing I'll say is this. It has a complete living quarters on the top floor. Kitchenette, storage area, two bedrooms, and two bathrooms. It's self contained. You could live onsite, so whatever you're spending on rent, you wouldn't need to spend anymore."

And I wouldn't be leaving the dogs and cats all alone every single night. Sometimes I wake up in a panic, sure the shelter's on fire. Then again, the barking if they hear something would probably go on all night. "It's not a fit for me now," I say.

"Oh, come on," Emerson says. "Let's just take a quick peek at the upstairs. That apartment sounds cool."

"It was all soundproofed," Bernie says. "Since it was an inn."

Gah. "Fine," I say. "*Fine.*" I can't argue with both of them.

But from the moment I step inside, I know I was right. The floors downstairs are all tile. Easy to clean. Nice on paws. They have lots of small rooms that would be easy to convert to sections for the dogs and cats, and there's already a room with tables that were probably used for food prep or something, but it would make a great infirmary.

The sunny kitchen's large and inviting, and it would be a perfect break room for volunteers, or an area for people to meet their possible new pet. I could totally see myself signing adoption paperwork right here.

"I hate it," I say.

"You do?" Emerson asks. "Because it looks like you love it."

When we get to the second floor, I finally have a reason to turn it down. "See, none of this space is necessary," I say.

"I had an idea," Emerson says. "Didn't one of your brochures list friends of yours who do pet related things?"

"Huh?" I blink.

"There was a green paper," he says. "It was close to the door."

"Oh, you mean the new pet owner paperwork?"

"Yes," he says. "Referrals for pet services."

"Sure," I say. "Yes."

"What if. . ." He clears his throat. "What if you rented this second floor to the grooming service? You could refer them, and then the owners could bring their pets back up here for grooming. They would clearly know where the shelter was, and they'd have to walk back and forth in front of the pets each time they came—if they chose one dog, maybe they'd adopt another."

"That's diabolical," Bernie says. "You're an evil mastermind."

"Maybe," I say.

"Or you could offer a dog boarding service up here, on the second floor," he says. "You already have people who are here daily. They could take care of these dogs, too."

"But they're volunteers. They don't want to run a dog boarding facility."

"They're volunteers," he says. "They're volunteering to help, and if boarding pets helps pay for the shelter. . . It would be another revenue stream."

I shake my head slowly. "I'll think about it."

Emerson shrugs. "Maybe it wouldn't work, and that's fine. I'm just saying, there are options here."

When we finally reach the third floor, I really fall in love. Whoever ran this inn loved these rooms—it's clear to see. The details are stunning. Tiny, hand carved birds and insects on the hand rails, and what look like unique and imported light fixtures in each room. The bathroom has a large soaking tub *and* a big shower.

"Did you see this?" Emerson's in the second bedroom. The one that doesn't have its own bathroom, which I haven't yet seen.

When I follow him in, I'm struck by the amount of light, even with the fading sun. But when I follow his eyes, I see what he's looking at—it's a big, tall, running sorrel horse. And he looks so much like Hottie that my heart just stops beating. A tear rolls down my cheek.

"Oh, no," Emerson says. "What's wrong? I thought you'd like it."

I shake my head. "I do like it."

"You *look* like you don't," he whispers. "Are you sure you're alright?"

"It looks like the horse I just sold." I swipe at my face and remind myself that it's just an artist's rendition, but it's a talented artist. This isn't someone who said they could paint a horse and slapped both eyes on the front of his face. This is someone who spent a lot of time around horses. It captures the wide nostrils, the startled look, and the illusion of movement in every line of his body.

"I do love the apartment up here," I say.

But like I knew it would, looking at the inn makes me profoundly sad. If I'm being honest with myself, I've been wondering whether the last six years have all been just a waste of time. I've been funding my entire life, my whole goal, with my own savings.

And now they're gone.

Am I going to buy a dump somewhere, be unable to pay the mortgage, and go belly up *again*, but this time, without a horse to sell to pay the piper? Or you know, the bank?

Ugh.

I'm such an incompetent loser. Why did I think I could run a shelter? I can't keep pets safe. I can't even run my own life.

"Elizabeth," Emerson says. "I think you should get this place. I'll help you fundraise or whatever you have to do, but think of how great it would be."

His happy face should cheer me up, but all I can think about is how, any day now, he's going to convince his grandmother to accept him no matter what. . .and then he'll dump me for Lisa. The girl he really wants. He's a nice enough guy that I'm sure he'll still help where he can. But any promises he makes me aren't worth much, because we aren't real.

"I appreciate the support," I say. "But I need to look at my numbers and decide what's viable. You were just saying that."

"But now, you look so happy in here," he says. "I just—"

Bernie chooses that moment to stomp through the doorway. "I know you didn't love that first place," he says, "but as you mentioned, you can set up a lot of outdoor kennels, and there aren't close neighbors. I think the vast majority of shelters utilize predominantly outdoor kennels anyway."

It's terrible in New York State, where half the year is so cold that the dogs are practically freezing, but they're much easier to clean—you just hose the kennels off into a main drain. And it was the right price point. Now that I'm not standing inside the rat infested, broken water-pipe-place, I'm not as bummed out. Maybe we could use those things to negotiate an even better price.

"I'll think about it," I say. "And I'll call you."

At that very moment, Emerson's phone rings. I shouldn't be worried about it. I mean, if it *is* Lisa, so what? I don't actually have any right to tell him who he can and can't talk to. My suggestions to get her interested again worked, and he has to take it from here. Even so, when he answers, I can't help listening. Maybe a little too intently.

"Hey. I'm almost done."

Almost done? Is he meeting someone else?

"No, it's fine. I can come to you."

To *who?*

"Who is that?" Bernie asks. Bless him.

"I mean, I'm not in the city either, but—"

"Is that your dad?" Bernie asks.

Emerson's ignoring him, the jerk. But *could* it be his dad?

"No, that's Bernie." Emerson rolls his eyes. "I'm with a friend—she's looking to buy a—" He sighs. "No, she doesn't want to come to dinner."

"Actually, I'm starving." I hate myself for saying that so loudly, but it's too late. I've already done it.

Emerson looks at me sideways. "You are."

I nod.

He mouths, "It's my mom. You want to eat with *my mom?*"

I shrug. "Why not?"

Emerson looks absolutely floored, but he cuts his eyes toward Bernie, clearly reminding me that he can't say anything real. We have company.

"Don't worry about having to invite me," Bernie says. "If I'm not home on time, Nance will shred me. She's making lasagna."

"Alright," Emerson finally says. "I'll bring my friend Elizabeth." He chuckles. "No, she's not like us." Then he hangs up.

"I'm not like you? What does that mean?" I'm trying not to be offended.

"Vegetarian," he says. "Dad and Mom have been squaring off for years, and I'm the only kid they've taken in who gave up meat. She's always recruiting."

"You'd think I'd be vegetarian," I say. "I do save animals for a living."

"Why aren't you?" Bernie asks.

I shrug. "Steak's more delicious than I am strong?"

He nods. "Me, too."

"Alright," Emerson says. "Well, Dad was going to grill, but they wound up shopping, so we're going to our favorite Mediterranean place instead. They have lots of vegetarian options and plenty that's not."

"It's *not* Mediterranean," Bernie says. "That place is an abomination."

"Where?" I ask.

"It's called PopoJito," Emerson says. "It's Mexican Mediterranean fusion, and you'll love it."

"Maybe I'll try avoiding meat tonight," I say.

"Don't do it for me," Emerson says. "Dad says their tacos are to die for, and I love plenty of meat-eaters."

Love? Is he saying he'll *love* me even though I eat meat?

It's just a figure of speech. I'm being stupid.

By the time we reach PopoJito, I'm a nervous wreck. What if his parents don't like me? What if he introduces me as his friend and tells them he's about to get back together with Lisa? I mean, technically it's true, and they do appear to be entirely disconnected with his grandmother.

Except for Bentley, who has now contributed to my shelter.

"You can't tell them it's fake," I blurt out as Emerson's parking.

"What?"

"Our dating," I say. "They know Bentley, and he knows everyone else."

Emerson blinks. "I wasn't going to."

"But you didn't say I was your girlfriend on the phone," she says.

"I *just* told them I broke up with Lisa," he says. "I didn't want to blurt it out over the phone. I figure the whiplash isn't as bad if they meet you first."

"Oh."

"Is that fine?" He's looking at me like you stare at the person on the corner who's batting at nonexistent ghosts.

"Of course." I climb out and bolt for the door.

"Easy there, Seabiscuit," he says. "We're not in a race, and I promise not to bite."

"What if I like it when men bite?" Oh, no. That was too much. What's wrong with me?

"Oh, please tell me Emerson doesn't ever bite," possibly the most beautiful woman I've ever seen says. She's walking arm in arm with a pretty handsome guy. .

.and I have a sinking feeling that they're Emerson's foster parents.

They can't be more than ten years older than him.

"I'm Seren." She's smiling now, and if it wouldn't sound like I was fangirling, I'd tell her that she's even prettier when she smiles.

"And I'm Dave. Don't worry. Emerson's a pretty open-minded guy."

Seren's eyes widen and she slaps his arm.

"Hey guys. This is my girlfriend," Emerson says, "Elizabeth Moorland."

"Well, she's lovely," Seren says. "And I already like her more than that horrible girl who wouldn't tell her father that you were dating, even after more than a year."

Emerson glances my way slowly.

I think he's hoping I'll save Lisa's reputation. *Not a chance, buddy.* I throw her under the bus so fast that I can practically hear her bones crunch. "Actually, my parents love him. They met him last night, and my mom's checking out wedding venues today and sending them to me via text." I actually wish that was a joke.

Seren's laughter's like the pealing of tiny bells. I could listen to it all day.

"I think I love your parents," I say without thinking.

Emerson flushes bright red.

"Well, let's go have some meat, shall we?" Dave beams at me. "I hear you're as selfish as I am."

"Actually, I've been thinking of going rogue too," I confess.

"Wait at least one night," Dave says. "Before you wave the white flag, try the tacos here at least once."

I'm eating my last taco—why is pulled pork so delicious?—when Seren asks, "Did you invite us to dinner to introduce us to Elizabeth?" She smiles at me.

"Not exactly," Emerson says, "though I'm glad you met her."

"Oh." Dave wipes his mouth. He ate his tacos as fast as I ate mine, and he had one more than I did.

"The thing is. . ." And Emerson fills them in on the drama. The funeral. His grandmother's offer. Moving in with her. Meeting me—how I thought he was a caterer. . . And then found out that he really was.

"You haven't been dating long then," Seren says.

"But sometimes you just know." Dave's smug smile has her blushing. It's so stinking cute.

Emerson clears his throat. "But here's where things went south."

South? I'm not sure I have any idea what he's talking about. "Is something wrong?"

Emerson inhales and looks at his hands. "While I was trying to find a way to help Elizabeth's shelter, I stumbled on a way to save Richmond Steel a lot of money. But when I pitched it to Grandmother last night, she got pretty upset. She was angry I talked to Uncle Bentley about it, and then she got angrier when I tried to explain my idea." He sighs. "I mean, I get it. I know that I really know nothing compared to all of them. And maybe there's a reason my idea's stupid, but she didn't even listen to it."

"Emerson." Seren reaches for his hand across the table, but he pulls it back.

"It's fine." He looks down at his plate, and I realize he's hardly eaten anything. "I felt like a failure in school right after Mom died, you know. It's how I felt my first year in college, too. And my first year at my new job, when I started working full time. But I felt that way because each of those times, I was behind. Everyone around me knew more than I did. I should be keeping my head down, learning, and listening like I did back then, not digging around and trying to tell Grandmother how to run her company." He looks up then, his eyes a little haunted. "It's fine. I guess I just wanted to tell someone about it."

Seren looks like she has something she wants to say, but a few minutes later, she gets up and goes to the restroom. Maybe her stomach hurt or something. By the time she gets back, Dave has ordered everything on the dessert menu, and she's laughing when she sits. "I've already had all of these."

"But Elizabeth hasn't," Dave says. "It's a tradition. We have to let the women decide which ones they like the best."

"David Fansee," she says. "You're ridiculous."

"We Fansee men know how to spoil our girls."

"I'm really not that fancy," I say.

"Ah, poor Emerson," Seren says. "Now you have *three* last names."

I'm so confused.

Emerson smiles. "My mother's last name was Duplessis. And then I joined the Fansee family." He spells out the letters. "F A N S E E. And now I've found out that my dad's family is named Richmond."

"It's a lot of names," I say. "And I think I like them all."

"Me too," Emerson says.

As we walk out, he takes my hand in his, and something inside of me thrills just a bit. He doesn't have to do it, but he is. Did he. . .did he have fun? We're almost to the car when it starts to drizzle.

And, that's when I notice that I left my phone inside.

"Aw drat," I say.

Emerson unlocks the car. "Hop in! It's barely raining, but it could start really coming down."

"I left my phone."

"I can drive you over."

But I need a minute to clear my head, and the rain actually feels kind of nice. I toss my purse in the car and shake my head. "I'll run grab it. Be right back."

"Wait." Emerson hops in and turns the car on.

But I keep heading for the restaurant on foot. I imagine he'll come pick me up at the front.

Luckily, I find it right away. It's on the table, right under the basket of hummus. No wonder I didn't see it. I'm darting back out when I hear Emerson's name. My head snaps sideways. Seren's standing outside the bathroom door, talking to Dave.

"I didn't know if she'd even see my email, much less reply, but she did, and I'm going to go."

"You should ask Emerson first," he says. "He may not want you getting involved."

Seren straightens, her brow furrowing, and her eyes flashing. "Well, she shouldn't have made him feel like that, then. She may be his grandmother, but that doesn't mean she can make him feel small."

Dave laughs. "Uh oh. Mama Bear coming through."

She hits his chest. "Stop. I'm being serious."

"Then I'll come too, just to make sure you don't go too crazy."

She rolls her eyes.

When Dave hugs her, I see my window and dart past, wondering on the way to the car whether I ought to mention it to Emerson. I don't owe Seren anything at all. It's Emerson I should be loyal to, not her.

But when I think about my own mother, when I try to imagine her emailing the great Catherine Richmond and setting up a meeting to bawl her out on my behalf,

I can't even conjure up an image. The only way I could ever see my mom behaving around Catherine Richmond is obsequious. She'd bow, compliment, and scrape.

There's no world in which she would rant. Not a single one.

It makes me love Seren even more in that moment. Emerson may have had a bumpy start. His grandmother may be a terrifying piece of work. But having a mother like Seren and a father like Dave, it's not nothing.

When I get into the car where Emerson was waiting for me right outside, I look him in the face and smile. "Thanks. It was right by the hummus."

And I don't tell him another single thing.

❧ 16 ☙

ELIZABETH

Every year when I was growing up, it was a mad scramble to find a place to stay at the Hamptons for the summer. When you live near NYC, that's where all the business chats happen.

Anyone who is *anyone* has a house in the Hamptons.

So of course, we never had one. But we would always rent one, and if my parents got really lucky, they'd run into people they wanted to chat with at the beach. Easton and I were necessary accessories. A lot of their friends had kids, and plenty of them were close to our ages. But one year, when I was barely old enough to read, Easton had made great friends with a kid who was a year or two older than him. That kid had a sister, and Mom and Dad really wanted his dad to invest, so we were told to play perfectly with them—not one squabble. Not one demand. We were basically told to keep those two kids happy.

Only, the sister was two and a half years older than me, and she loved to swim out as far as she could in the ocean. Which was fine, except I wasn't the strongest swimmer. Mom handed me arm floaties, which was already embarrassing enough, and then told me to go have fun.

I struggled the first few weekends, but about halfway through the summer, I got the hang of swimming in the waves, and I had a lot of fun swimming way out with the other girl. That's when I stopped wearing the floaties. Mom never noticed. And one Saturday afternoon near the end of the summer, I caught a wave wrong.

I still remember how it felt—I couldn't breathe. Salty water flooded my nasal canal and throat, burning, and when I flailed around helplessly, my eyes got all blurry, too. As soon as I managed to spit all the water out and surge to the surface, another wave would hit me in the face. By the third or fourth round, I felt weak. I was probably pretty oxygen deprived.

I remember thinking that I was going to die.

I didn't, luckily.

Easton noticed I was thrashing and had the presence of mind to bring two boogie boards when he came after me. I clung to that boogie board desperately as my brother towed me back.

This morning, when I finally get my friend Kristy on the phone, it feels like another wave slapping me in the face. "I can't take all the animals back," she says.

"But you're an open intake shelter," I say.

"You didn't let me finish." She sighs. "I can't take them all next week. If I do, they'll all be euthanized in a three-day period."

"What? Why?"

"You need to bring at least forty of them over today."

"*Today?*" I ask.

I'm not ready to surrender them yet.

"Look, here's how our system works." She proceeds

to explain some thing about quotas and total numbers and bylaws about intake from other shelters versus private citizens.

"But if I bring forty today," I say.

"And if you bring the other forty-something next week, that's low enough that it won't trigger the shelter surrender clause." She grunts. "And then they'll go into the normal thirty-day queue."

Which gives me thirty days to go back and save the ones who aren't adopted over there. That means I need to close on a new place and get it in some kind of shape quick.

"Thanks, Kristy."

Only this time, unlike that summer, there's no one to bring me a boogie board. I think about calling Easton, but I know he's already drowning, trying to get his company ready to go public. I could call Victoria and Rhiannon, except they're both at a show today. As a good friend, I really should go watch and cheer. Only, they know the shelter's closing, so they won't be mad if I miss it.

I call my best volunteers, the ones who often sacrifice weekends, and two of them come. "You're lucky I have the minivan today," Belinda says. "My ex is doing the carpool in his truck, so I'm free."

Between the two of them making one run each, I only have twenty-three animals to take myself. I'm crying as I load up my first batch into the shelter's van—cats this time. As I slide my key into the ignition, another car pulls in. It's one I recognize, but it's still a surprise.

I open the door and stand up. "Emerson?"

He's peering into the windows of the van. "Where are you going?"

I explain the situation as quickly as I can.

"So that's why you were crying." He tilts his head sympathetically. "How can I help?"

I shake my head. "There's nothing you can do."

"Then I'll just ride over with you."

Now I'm really going to start sobbing.

"Hey." He circles the van and pulls me against him for a hug.

"They may all die," I say. "If I'm not fast enough, if I can't get another place lined up. . ."

"Have you asked Bernie about rentals?"

I can't help my ragged laugh. "Yes. He thought it was a joke—no normal person would rent a space to an animal shelter. Only my parents." I don't clarify that I was paying them exactly nothing.

"Well, look." He grabs my shoulders and backs me up a bit. "You have done and you are doing everything you can. No one can fault you, and what's more, you shouldn't fault yourself. Okay?"

If he knew how much I was regretting selling my horse right now—if they're going to die anyway, did I sell Hottie for nothing? I'm such a selfish jerk, but I know he's showing right now in the Grand Prix I wanted to ride in, and I'm here, carting animals over to be put in line for extermination.

But today, Emerson's my buoy. He holds me up, he bobs back and forth, and he wipes the tears off my cheeks whenever my eyes leak, as he keeps calling it. We're on our way back from the last trip when it occurs to me to ask. "Did Bentley say how Lucky's doing?"

He frowns. "He didn't mention her." He whips out his phone. "I should check in."

Luckily, he puts the phone on speaker.

"Hello?"

"Hey, Uncle Bentley. It's me, Emerson."

"Was Catherine impressed?"

"Not exactly," Emerson says. "But that's not why I'm calling."

"What? How could she not be—"

"I wanted to see how Lucky's doing," he says. "The shelter's closing, so if she's not a great fit, we need to make a plan for what to do with her."

"Ah, right. Of course." He sighs. "She likes running way more than I do. She also likes to jump up on all my furniture, including my counters. I was going to bring her back, but I've been too busy to do it."

It bums me out, I'm not going to lie.

But then, Bentley keeps talking. "But then, whenever I thought about calling you, I got kind of. . ." He coughs. "I can't explain it really."

"You got sad?" I ask.

He grunts. "Is that Elizabeth?"

"Yep," Emerson says. "She's in the car with me."

"Right. Well, that's the thing. I was thinking. I have no reason to keep her. She's a mess. She breaks things. She's super, duper high energy. But then I look at her pathetic tail stub, and her desperate little eyes entreating me to love her, and I don't know."

"Well, there's no huge rush," I say.

"I thought Emerson said—"

"You can keep her a few more days yet," I say. "We'll call you back and check in then."

"Alright. Well, if you're sure."

Oh, I'm totally sure.

Emerson's about to hang up when Bentley asks, "Did it really not go well with your grandmother?"

"Let's just say she didn't hear me out with as much patience as you did."

"Huh. Well, let's hope the meeting with your parents goes better."

"The meeting with—what?" Emerson steps on the brake, and cars behind us start honking. Thankfully, he pulls over to the side of the road. "What are you talking about?"

"You didn't know Dave and Seren were going to the Richmond Mansion for lunch today?" Bentley asks. "I thought you set it up."

All the blood drains away from Emerson's face.

"Hey, can we call you back?" I ask.

"Oh, sure," Bentley says. "No rush, but if you need anything, call right away."

"Will do," I say.

Emerson's still staring out the front windshield blankly, and I recognize the news for what it is.

It's a wave to the face.

So I do what he's been doing for me for a while now —I hand him a boogie board. "Let's drive over there right now," I say.

"Right now?" He turns toward me slowly. "This could be pretty awkward. Actually, I'm sure it will be."

I slide my hand on top of his where it's resting on the steering wheel. "I'm pretty good with awkward."

His laugh's pretty dry. "Well, that's good. I feel like that's all you've experienced around me."

Only, this moment isn't awkward at all. In fact, it feels pretty authentic to me. I'm just too afraid to tell him.

EMERSON

I might not have been thinking very straight when I decided to drive what looks like a creeper-van-extraordinaire past the Richmond Estate guard tower and park it in the circular drive. There's a service entrance for stuff like this, and I might've been able to sneak up on their conversation had I used it.

Only, I'm not really thinking very clearly. Not at all.

My grandmother's a difficult woman. Actually, that may be putting it a little mildly. She's a terrifying snob who also happens to be a bully. I really didn't want to subject Seren to her. Ever.

Probably because for basically my entire life, I've been disappointing poor Dave and Seren, starting with the day we met. Seren's first impression of me was trying to save me from the police after I robbed a hardware store.

A few months later, she asked to adopt me and I turned her down.

Or rather, her husband Dave asked, but either way, I said no. In all the years in between, I've regretted that a dozen times at least, but at first I was too proud to say anything, and then I was too old to do much about it.

It's not like people adopt twenty-year-old kids.

So here I am, standing at the front door, staring at a butler with a big white van behind me and Elizabeth at my side, unsure what in the world I can do to stand up for the parents I don't deserve when they've invaded my grandmother's army camp.

Unarmed.

Because Seren is *always* unarmed.

That's just who she is—vulnerable right down to the ground.

Most people, in the wake of a terrible tragedy, armor up. Most people protect themselves from being hurt again. Most people shut themselves off. They become insatiable shoppers. They drink. They do drugs. They steal. They become cold and hard.

Seren asks little thieves to become her kids.

She invites con artists into her home and then she loves them utterly and entirely without reservation.

When the mayor has abandoned his own grand-daughter, when her parents don't care about her either, when the state is offering exactly zero dollars for her care, and the little girl spits in her face, Seren opens her arms and says, "Come here, you tiny little angel."

What in the world is going to happen to my darling mother in the lair of the Richmond Steel dragon herself? She's going to be reduced to a pile of ash.

That's what.

Unless I can get there with a shield in time.

So I finally square my shoulders, and I stop shaking in my non-boots, and I force myself to wade into the fray to try and keep her from being roasted.

Only, I'm too late.

When I get closer to the dining room, Elizabeth on

my heels, I already hear shouting. I should speed up, but instead I find myself slowing down. . .

Because something very, very strange is happening. It's not Catherine Richmond who's yelling. No, it's the voice of an angel. An avenging angel.

"That little boy has been through hell and back, because of *you*, so how dare you—after abandoning him *and* his mother—not even listen to his ideas? How dare you make him audition to be part of your stupid, greedy, ugly, and frankly, *lonely* family? You don't deserve someone half as good as Emerson, and I think you already know it."

Holy cats in high heels.

Mom's *furious*.

"Well. If you're quite done." Now *that* is the dragon I expected.

"Thank you for asking," Mom says, her tone entirely flat. "I'm not." She huffs. "I'm just getting started."

"I think I've listened to about all I plan to hear." I can imagine my grandmother sharpening her finest, most withering glare. "And until you've dealt with the sort of tragedy that I'm currently enduring, I'll continue to ignore your blunt-tipped accusations."

"Until she's dealt with tragedy?" Dad says. "Let me tell you what my wife knows about tragedy."

"It's alright," Mom says. "She doesn't know who I am or what I've been through. The relevant part is this. When I was much younger, I lost a lot of people. I blamed myself when it happened, but that wasn't quite right. It wasn't my fault they died." Her voice softens. "I didn't cause the death of any of the people in my life that I loved. But you? You *almost* did. I'm not sure how much it hurts for you to look at that darling little boy and know that he almost didn't exist because of you, but that pain must be pretty sharp."

She's not railing now. Mom's so quiet that I can barely hear her.

"That's why I'm not yanking that stupid decorative sword off the wall to carve your tiny, shriveled heart out of your chest for hurting my darling, perfect, shining little boy. Because I think you're in more pain than he is, and I've always cared about people who are hurting."

"I'm not hurting over anything that happened twenty-seven years ago," Catherine says.

"Lying to yourself may be the worst sort of lie," Mom says. "Believe me when I say that I know the truth of that. But in life, you reap what you sow, and that means you can't plant brambles and expect a harvest of delicious fruit. You didn't earn a kid like Emerson. The fact that you want to change him, when he's already such a startlingly beautiful soul, that's the real tragedy." Mom quiets for a moment, and I wonder what's happening. "Let me make you a final promise," she says.

I wish I could see her. I imagine she looks magnificent.

"If you can't stop trying to change my boy, if you can't let him shine like the star that he is, then I will ensure that you can't hurt him ever again. If that means I need to have a nice long talk with Emerson, I'll do it, and so help me, if it means I need a sword and a shovel, well, I'm stronger than I look, and you're pretty old. I doubt many people will miss you."

Ten seconds later, Mom almost runs right into my chest.

"Oh." She startles. "Emerson."

She's brighter than the sun at midday. She's stronger

than a team of Clydesdales. I love her more than I've ever loved anyone, even my first mom. I feel horrible thinking that, but I realize that it's true.

"Did you just threaten to kill my grandmother?"

"She did," Catherine says from a few steps behind Mom. She's standing in the doorway of the dining room.

I wrap my arms around Mom and I hug her, and then I say, "I love you. More than you know." And then I release her, because I realize that I've been scared. This entire time, I've been afraid, and not that I wouldn't inherit Richmond Steel and Grandmother's money. That was the obvious thing at risk, but it's not really the scary part. Since meeting Mom and Dad, I've never gone hungry. I've never had to move because rent was due.

But my entire life, I've known my biological father didn't love me.

Ever since my mother died and I had no father to turn to, I've been afraid that it meant that I wasn't really lovable. But in the face of what Mom just did, of what Mom just said, I realize that although I wanted Catherine Richmond's approval. . .I don't need it.

I know I'm loved.

Deeply. Unequivocally. By someone who knows how to love. By someone who won't change their mind. By someone who would risk going to jail to make sure *I* know how special I am.

I thought Mom had no armor, and that meant she was at risk of being injured. I guess the truly brave warriors just don't need it like the rest of us do.

But now it's time for me to face Grandmother. The woman who loves me. . .if I become what she wants. The woman who has strings attached to all her gifts and armor covering every part of her soul.

"I appreciate the offer you made me," I say. "It was really generous of you to invite me into your life. It was great that you were willing to teach me, to train me, and to help me repair all my flaws. But the thing is, I've realized today that I don't want any of that. I don't need Richmond Steel, and I don't need billions of dollars, and I don't need love that comes with clauses and contingencies. I already have the kind of love that comes with no strings at all."

"You don't even have a job," Grandmother says. "You're not afraid about that?"

"I'll call Uncle Bentley," I say. "I bet he can help me find one, and I bet he'll do it without making me promise to change my wardrobe, my girlfriend, or my educational background."

Of course, after I spin around on my heel and follow Dad and Mom out the door, I realize how brash that was. Three billion plus dollars, and I just threw it all away. I've lost my ever-loving mind.

Bea is going to kill me.

Lisa may not even like me.

But it's fine.

I was right when I said I don't need it.

Any of it.

"Are you really going to call Bentley and ask for a job?" Dad asks.

"Probably not," I say. "I have a little pride left."

"So you don't practice what you preach?" Mom asks.

I roll my eyes. "Telling her what she *should* do doesn't mean that I *need* to get help. I have a degree and a great resume."

"You're as stubborn as your mother." Dad picks up his phone and presses a button.

"Wait."

I freeze, realizing that I came here in Elizabeth's white van. She came inside too, but somehow, during either my monologue or Mom's she must have left. She's sitting inside the van now, staring at the steering wheel. She looks a little shell-shocked, and I feel like a legitimate jerk.

"Hey, Bentley," Dad says. "Well, Emerson just told off that grandmother of his, and now he's out on his ear. Before he gets snatched up by another snooty accounting firm, I thought I'd give you a chance to make him an excellent offer."

It's like two trains are barreling down the line, both of which I need to deal with, and I'm not sure what to do with either. I should be stopping Dad, and I should be apologizing to Elizabeth. I was just telling her that I'd help her, but then I burned down the bridge I would have needed to take to get her help.

I suck.

It was a selfish thing to do. I should have bitten my tongue, at least until she had a couple decent donors. I know I'm only a fake boyfriend, but I'm still a terrible one.

"He wants to talk to you." Dad shoves his phone at me.

"Emerson," Uncle Bentley says. "I offered you a job right out of school, and you turned me down."

"You said yourself at that party that you don't hire the children of people you know."

"Society fops," Uncle Bentley says. "Not my nephew."

"Still, I can find a job," I say, but it sounds half-hearted, even to me.

"You're not listening. After that catch you made for your grandma—the one she didn't even listen to—I really want you on my team. That's exactly what we do.

We find redundancies and eliminate them. We streamline. We repair and improve. I bet you'd be great at carving out the salvageable parts of companies, too."

I grunt.

"Look. You didn't listen to *me* the last time, but I mean it this time. I'd love to double your salary, and I'll even include a performance bonus. Come work for me."

Is it a bad idea to work for family? It didn't work out well for me the last time, that's for sure. But maybe what I said was true. Bentley's real family, even if we're not related. He's more of an uncle than anyone else has ever been to me. "Okay," I say. "But I want my bonus to go to Elizabeth's shelter."

"Done," he says.

"Text me where to come Monday. And Uncle Bentley—thanks." I hand the phone back to Dad.

"It's going to be okay." Mom hugs me tightly, and then she shoves me toward the van. Before I can even wave goodbye, she and Dad are briskly walking toward their car.

Elizabeth's still staring at the steering wheel.

Even when I open the creaky passenger door, she doesn't move.

"It was pretty heated in there," I say.

She's still staring. I'm beginning to worry that she might be in shock.

"But listen, Uncle Bentley actually did hire me, and I told him I want my bonus to go to the shelter." I wince as I say it. As if some year-end bonus will somehow help her right now, in her time of ultimate crisis. "But, like, I know that's not really what you need," I say lamely, closing my eyes and trying to figure out how to fix this.

She inhales sharply.

I open my eyes and watch.

Her hands tighten around the steering wheel. "You told her just exactly what you should have, and now you're free." She turns toward me, a smile plastered on her face. It's clearly fake.

"It was selfish, and I'm sorry."

She frowns, the fake smile thankfully melting away. "It was actually the opposite of selfish." This time her kind smile is real. "It was a pretty moving monologue. You and your parents know more about family than she does, that's for sure."

"I walked away from all that money, and I told off a grieving mother."

"I'm not sure Catherine Richmond has a heart under there to grieve with," Elizabeth says. "If you opened her up, they might just find an account ledger."

That image makes me laugh. "I think her heart has just been unused for a while."

"Well, either way, you're *free* now." She isn't smiling, but she looks resolved. "Which means. . ."

"I can't really help you." I feel awful. "I'm so sorry. I swear I didn't think about that."

"Emerson," she says. "That's not what I'm saying. My problems are my problems. What I mean is, you don't need to fake date me anymore. You can call Lisa and you guys can get back together. Finally." Her smile's forced again, but her words sound real. "I wish you all the best."

Because there's no reason for she and I to date any more. Obviously.

"Right. Of course you do." I nod woodenly. "And of course I wish you the best, too."

"You don't need to give your bonus to the shelter." She starts the van, and she pulls into the drive, headed out. "It's such a nice gesture, but it's not really practical. You'll probably need that money."

"I will?"

"For the wedding." Her lip's twisted in humor. "I doubt Lisa will be satisfied with a small, low-key wedding."

"I guess not." I hadn't even thought about a wedding. Geez. Thinking about that gives me major anxiety, but I'm not sure why. I doubt it'll be *that* expensive. Doesn't the bride usually pay for that?

Elizabeth keeps talking about the wedding, all the way back to the shelter where my car's parked. She asks me if we have a lot of friends in common. She asks if any of my siblings have gotten married—no way—and whether I'd want them to be in the wedding party. *What the heck is a wedding party?* The more she talks, the more panicked I feel. Probably because I haven't even talked to Lisa yet. That's surely why.

Only, when Elizabeth parks, I get this terrible feeling in my stomach. I feel. . .sick. Like maybe we ate something bad. Maybe it's that I'm hungry. We skipped dinner.

"Did you want to grab something to eat?" I ask. "I'll pay."

She shakes her head slowly. "Nah, you don't have to do that."

"I want to," I say.

When she whips her head toward me, her eyes look resolved. Like she's come to some kind of conclusion. "Emerson, you were great. And the idea we had, well, it wasn't a bad one."

"I didn't really help—"

"Pshaw," she says. "You got me not one, but two ten thousand dollar donations I'd never have gotten otherwise."

"But you need—"

"Emerson."

"Yeah."

"Get out of this car and go talk to that girl you're crazy about."

Lisa. She's talking about Lisa.

"You've had to hold off, but now you don't. Okay?" Why does she look so weird?

"How much more would you need—"

"I have most of a downpayment, thanks to Hottie," she says. "And I have two more cash donations that will pay for the rest. I have a job now, and that will be enough to look like a steady prospect to a bank. As long as I'm smart and wait for a good place, I'll be just fine."

Waiting for a good place means all those animals we just took. . .

"Emerson, I know what you're thinking, and you can stop. Your conscience is clear, I swear, okay? You were right. I can't be responsible for the world. I do what I can, and the rest is what it is." She tosses her head at the door. "Go already."

I finally listen, but I'm preoccupied the whole way home. Elizabeth sold her horse—the one she loves. She has no one to ride. Some rich lady has him. She lost her shelter. She's working half the day so she can get a loan to buy a new one that no one can just take away, but she has no real plan for funding it beyond that. Is she just going to be stuck paying for it out of pocket?

I'm still worrying when I get back to my apartment. When I walk up the sidewalk leading to our door, I slow down. Because the strident voices up ahead are ones I'm very familiar with.

Bea isn't shouting, but she's not happy. "I told you. I have the same cell phone number for him that you do. I don't know the address of his grandmother's house, and it's not listed. So unless you're planning to pay rent and sublet his room—"

"You're saying that you're his sister, but you can't even reach him?" Lisa sounds pretty miffed.

"I'm saying that when I call my brother, he calls me back. Presumably that's because he wants to talk to me. If he's not calling you back, maybe take the hint." Wow, Bea is always nice. She must be royally ticked.

"Hey, guys," I say. "No need to worry about my address—I'm moving back in here today."

"You are?" Jake's head pops up behind Bea. "So does that mean I have to move all my crap out of your room?"

I hope he's kidding.

"Hey." Lisa looks nervous when she turns around to face me. I wonder why she would be. "You haven't been answering your phone."

I smack my forehead. "It didn't charge last night for some reason. It must have died. It's been a long day."

"It has?" Lisa steps toward me. "Have you eaten? We can talk about it over dinner."

"I guess," I say, suddenly not feeling very hungry.

"But, like, are you really moving back in?" Jake's still hanging on the side of the doorframe.

"Yes," I say.

He swears under his breath and disappears. Sometimes he really makes me angry. Was he actually using my room as a storage space? I don't even want to think about what kind of stuff he's slung in there. Or worse, which of my things he's rummaged through. I should have bought a lock for the door.

Actually, he'd probably just have picked it. The guy's actually a criminal.

"Make sure it's clean when I get back," I tell Bea.

She's laughing as she closes the door. I'm not sure whether that means she won't be able to, or whether she won't need to do much and I'm worrying over a joke. . .

"Em?"

In the two years we've known each other, Lisa has never once called me Em. "Yeah."

"You ready?"

She's being really strange. Usually she kind of orders me around. Now that I think about it, it's a little odd that I liked that. But she's never been nervous or tentative like this. Maybe it was the confidence that I liked and that's what's bugging me right now. "Let's go."

We're nearly to my car when she says, "Why are you moving back in?"

"Oh." I take a few steps to the car and turn, leaning against it. "It's been a really weird day." I exhale. "It feels almost like I've been running all day."

"What happened?" She rearranges her purse strap so it lies flat and tilts her head.

"I spent the morning helping Elizabeth."

Her entire body stiffens.

"The shelter's closing, and she had to surrender all the animals to a bigger shelter in the city. It wasn't very fun."

"Distasteful," she says.

"I mean, it wasn't that." I'm not being very clear. "She loves those animals. She calls them all by names, and she wanted to find them homes. So surrendering them all. . .it was really depressing."

"Why did you have to go?" Her frown bugs me for some reason. "It's not your shelter."

"I didn't *have* to go, but I felt like I ought to lend a hand."

"Meanwhile, I haven't heard from you at all."

"Elizabeth's my girlfriend, though." Although, technically, she never really was, and now she isn't at all. Still. "Then, after that, I heard from Uncle Bentley, and he said Mom and Dad were going to talk to Grandmother, and I rushed over to avert a disaster, and. . ." I sigh. "I was too late."

Her eyes widen. "Oh, no. What happened?"

"Actually it was really good." I nod slowly. "It was what needed to happen. I realized that Grandmother was using her money as a way to order me around. I mean, I knew that? But I guess. . .she wasn't even listening to me. I'm not sure she ever would have."

"But Richmond Steel is a really massive company," Lisa says. "It might be worth letting her order you around a little to learn how to manage it."

"Sure, but she was telling me who I could date, and what I had to do every day, and when I found a way to save the company money, she didn't even listen."

"You found a way to manage her company better?" Lisa arches one eyebrow. "Really? Because that sounds kind of. . .condescending. I can see why she didn't want to hear that from you."

"But I was right," I say. "Uncle Bentley thought it was great, too, and he would know—that's literally his job."

"You talked to someone else about her company?" Lisa cringes.

It feels like I'm being audited or something. "Yes, about my *family's* company, before going to her about it, to make sure I wasn't wasting her time."

"Emerson. You just haven't ever really had a family, so you don't know, but that was really disloyal."

"I've never had a real family?"

"Not until now," she says. "I can talk to her if you want. I can explain."

"I don't need you to explain," I say. "Actually, I just straight up think you're wrong."

"So your grandmother was fine with all this, then? With you telling her what to change about the company?"

"No. She was really upset." I fold my arms.

"Forget dinner. We need to go over there right now. You can introduce me to her, and we can apologize."

"I'm not going to do that," I say. "She doesn't need to meet you."

"Okay, that's fair. She doesn't have to meet me yet —no reason to upset her further on the same day. But you need to tell her that you were sorry and convince her that you're learning."

I shake my head.

"Emerson." She steps closer, her arm outstretched. "Look, this is confusing and it feels suffocating too, maybe, but that's what family is."

"No." I knock her outstretched hand away. "That's not what family is. Dave and Seren have never suffocated me. They've never tried to tell me what to do or who to date." If they had, I'm guessing they'd have had their opinions on Lisa, who hid that we were even dating from her parents.

"Well, when you have a real family, it's different. Trust me."

A real family. That word again. "I have a real family," I say. "I have a healthy family, and I have a strong one."

"Your so-called *brother* just co-opted your room and doesn't want to give it back." She snorts.

"That may be the most real thing any family member can do," I say. "That's what siblings do. They get all up in your face and they bug you and they badger you." I realize, as I say it, that it's true. I get really frustrated with Jake—but he is my brother.

"What you have is a cobbled-together band of misfits, and it was really nice of Dave and Seren to take you all in, but with your grandmother, you have a shot at a real, stable family."

"My family *is* stable," I say. "And my grandmother isn't really much of a grandmother. I feel like I'm being recruited for a sports team, and if I don't do what they say, they won't sign the commitment letter."

"That's not how that works," Lisa says.

"Whatever," I say. "The point is that I told Grandmother I was done with her ultimatums. I said I'm not a performing monkey, and then I quit."

Lisa grabs my arm and tries to turn me toward the car. "We can still fix this."

"No." I shake her arm off. "And I'm just now realizing that I can't fix *us* either." I can't help my dry bark of a laugh. "Actually, there hasn't really ever been an us, has there? You wouldn't tell anyone about me, and you weren't too excited to date me until you found out I could be rich."

"That's not at all—"

I shrug. "The ironic part is that I just ended my real relationship." Because I thought it was the fake one.

I'm monumentally stupid.

"If you don't go with me over to your grandmother's right now, then we're through." Lisa glares.

"Oh, good," I say. "You promise?"

Her face is priceless.

But when I finally get her to leave—she does not storm off like she said she would—and I go inside, Jake isn't even *close* to having his crap out of my room.

"Teddy bears?" I ask. "Really? And what are these weird t-shirts?"

Bea tackles me from behind with a huge hug. "Thank goodness you're back. Jake's fans keep sending him crap, and some of it is really, really weird."

Oh, good. Someone with a stranger life than mine.

"She kept threatening to kick me out if you moved back in," Jake says.

"You and I can split the rent," Bea says. "Then we can share that extra room." She points at Jake's room, and then she turns to face him. "Once we get it disinfected."

We both laugh.

"And I wasn't kidding," Bea says, turning toward Jake. "You need to go find some place with a guard or something at the front of the building. I can't keep dealing with your crazy fans."

Jake immediately starts complaining about her never-finished laundry. Bea launches into a diatribe about his inability to ever wash a dish. And within two minutes, they've forgotten about cleaning his crap out of my room, and they're practically coming to blows about leaving the windows in the family room open or closed.

I start shoving boxes out of my room and into the hall, and I can't help my goofy grin. Yes, they're annoying. Yes, when Jake's not filming, we bicker all the time.

And that's what real family is. It's the love behind the bickering.

Lisa never got that at all, but I think maybe Elizabeth does.

And I'm going to do my very best to find out.

❧ 18 ❧

CATHERINE

When I was a child, most of the children of my parents' friends played together after school. They had dolls. They went to parties. They swam. They played sports, some of them.

Not me.

I learned Latin, a totally useless language. After private school classes ended each day, my tutor came to teach me French, Spanish, and Italian. I played piano, taught by the best piano players of my time—I was one of the first women invited to teach at Juilliard.

No moment of my waking time was wasted.

Because I knew from the time I was born—my birth killed my mother, as I was repeatedly reminded—that the responsibility fell to me to captain the Richmond Steel enterprise. Eventually, even my marriage was planned by my father. He found someone who would take my name, who brought efficient and intelligent planning expertise to the table, and most of all, someone who would listen to me in a time when women were not often allowed, much less encouraged, to run companies.

My father always treated me like I was the son he never had.

And I took my responsibility seriously.

I learned what was taught. I worked, and worked, and worked ceaselessly to turn Dad's large company into the unparalleled empire that it is today. When the time was right, I gave birth to a strong and healthy little boy. And then, I did for Alistair the exact thing my father did for me. I molded him, like unformed clay, into the perfect successor. He learned four languages—and more useful ones than I had. He spent his time on robotics projects, on developing science and technology areas where I always felt reliant on engineers to translate for me. I made the knowledge of running a business paramount, but the underlying technology wasn't a puzzle to him.

He became exactly what Richmond Steel needed—what I shaped him to be.

All my efforts were nearly derailed while he was in high school, because of a girl.

I called my dad and asked him what to do. He said that having a child while my son was a teenager would be catastrophic. Not only to his reputation, but also on his focus, on his ability to learn, and in his capacity to work. Richmond would suffer. Our legacy would suffer. I was undecided before then, but galvanized by my father's words, I took care of the problem ruthlessly.

Or, I thought I did.

The one area on which I didn't spend enough time, because focusing on it was diametrically opposed to my plan to make him a perfect successor, was ensuring that Alistair had a proper diet, exercised enough, and had low stress. I've since discovered that those deficiencies are the leading causes of heart attacks in men under fifty, and that's what ended his life.

Which means that I killed my own son.

I took identical steps to those my dad took with me, but instead of living a long and healthy life as I have, Alistair died early. All that effort, all that push, and all the misery I inflicted on him were utterly pointless. And worse, I had absolutely no one to take over the one thing I'd done right—no one to manage the Richmond dynasty.

Until I met Emerson.

He was twenty-seven years behind, but he was clearly my grandson. He was bright, eager, hard-working, and competent in the things he had managed to learn. He hadn't been raised as he should have, but I thought I might be able to repair the damage. I was making progress—more than I expected, frankly. He was receptive to dating the right people, and I didn't even hate the girl he chose. Her family wasn't the best, but she had a basic understanding of what would be required of her. She seemed fairly competent, and she was clearly gifted in guiding him. If she was obsessed with saving mongrels, well, everyone has some flaws.

She was nice enough looking and reasonably intelligent.

But then. . .Emerson thought he had come up with something that would transform Richmond Steel. I could barely contain my laughter. He had the audacity to invite outsiders to evaluate *my work*, and when I rightfully dismissed his ideas, his *parents* showed up to yell at me. It was absurd in the extreme. I should be relieved he's gone. Clearly the progress I thought I was making was false. It couldn't have been real, not with that sort of delusion.

And yet.

I keep wanting to pick up my phone and *call him*. Not for any particular reason, but I just. . .seeing him made me feel better somehow. My chest wasn't tight. My lips kept wanting to turn up in a smile, like I was a soft-headed idiot. And now that he's gone, I feel. . .sluggish. Perpetually disappointed with everything.

"So you don't like the updates to the plans?" The CEO looks like he might have already asked me that.

I snap my head down at the plans in front of me. "No."

"What didn't you like?" He looks like he's worried I'll maul him. What's he so nervous about?

"They're fine, I said."

"Oh." He blinks. "Alright. Then if you could sign off on them."

I stand up. I clearly can't sign off on anything right now. I wasn't listening to a word he said. "Send a copy to my office. I'd like the chance to look over them a little longer." When I'm not so distracted thinking about The Great Disappointment.

"To your—okay. I'll do that."

"Thanks."

I'm nearly to the door, my hand reaching for the knob when he says, "And by the way. That suggestion was one of the best I've seen. I'm interviewing people for the proposed position internally first, and if we don't find a suitable candidate, we'll post a listing."

I freeze. "What?" I pivot on my heel and pin him with a stare.

He clears his throat. "Did you want me to post it externally first?"

I shake my head. "I have no idea what you're talking about."

"The cost savings proposal you sent over? It came at the bottom of that stack of materials on the shipping contracts and the warehouse design, so I didn't see it until this morning."

It's like he's lost his mind. "I didn't send any cost savings proposals."

"The one your grandson authored?" He tilts his head. "I assumed you had written most of it. It was one of the most clear, most impressive memos I've seen, and it's one hundred percent right—with the hand-written corrections. Surely those came. . .from you?" His brow's furrowed.

"Oh, yes." I nod. "The hand-written corrections."

He exhales. "Thank goodness." His mouth turns up into a smile. "You were kidding. It's not like you to make jokes like that. For a moment I thought I misunderstood."

"Can you tell me about the proposal in your own words?" I ask. "Just so I'm sure we're on the same page with the interviews?"

"To be honest, I was floored. I had no idea we had such a huge cost latency in the company profile. To think that we had that many million in wasted rental payments—ten times the cost of the equipment over a term of years." He whistles. "What even made him think of that?"

"I've just realized that I sent you my only copy. If you could make copies for yourself and send it back to me, that would be great."

"For sentimental reason." He bobs his head. "Of course. I'd want to keep that too—your grandson's first save ever." He chuckles. "His projections were showing close to ninety million, but I'm embarrassed to say that now we're digging through the figures, it'll be closer to a hundred million."

A hundred million. . .savings? From Emerson's memo?

"And boy, if anyone was wondering whether he really was a Richmond, initiating a new position in the company that will save that kind of money in his first week here?" He smiles. "Impressive."

I practically race back to my office and tap my fingers until I get the original proposal back.

The one I ignored.

The one I mocked.

The one my CEO says is the best save he's seen.

I read it myself, and I realize that Emerson was dead on. How did none of our accountants see this?

How did *Emerson*?

It's hard—my hand shakes as I press the buttons—but I call him.

He's ignoring me.

I hate doing it, but I actually cancel my meetings, and I drive to the address he wrote on the file. I knock on the door of his shabby little apartment, shuddering at the thought that he lives here.

Some girl answers the door. It's most definitely not Elizabeth. "Hello," I say. "I'm looking for Emerson."

"You must be the grandmother." The small girl with dark hair tilts her head. "You look just as mean as he said."

"Excuse me?"

"Emerson's at work," she says. "Maybe leave him alone, yeah?" Then she slams the door in my face.

I wasn't wrong about his horrible family, at least. But he's *at work*? He had just been fired and was working as a caterer when we met. Then he spent every day with me, shadowing me through business operations. Where else could he have gotten a job in two days? It must be Bentley Harrison.

I try calling his office as well, but infuriatingly, his secretary asks me to leave a message.

Well, I'm more tenacious than his sister thinks. I can wait around. It's three-thirty. How late could

Emerson possibly be coming home? I notice a bench across the parking lot, and I walk over and sit down at it. A few moments later, a horrible, squelching, burping bus stops in front of the bench.

"You getting in?" the driver asks.

Horrified, I shake my head. "No."

The driver shrugs, closes the door, and the horrible bus blasts its way down the road, making an already muggy day even hotter. A few moments later, I notice someone heading for the apartment door. I spring up and dash across the street, but when I get closer, I realize it's not Emerson.

It's another young man—possibly the dark-haired girl's boyfriend? He doesn't bother knocking, though. He simply grabs the knob and barges into the apartment. Is Emerson's place some kind of young person waystation? I wait, and then I wait, and then I wait more, and he's still not here at half past six.

I should leave. Surely the appallingly poorly mannered dark-haired girl will tell him I came by. Or he might notice the several missed calls from me. Either way, he'll probably call me back soon.

Or will he?

I can't help thinking about what he said to me again. It keeps coming back to me, over and over. *I already have the kind of love that comes with no strings at all.*

I don't even really understand him. What kind of love has no strings? Not a good kind. Everything has strings. If you want to have lots of money, you have to work for it. If you want to run a company, you have responsibilities. If you want your spouse to respect you, you earn that respect. Nothing in life is ever free. Similarly, love isn't love if it doesn't have obligations.

Love always comes with strings.

He's just too young and naive to understand that.

But finally—*finally*—he comes home. I watch him park his old, tired car, and I stand. He looks backward, seeing my movement, and his eyes widen alarmingly. "Grandmother?"

That's a little satisfying, at least. He didn't expect to see me.

I can't help but notice that he's cut his hair. When we met, it looked almost dopey. Long, block-cut, and not at all what an heir of the Richmond empire should have. One very expensive haircut later, he looked the part. He should have been delighted with his appearance.

So why did he essentially shave all his beautiful hair off?

I take a step toward him, but he jogs toward me. "Are you alright?" He's looking me over for signs of injury, but other than being a bit stiff from spending hours on a bus bench, I'm fine.

"How long have you been here?" His brow furrows.

I want to lie, but I'm worried that little girl would out me on it. "Since earlier this afternoon."

"Why?" He sits on the bench and gestures that I can join him.

Of course a bus pulls up right then.

We both wave it on—I've gotten good at that—and he stares quietly, waiting for me to explain. Now that he's here, I wish I'd spent more time thinking about what exactly to say.

"You cut your hair."

He shrugs. "That expensive haircut wasn't me. This one is."

"Maybe they're both you," I say.

"Did something happen?"

"You left your clothes," I blurt out.

"My. . .oh, that's okay. Maybe you can return them. I barely wore any of them."

I didn't expect that. Those clothes are expensive, and he walked away from a lot of money. Surely he would at least want the clothes so he could resell them or wear them or whatever.

That's when it hits me—that's what he means by strings. I thought he would appreciate the clothes, but he didn't want them in the first place. He didn't want Richmond Steel enough to let me tell him what to do. For a split second, I wonder.

If I'd met my dad at age twenty-seven, what would I have thought about his orders about what I should study? What I should learn? How I should apply myself? Would I be upset? Would it chafe?

"I'm pretty tired," he says. "And I was going to go shower and try to see someone."

"The old girlfriend." I sigh. "Right? The one I wouldn't let you date?"

"Actually." He shakes his head. "She turned out to be. . . disappointing."

"She did?"

He nods slowly. "I'm not sure it's any of your business, but I want to go see Elizabeth Moorland."

I can't help a smug smile. I know it's not helping me, but. . .he likes the type of girl I wanted him to like. "Well, that's interesting."

"It's not, really. I'm sure if you knew more about her, you'd be just as disapproving of her. Her parents are selling you the shelter because her dad's business is dying. They're broke."

"I know."

"Wait," he says. "You do?"

I can't help my laugh. "I always look into the

finances of people when I enter into a business transaction. The Moorlands have been struggling for a while."

"Oh." He looks floored. "And Elizabeth blew her entire trust fund saving animals."

I nod. "Knew that too."

"Well."

"You wanted me to fund her shelter."

"I did, but you said no." He folds his arms and shifts away from me. "You said she's not your family."

"But if my family cares about her, maybe I was wrong."

"Maybe?"

"Do you?" I ask.

"Do I care about her?"

I nod.

"Yes. I do."

I suppress my grin. She may be broke, but she's bright, beautiful, and she's well-heeled. She's everything I need for my future great-grandchildren. And she *understands* what's expected.

"Grandmother?"

"Yes."

"Why are you here?"

"I might have been a little hasty," I say. "My CEO found your proposal, and it was good."

He huffs. "It was."

"I underestimated you," I say. "I'm sorry about that."

He stands. "Well, I'm glad we got that cleared up. No hard feelings now, right?"

"Wait." I stand too. "Come back and live with me again."

He shakes his head.

And my heart twists in my chest in the same

painful way it did when I found out that Alistair died. "Why not?"

"I already told you. I have a family." His face softens. "I'm not trying to hurt you, but you're not it. I thought you might need someone—I thought we might need each other, but you don't need anyone. And I won't live my life as some kind of untouchable statue. Mom and Dad have taught me better than that."

I hate it. How could he turn around and walk away from the Richmond name? Our estate? "I'll write you in," I say. "No strings."

He laughs. Not forced. Not stilted. Not nervous. "I'm still passing."

"Why?" I hate how brittle my voice sounds. How unsure.

"Grandmother." He sighs. "I didn't know my father—because of you, because of your machinations. My mom and I were alone. We were poor. We struggled. You didn't owe my mom anything, and she never talked about you or Dad. For some kids, that might be enough. I still wanted to know you. But." He shrugs. "It's not healthy, and I know what I want now. It's not running Richmond Steel."

"What is your new job?" I hope it's a good one for his sake. I hope it's horrible for my own—then maybe he'll recant and come back.

"I'm working for Uncle Bentley. He offered me a position before, but I turned him down."

"I forbid it," I say. "You have to work for me, not him."

"Grandmother." His eyes are so sad.

And they look just like Alistair's.

That's what gets me, in the end.

Something inside of me snaps, and for the first time in a very, very long life, a tear rolls down my cheek in public. As if that somehow freed the floodgates, I'm suddenly sobbing like a complete nitwit at a *bus station*, as if there could be a more pedestrian, a more embarrassing place to cry.

"Oh." Emerson steps forward and pulls me against his chest. "Oh, Grandmother." His arms wrap around me, and his hands pat my back stiffly. "It's okay."

"Nothing is okay," I say. "I messed up, and your father died. And now I've done it again."

"Everyone screws up," he says.

"Not Richmonds," I say.

"Well, I have news for you. If you want this kid to ever use the Richmond name, even Richmonds will screw up."

I'm laughing now, which is so weird, because it's not even that funny. But with every laugh that rockets through my body, the tears abate a little more. And suddenly, I'm laughing, and laughing, and Emerson releases me, and he's laughing, too.

"I'm arguing with you at a *bus stop*," I say.

Just then, a bus pulls up, and a hunched old woman climbs off the bus. "Don't get on that one," she stage-whispers. "I just ate a bean taco that I should *not* have eaten."

Emerson meets my eyes. "Should we talk at your house?"

"You mean *our* house?" I hate how much hope there is in my voice. In my *plea*. But it's there nonetheless.

My beautiful, brilliant, talented grandson half-smiles. "I guess that's what I mean."

For the second time in more than sixty years, I'm crying in public, at a bus stop. But this time, the tears feel different. Beautiful, somehow.

"Uncle Bentley is going to kill you if I quit my job. I just started."

"I'm willing to risk it," I say. "Bentley Harrison is a smart guy, but he's a creampuff compared to your grandmother."

Emerson wraps his arm around my shoulders. "Let's go, creampuff."

"No," I say as he drags me toward his car. "Bentley's the creampuff."

"Right," he says. "Now let's talk about what the terms of being written back into the will are."

"No terms," I say. "Unless you want a formal apology from me first."

"It would be nice, but I'm not all that demanding," he says. "An informal one would be fine, too."

My heart swells, then. Like the surf frothing its way toward the sandy shore, it grows and grows, expanding until I'm worried I'm having a heart attack like Alistair. But this never hurts—it only feels better and better.

And I wonder if this is what it feels like to love without strings. "I may be an old dog, but maybe Elizabeth will say that even some old dogs can learn new things."

"I think she'd agree with that," Emerson says. "Or at least, now I bet she would. If she was still talking to me."

"Oh, no," I say. "Did you mess up too?"

He kicks at an anthill on the edge of the parking lot. "Well, I did tell you that Richmonds made mistakes."

"But when we do," I say. "We do whatever it takes to fix them."

19

ELIZABETH

On the day I opened the shelter, Rhiannon and Victoria brought a huge, red velvet ribbon. I have no idea where they found it. It didn't wrap all the way around the building, of course, but it was large enough to tie from one end of the front to the other, and the bow at the center was massive.

I had selected five pets to start, and after cutting that ribbon, we brought them inside the building Mom and Dad had said I could use.

The barking, and the screeching, and the meowing wasn't very regal, but it was a good precursor for the chaos to follow. Only, now that I'm officially closing down the shelter after more than six years, I'm not sure how to commemorate that. Or if I even want to.

"Have you found a new place yet?" Rhiannon asks.

My laugh sounds more like a wail. "Not really. Not unless I want to take up home renovation—or, shelter renovation?" I sigh. "Every place in my price point is a total dump."

Victoria picks up a broom. "I feel bad walking out without cleaning at all."

"Like you've ever cleaned in your life," Rhiannon says.

"Not true," Victoria says. "I always clean up the crossties when I'm done tacking up or down. And I scrub the bathrooms at the barn every week."

"The girl can sweep, ladies and gentlemen," I say.

"And scrub," Victoria says.

I scrunch my nose. "Have you seen your bathrooms? I wouldn't advertise that you're in charge of keeping them clean."

"It's so quiet now," Rhiannon says.

I look around then, slowly. We took the last pets to Kristy this morning, and now I have to lock up for the last time.

"They're demolishing it?" Victoria shakes her head. "It seems like such a waste."

"Tell my parents that," I say. "Believe me. I have."

"They really don't care?" Victoria looks like she'd gladly punch them for me.

But I can't really fault them. "It is their building, and they need the money."

"Like the world doesn't have enough warehouses," Rhiannon says. "Just, ugh."

"Richmond Steel," Victoria says. "I still can't believe that handsome boy hasn't ridden in on a white horse yet—"

"Forget a white horse," Rhiannon says. "Her horse just won its first Grand Prix, and she wasn't even riding him."

"He won?" I had specifically not looked, since I didn't get to watch him myself. My heart lurches a little, but I shake my head. "I knew he would do great. I'm proud of him."

"You made that little horse into what he is. You took something broken, and you turned it into a shining star." Victoria beams. "That's kind of your thing. That Emerson kid was a wreck, and now he's telling off his grandmother and working for his rich uncle."

"And marrying some other girl," Rhiannon whispers. "Maybe ease-a up-a on-a eh-they Emerson-a."

"Pig Latin was stupid when we were kids," Victoria says. "Please don't accost my ears with it now."

"It's better than actual Latin," I say.

"Which we can only read, and then, just barely." Rhiannon shudders.

I got a F in that class, but no one mentions that, blessedly. "Well, then, what do we do to commemorate closing the shelter?"

Victoria skips toward the door, leans down, and snatches a bag off the floor. "I brought wine."

Rhiannon laughs. "That seems fitting."

We drink the first two bottles. By the end of the second one, I'm not quite as depressed, which is nice. "I mean." I stand up and hug the column near the door. "I don't have a boyfriend."

"You never wanted one," Rhiannon says.

"Plus, you just told us he wasn't really your boyfriend," Victoria says.

Crap. I did?

Well, I couldn't tell anyone it was fake before, but now that we've broken up, it's not like I'm breaking rules. "Right. It was never real."

"So, then you're better off without him," Victoria says.

"I don't have an animal shelter anymore," I say.

"Hey, we haven't even left yet." Rhiannon's slurring

a little. "It's still yours. Your horrible boyfriend's grandma hasn't stolen it."

I shake my head. "He's not my boyfriend, and he's not horrible. She is."

"That's what I said," Rhiannon says. "Geez."

"You said my horrible boyfriend, but he's not horrible," I say.

"We should've left the animals here," Victoria says. "Then you could have climbed into a tree and refused to leave. Or if they bashed the building, they could run free."

I think we may be mixing metaphors. But she does have some good ideas. "Only, now it's too late for that," I say.

"Ooh, call him and yell at him," Rhiannon says.

"At who?" Now I'm really lost.

"At the boyfriend," Rhiannon says.

"For what?" I blink. "Plus, I said he wasn't horrible."

"For not saving your shelter. Duh." Victoria swipes my phone. "How did you have him saved?" She holds my phone up to make my own face unlock it.

"You know, this face technology is pretty lousy." I've never thought of this before, but it's how I know I'm not drunk. I'm having these big thoughts I've never had, and you don't get smarter when you're drunk. "If I got kidnapped, the napper could just use my own face to open my phone." I shake my head. "Dumb."

"You're not a kid," Victoria says. "You can't get kidnapped."

"Man, we are so smart," I say.

And I hear a phone ringing. "Hello?"

Victoria has it on speaker. That's better.

"Elizabeth?"

"I like how he says my name," I say.

They both giggle.

"Elizabeth, are you alright?"

"She's ticked at you for being a horrible boyfriend," Victoria says. "Her horse is sold. Her shelter is gone. And now she doesn't even have a hot boyfriend anymore."

"Wait, am I horrible or am I hot?"

I could listen to his voice all day. "Both," Victoria says.

"Who thinks I'm hot?" he asks.

"We all do," I say. "But mostly me."

"Is that you, Elizabeth?"

He said my name again. That makes me smile. "Yeppers."

"How much have you had to drink?"

"I have to surrender the shelter today by five p.m."

"That's an hour," he says.

"But we might climb into a tree," Victoria shouts. "We could refuse to leave."

"There aren't any large trees on the shelter property." Emerson's so smart. So, so smart.

"How did he even notice that?" Rhiannon shakes her head. "No trees at all."

"We need a new plan, then," Victoria says.

"We'll think of something to save the shelter," I say, "but Emerson."

"Yeah?"

I have no idea what I was going to say.

"Emerson, Elizabeth's too scared to ask, but if we save the shelter, can you come here and be her boyfriend again?" Victoria asks.

"Hey." I can't believe she just said that. But then I really want to know what he says. I crawl closer to the phone and press my ear close to it.

"I thought you said I was horrible," he says. "Why would she want me back?"

"Well, you didn't save her horse or her shelter, but you are hot." Rhiannon chuckles.

"He is hot," I say.

"And what about her horse?" Rhiannon asks. "Who's going to buy her horse back if you don't?"

"Or buy a nice big white one," Victoria asks. "That might be better."

"Shh," I say. "He has to answer about the boyfriend thing still."

But when I look down at the phone, somehow the call has disconnected. "Hey." I poke at buttons, and then I realize my battery must have died. Nothing is lighting up.

I swear under my breath.

"Hey, we should clean up," Victoria says. "There are, like, trucks pulling up outside."

"In the afternoon?" Rhiannon's muttering swear words under her breath. Someone as posh and classy as her should *not* use words like that. It makes me laugh.

We gather all the trash into one bag, and then we manage to get all our stuff together. Finally, we're ready to leave the shelter. In a bizarre moment of clarity, I realize that I can't just get sloshed and walk out. It's not a fitting departure.

"Hey, is there any wine left?" I ask.

Rhiannon clutches the bottle against her chest. "Just one, and you can't have any. You definitely won't be able to drive."

Driving. Well, that sucks. I doubt any of us can drive.

"It's fine," I say. "I'm not drinking it. Here." I hold out my hand and wiggle my fingers. "Hand it over."

Rhiannon glares, but eventually she passes it over. I

open the front door and dance onto the porch. And then I spin round and round and round and smash the wine into the support beam that Richmond Steel is going to knock down tomorrow.

The bottle actually breaks, and wine splashes all over.

"Whoa," a man says.

I spin around, and I realize that right behind me, Emerson was climbing the stairs to the shelter. I've just soaked him.

"I guess I deserve that," he says.

"What?" I blink.

"The first time we met, I covered you in champagne." His eyes are sparkling.

"You did."

He nods. "And now we're even. The first time you see me after our breakup, you soak me in wine."

"It was an accident," I say.

"I noticed that too." He shakes his hands and wine flings all over.

"You're not even supposed to be here," Rhiannon says. "And you cut your hair. You were hotter with longer hair."

He laughs. "Duly noted."

"I agree," Victoria says. "But you're still okay now."

"You two are a fun bunch of friends." He looks back at me. "I thought, in the interest of the trees in the neighborhood, I should come by." His smile's adorable. He's way, *way* better looking than I remembered, even with short hair.

And I remembered him as being really handsome.

I swear under my breath again.

"What?" He steps toward me, his eyes searching for the problem.

"You're hot," I say. "Way hotter than I remembered."

He starts to laugh. And he steps closer yet again. So close I can almost feel the heat from his body. And even though it's hot, I still like it.

I lean just a hair closer, and I breathe in deeply. "You smell good."

"I do." His voice sounds disbelieving.

"Like that cologne I love, the oceany-floraly-one. And also like grapes."

"Fermented grapes?" he asks. "Because I think that part came from you. . ."

"Right." I bob my head.

"How about I give you three a ride to wherever you want to go?"

"A knight in shining. . .wine." Rhiannon laughs uproariously at her bad joke.

"You're not very funny," I say.

"You're all delightful," he says.

"Then why don't you sit down and have a drink with us," Victoria says.

"I see two issues with that," Emerson says. "First, we have no more wine. I think I'm wearing the end of it."

"And?" Victoria says.

"And they're all waiting for us." He points.

As if they appeared out of *nowhere*, I suddenly notice not one, not two, but three different groups of men, and a few big trucks, hovering.

"What's happening?" I ask.

"The ownership changes hands at five p.m.," he says. "And that's three minutes away."

"Are they really tearing it down *right now*?" It brings tears to my eyes. I knew they'd tear it down, but I don't want to see it.

Emerson drags me toward his chest, and I collapse, breathing him in. Grapes and ocean and a surprising amount of muscle on a lean guy. "Do you work out?"

He laughs. "Only as much as Jake badgers me into doing. Mostly I play soccer."

"It's fine," I say. "I like slender guys when they're smart."

He chuckles again. "Why don't you come with me, Elizabeth. I'll get you three home."

And he does. But by golly, I wish he'd just have come home with me. If anything, time away from him has only made me miss him more.

20

EMERSON

The best things in life take a lot of effort. But some things in life that take a lot of work aren't worth it. This is clearly one of those.

"If I had known when you called and asked me to come over that you wanted to go running, I would have hung up and gone back to sleep," I say.

Uncle Bentley's waiting at the door when I arrive, already holding Lucky's leash.

"You know what sucks less than running?" Uncle Bentley asks.

"Not running?" I look down at my sneakers, wishing I'd worn loafers. Then at least I'd have a better excuse to bow out.

"I was going to say running with someone else," he says. "But I guess yours is truer."

"You hate running," I say. "Why on earth are you doing it?"

"So when you get old—"

"You're barely forty," I say.

"When you get old," he says, as if I never interrupted, "you have to go see doctors. They check levels for things."

"Like what?"

Lucky's now spinning around and around, the leash getting all twisted up around Uncle Bentley's legs. And. . .now she's chewing on it.

"Your dog's kind of crazy."

"She's not my dog," Uncle Bentley says. "She's a loaner."

"I don't think dogs work like that."

Lucky sits down on her haunches, her head pointed straight up at Bentley like a heat-seeking torpedo, her eyes focused on him, her tongue lolling, like the only thing in her world is Bentley. "You're a good girl," he says.

And she goes berserk. She spins. She leaps. She tries to lick his face, while he's standing and she's on the ground. She gets closer than I'd have thought possible, between the leaping and her giraffe tongue.

"Alright. I'm headed back home." I turn to leave.

But Uncle Bentley's already out the door and jogging alongside me, Lucky pulling and whining, her nails clicking on the tile floor of the hallway outside his posh condo. "I'll come with you."

"To my car?" I ask.

"I had an idea."

"For what?"

"Well, remember yesterday, when you were saying you weren't sure how to approach her, now that it's done?"

Oh, right. Elizabeth. "Sure."

"She lives near the old shelter, right?"

I nod.

"Let's go for a walk over there."

"I'm not ready to call her yet," I say. "I need to make a plan first."

"You and your plans," Uncle Bentley says. "Not everything needs a plan."

It's like he's talking gibberish.

"The world isn't won with plans. The world is won by the bold. The brave."

"So you're saying people like me don't ever win?" I might kick my uncle.

"When you realized you didn't like Lisa, did you plan that?"

I hate him.

"What about when your grandmother showed up on your doorstep and apologized? Was that planned?"

"For her or for me?"

Uncle Bentley throws his hands up in the air. That frees Lucky though, and now she's racing back and forth in the hallway outside my uncle's place like a greyhound, her ears flattened to her head. It takes us a solid two minutes to catch her again, since she thinks it's a really fun game.

"So, was that little interlude planned?" I ask.

Uncle Bentley throws the leash at me. Thankfully I catch it, or we'd have been at it again.

"Hey."

"Emerson, you want a plan because you lost your mom."

"So what?" There's nothing wrong with having a little predictability.

"Be spontaneous."

"What are the odds she'll even be outside?" I fold my arms.

"It's a gorgeous late spring day. Everyone's outside."

I roll my eyes. "That's not even close to what I asked for."

"Fifty fifty," Uncle Bentley says. "How's that? I bet we run in to her. Call it a hunch."

"And if we don't, our trip over there will be a total waste."

"It'll be fresh air with my favorite nephew and a nice walk with my dog."

"What happened to the jog?"

"I'm being realistic," Uncle Bentley says. "Jogging sucks."

I can't help laughing at that, because he's right, but. . . "Then what are you doing with a border collie? They love to run."

"The heart wants what the heart wants, Emerson. So if my heart wants a dog that loves to run, and her heart wants an owner who doesn't, well. We'll figure it out."

"Your romance finally happened. With a dog." I can't help laughing about that. My handsome, brilliant, rich uncle whom people love to talk to, and the closest he's gotten to a girlfriend is this maniac dog.

He points at himself. "I should be your motivation. If you miss your moment, this happens." I know he's kidding, but there's an underlying note of sadness that's not fake.

"Alright." I nod. "Let's go."

An hour later, we're still walking around, and I want to strangle Uncle Bentley and his stupid fresh air. "My toe has a blister on it," I say. "And so does this space between my thumb and my index finger where your dumb dog's leash has been pulling this whole time."

"It's a good thing we didn't see her," Uncle Bentley says. "Because all you do is whine. You're a major downer. If I were her, I'd turn you down flat."

It's been more than two weeks since I realized that I like Elizabeth. It's been nearly two weeks since I showed up at the shelter and found her and her two friends drunk. I've been searching and working and focusing on making a plan, but I keep getting stuck.

Because we met in such a weird way, nothing between us was ever real, and I'm not sure how to bridge that gap.

Anything I say will feel. . .contrived. I know I can't think about anyone but her. I know that she makes me smile—even the thought of her. I know she said most of the truest things I've ever heard. I know that I want her with me forever. And I also know that she won't believe anything I say. We lied to the world the whole time we were together, and I can't come up with a plan to fix that.

Plus, a little part of me worries that she only ever flirted as part of our deal. Or that, even if it was real, she was like Lisa. She liked the Richmond package more than she liked *me*.

Besides.

She lives right by the old shelter. She probably walks by it all the time. If she really liked me *at all*, wouldn't she have called? The obvious answer is *yes*.

And she never called.

We're finally headed back to the car when I hear my name.

"Emerson?"

Uncle Bentley throws me a little thumbs up and keeps walking.

"Is that you?"

When I turn around, Lucky notices I'm stopping and spins too. And then there's a cacophony of barking the likes of which I've never heard. Two tiny puffballs begin frolicking toward Lucky, and Lucky's shaking more than I've ever seen her, like she's having a nervous breakdown.

"Sorry," Elizabeth says. "I kept Lucky at my place for a while, so she knows my dogs."

"What are their names?" Uncle Bentley widens his eyes and sticks his chin out and tosses it at her, like he's tasking me to storm Normandy or something. Ugh.

"Fluff and Boba," I say. "I remember."

"Floof," she says. "But not bad for a fake boyfriend."

A fake boyfriend. Why do the words sting so much?

I cough. "So, have you found a new shelter yet?"

Her shoulders droop. "Poor Bernie. He must be really irritated. He keeps sending me things, but so far they've all been. . .disappointing. I guess I got spoiled with the one I had."

"He said you saw one really nice one," Uncle Bentley says.

Elizabeth shrugs. "It was double the price I could feasibly afford."

"Don't you ever go by the old shelter anymore?" I finally blurt out.

Why isn't she saying anything about it? Does she hate it? Was she mad?

She frowns. Then she shakes her head. "I think it would hurt too much."

"Isn't it, like, one block away?" How could she avoid it?

"I just loop around this way." She's pointing.

"But—you really haven't—" Uncle Bentley looks as confused as I am.

It means she has no idea what I did. Maybe that's why she didn't call. That's why my plan has stalled out. I should grab her arm and drag her. . .but then an idea occurs to me.

"Uncle Bentley, why don't you head home? I'll take an Uber."

"You'll—why would you do that?" His eyebrows rise. "From here—"

"I need to talk to Elizabeth." I clear my throat.

"Oh." He smiles. "Okay."

"How's Lucky doing?" she asks. "Looks like you two are still getting along pretty well. It's been, what? A month?"

"I mean, she's not exactly a perfect fit for me," Uncle Bentley says, "but I can keep her a little longer."

Elizabeth smiles. "I'll send over her shot records, just so you have them."

"That wouldn't be a terrible idea," he says. "It's probably time for her next heartworm pill too, right?"

"You could take her to the vet, if you wanted," she says. "Just as a temporary checkup."

"They have those?"

What a dope. "Sure they do," Elizabeth says. "For sure."

"Great."

"I'll email you." She's still half-smiling as he and Lucky head the other direction, both of them turning around every few steps.

"What are you doing over here?" she asks.

"Oh, you know, kind of trolling around, hoping to bump into you." I shove my hands in my pockets and look at my sneakers. This is *so* not the conversation I was prepared to have.

"Hoping to—why didn't you just call?" She looks lost.

It's now. I can't keep waiting. "Because I wanted to see your gorgeous face," I say.

Her mouth drops open a bit, and then she starts laughing. "You're so weird."

"I mean it," I say. "I'm not great with this stuff, but I like you, Elizabeth. For real."

"What about Lisa?"

"I mean, we broke up before you and I started dating."

"Be serious," she says.

"I am," I say.

Her dogs start popping up on her legs. One of them has a prosthetic back leg. How did I not notice that until right now? "Do you need to take them back?"

"They're fine." She picks one up, but that makes the other one cry.

"I can hold one," I say.

"You can try." Her smirk is fond. "They're very particular."

I crouch down. At first the white one just looks at me, but then it slowly creeps closer, sniffing my hand from a few inches away, and then licking my fingers. Finally, it lets me pick it up.

"Floof is blind on the right side," she says. "And usually she won't let strangers touch her. You should be honored."

It's a dog, but somehow, I still am.

"Look," I say. Floof bumps me with her nose, and I pet her with my free hand without thinking. "Lisa dumped me. I thought she liked me, and I thought we were right for each other, but I guess I didn't know her —or myself—as well as I thought. Because dating you felt more real than any of the time I spent with her."

Elizabeth and her tiny black Pomeranian are both staring at me with the same baffled expression, like I'm speaking Latvian.

"I know it was fake," I say softly. "But to me, the time we spent was the most real time I've ever had with someone."

"You haven't called me in weeks."

"My grandmother and I reconciled," I say, "and—"

She nods. "Oh. Now that she's done some digging, she realized I'm not suitable either." She chuckles. "You have a real knack, Emerson, for picking people to date that your grandmother hates."

I realize how I can find out whether she likes *me* or the Richmond estate. "We reconciled sort of, but not all the way. I'm not taking over Richmond Steel," I say. "I probably never will be. Nothing I do makes my grandmother happy. But I decided that of all the things in life I can have, of all my options, the only one that really matters is. . ."

"Is what?" She's staring at me earnestly.

"I don't know. Saying 'you' seemed suddenly cheesy and cliche."

"I'm okay with cliche," she whispers.

I step toward her, and I can't see anything but her mouth in that moment. Her lips, slightly parted, are a light, light pink. I reach for her arm, tugging her closer, and then my head lowers. I'm about to kiss her when something starts growling.

It's Floof—she's growling at Boba.

"They do that," Elizabeth says. "It's like a playing thing they do."

"Oh."

She sets Boba down, and she takes Floof from me and sets her down, holding the leashes loosely. "Bad dogs," she whispers. And then she smiles at me.

Her bright eyes. Her windswept hair. Her tiny, bouncy dogs, now hopping up on her legs and mine. It's not the perfect movie kiss, but it's the only one I want to have. This time, I grab her hips and drag her closer. "I will always have a good, solid job. I'll always take care of you."

Her smile looks almost sad.

"I may not be rich, but I'm steady." I sound even

worse than earlier. I groan. "It sounds like I'm trying to sell you a Toyota Corolla."

She grabs the collar of my shirt with her one free hand and yanks me down. "If you had been raised like me, barely able to make the Porsche 911 payment and using new credit cards to pay off other credit cards, a Toyota Corolla might sound pretty great." She yanks my head toward hers, and our lips miraculously collide.

I've kissed women before. Pretty ones. Smart ones. Greedy ones.

None of them were anything like this. Her mouth is warm and urgent, and her hand is persistent, holding me close. She's grinning against my face. "Even if being with me means you'll never be rich, you don't mind?"

There's less than half an inch between her mouth and mine, and we're both smiling. It's not hot, but it's exactly what I needed.

It's sunshine.

It's the promise of tomorrows filled with laughter.

Filled with a smiling Elizabeth.

"Not a bit," I say. "As long as it means being with you."

She starts laughing then, and she spins in a circle, the dogs racing around her feet in confusion. "Is this real?"

When she stops, her eyes are bright, and her smile is broad, and none of it looks feigned.

"What's going on?" I ask.

"Every night for almost two weeks, I've dreamt that you came to see me. That you told me that you wanted to date me for real."

I take the leashes from her carefully, and I drag my free hand down the side of her face, my fingers curling around her smile. "I should have come every single day, but I was waiting on something."

"Something?" She turns and presses a kiss against my hand.

"Real dating has a lot more kissing than fake dating did." I'm the one smiling now. "I like it."

"The fake dating was never fake to me," she whispers.

And my heart goes nuts. "Me either."

I almost drop the leashes when I kiss her this time. Luckily, the dogs are both so fixated on bouncing up on our legs, I doubt they'd have even noticed.

Finally, a honking horn from some enthusiastic onlooker reminds me that we're standing on the street.

"What did you want to show me?" Elizabeth bites her bottom lip that's now much brighter pink than before.

"How far can these guys walk?" I ask.

She frowns. "Not super far."

"To your old shelter?"

She shakes her head. "I don't really want to see—"

"Then let's carry them." I don't wait for her to ask. I just pick up Floof and start walking, Boba trotting along behind.

Elizabeth catches me pretty quickly and picks him up. "Seriously, Emerson."

But no matter how much she bugs me, I don't cave. I don't explain why we're going or what she'll see. I just keep walking, my toe blister complaining. I ignore it, and then we come around a corner, and it's there.

"Oh." Elizabeth stops. "It's not—they didn't demolish it yet?" She frowns. "I thought. . ." Then her eyes widen.

She's noticed the sign. "What's going on?"

"My grandmother and I actually did make up," I say. "But one of my stipulations was that she had to carve out the shelter and donate it to your charity."

"She had to. . .what?"

"She agreed, but only if we brought it up to standard. Since the warehouse will be right behind it, she wanted them to look similarly new and nice." I tilt my head, watching her carefully.

"To donate it. . ." She inhales sharply. "I'm having trouble keeping up, Emerson."

"Richmond Steel is proud to present the Posh Pets Richmond Steel Shelter."

"Wait."

"She *really* wanted it to say Richmond Steel on it," I say. "But she agreed to donate four thousand dollars a month for the next three years in exchange for that, so I thought it was worth it."

"But—"

"As the manager and owner of the Posh Pets Charity, you'll need to come in and sign all the papers for it to be official, of course, but it's all ready for your signature, and I believe you have. . ." I glance at the date on my watch. "Four more days until the first of the pets you surrendered would run out of time."

Tears stream down Elizabeth's face.

"I thought you'd see the sign and call me," I say. "But then you never did. That's why my plan broke down."

"That's why you waited."

"Well, it took a week or so to get things repaired and repainted, and getting the sign made, even expedited, was annoyingly slow, but then, yes. That's why I waited."

"You wanted me to come to you?" There's a new glint in her eyes.

"I mean, I thought it would be nice."

"But then, what was with the 'even if I never have money' nonsense?"

"When Lisa thought I was poor, she was pretty upset," I say. "I thought it was nice that you didn't seem to mind."

"I've never really enjoyed looking rich," she says.

"Underneath everything else, I'll always be a Toyota Corolla. No matter how many expensive clothes or haircuts or facials I get."

"It's a good thing I like Toyotas," she says.

"I guess it is."

After we go inside the shelter, she lets the dogs off their leashes, and I can finally kiss her without interruption. I shouldn't have waited an extra week, but it was worth it.

The next morning, after our first meeting of the day ends, Grandmother stops me. "You stay." Usually she digs through piles of paperwork before the strategy meeting at eleven. But when I frown, she points to the chair across from her desk. "Sit."

I listen. Because everyone listens to Catherine Richmond.

"Tell me."

I swallow. "Tell you. . .what?"

"Something happened. You've been smiling like a halfwit all morning."

"You really have a way with words," I say. "When you finally retire, you should try writing a romance novel. I hear grumpy sunshine is a really big trope these days—"

"Stop babbling." She presses her hands together in front of her and leans closer, her eyes focused. "You talked to Elizabeth."

Okay. "That's creepy."

"Or, maybe I have someone following you."

I shoot to my feet. "Are you kidding?"

She shakes her head. "I took them off you last week."

"Wait." I sit back down, unsure how upset to be. "So, you *did* have someone following me, but now you don't?" I arch one eyebrow. "You—no one would even believe this if I told them."

"What?" She leans back in her chair, her eyes never leaving my face. "That I would keep tabs on my greatest asset and my largest liability? It would have been irresponsible not to. The board could have had me dismissed."

I roll my eyes.

"So, what is it? Why are you so happy?"

I bite my lip.

"Are you really not going to tell me?"

"Are you asking as my grandmother or as my boss?"

She frowns. "Is there a distinction?"

Now I'm really laughing. Since I have a favor to ask, I turn around and walk out, shaking my head. I know her a lot better than I did, because exactly fifteen seconds later, I hear her stand. The clicking of her heels on the tile floor sounds exactly like I knew it would. "Emerson, wait."

I turn around slowly.

"Please tell me." She looks much nicer, now.

"I might need a favor."

"You're holding this information hostage?" She narrows her eyes.

I shrug.

"I'm proud of you." She nods. "Never give anything of value away for free."

I still don't reply.

"What do you want?" She circles back to her desk and perches on the edge of her seat. I know this face, too. She's ready to play hardball.

"You have to agree first," I say. "Telling you what I want will tip my hand."

Her sigh is significant. "What's the upper limit?"

"A hundred and fifty grand," I say.

She arches one eyebrow. "Fifty."

I shake my head, and then I slowly smile, since that's what baited her to begin with.

She slams her hand down on her desk. "A hundred."

"Done."

She scowls.

I should have made her work a little more. Shoot.

"Alright." She leans forward again. "Out with it."

"I need to buy a top level jumper."

"A top level—" She swears under her breath. "It *is* Elizabeth." Now she beams. "I should have known."

"Do you regret making our bargain?"

She shakes her head. "But I'll give you the original ask. We can't have our girl competing on a jalopy."

"Wait, there's a heart in there?" I lean against the doorframe. "I ran into her last night."

"And finally showed her the shelter, I take it?"

I nod.

"So it went well." Her smile is almost as big as mine was.

"It went really, really well."

Her expression returns to blank and she straightens, focusing on her paperwork, straightening it. "That's great to hear. Now, if there's nothing else."

I suppress my smile. She may not be great at expressing herself yet, but she's learning. I'm on my way out again when she calls out.

"Emerson?"

"Yeah?" I turn.

"Since I said I'd meet your initial ask. . ." She swallows.

"What?"

"If you happen to have any photos, I'd like one."

Her office is the most severe room I've ever entered. It's stark—black. White. Red. If rooms could cut, it would shred the people who come inside. "How about a photo right now?"

Her shoulders droop. "I don't understand."

But I'm already striding toward her desk. I circle to her side, and I pull her to her feet. Then I wrap an arm around her shoulder and snap a selfie.

It's the worst selfie I have ever seen in my life. "And now I have a new bargaining chip." I whip my phone around to show her.

Her eyes are sideways, her mouth half-open to protest.

"Emerson Duplessis Richmond," she says.

"You know, I've never had a middle name," I say. "But I was thinking. If we change my name, maybe Emerson Alistair Duplessis Richmond."

Tears well up in the corners of Catherine Richmond's eyes, and she nods. "That was my father's name."

That figures. It sounds like an old man. "I'm sure he was as horrible as you."

"Worse." Now she's laughing. So I snap another photo.

This one's pretty good.

I text her that one and a few of Elizabeth and me from the night before. "That should get you started."

"Think about what you might want from me to convince you to pose for some actual portraits," she says.

I lean over her desk. "Grandmother."

She meets my eye.

"I'd need you to ask. That's what family is, remember? The whole bargaining thing was a game. Right?" I lift my eyebrows and compress my lips. "It's all for fun."

For some reason, her eyes well with tears again, but she nods. "Yes. You're right."

"Name the day, and I'll be there. But only if you're in them with me."

"You could bring that David and Seren too, if you really wanted to."

I consider asking her about the siblings, but just including Mom and Dad is already a big concession from her. "Sure. That would be nice."

When I leave, I pretend not to see her wiping her eyes with a tissue.

But when I reach my office, I have no chill left. I call the number I got from Victoria right away.

"Hello?"

"Hey," I say. "My name is Emerson Du—Richmond."

"Hello, Emerson DuRichmond."

I laugh. "Just Richmond, actually."

"Catherine's young grandson?"

"That's me," I say.

"Do you know who you're calling?"

I sigh. "It's a strange call, and I'm sorry if you find it upsetting. But you see, my girlfriend sold her show horse because she had no other choice."

"Elizabeth Moorland?"

"Exactly. I heard you won on him a few weeks ago, and I'm sure you love him, but I'm hoping you're willing to sell him back to me, because—"

"Emerson."

"Yeah?" My heart sinks. The way she said my name wasn't exactly encouraging.

"I have some bad news, son."

Why do rich people always call me son? "I don't like bad news. Could we skip it and go straight to the good news?"

She sighs. "I'm afraid in this case, there isn't a lot of good news."

"What is it?"

"I can't sell you Elizabeth's horse, because there's been an accident. Hottie can't jump anymore. In fact, I've pretty much decided the best thing is to put him down."

21

ELIZABETH

One year, when I was sixteen, Dad had invested heavily in a friend's company. It collapsed right before Christmas, and we were really casting around trying to figure out how to keep the Moorland house of cards from collapsing.

That didn't stop Mom from throwing her annual holiday party, obviously.

She decorated our enormous Christmas tree in the entry hall. She hung the garland, the tinsel, and the lights. We pulled out the blown glass ornaments imported from Italy. We put the human-sized nutcracker soldiers on the porch. The lions on either side of our front gate got fresh pine wreaths around their necks.

And under the tree, where we definitely didn't have any money for presents, Mom placed empty boxes, wrapped with the most beautiful paper and bows you've ever seen. The only people who knew they were empty were me, Easton, Mom, and Dad. Mom even put books, bricks, and used clothing in some of them so no guests would kick one and accidentally realize they were fake.

I've often thought it was a pretty good analogy for my life.

Stunning from the outside. Shiny, beautifully wrapped, and lovingly tied, but entirely vacant on the inside. No boyfriend. No parental support or interaction. No polished education. No real job. No value provided at large to the world.

Just an empty box.

I felt full when I was with my horses. I felt full when I was saving animals. It was pure. It was honest. It was mine. So when that was taken from me, when I lost Hottie *and* the shelter, I'd never felt more useless in my life.

Those intervening weeks were hard.

The person who stood at my side for most of it was Emerson. When our fake dating died too, instead of staying empty, I felt gutted. If I hadn't had a part time job to go to and tiny dogs to feed, I might have just stayed in bed all day and all night.

But now I wake up bursting with excitement. I've even made a few suggestions at work this week that Ace said showed some promise. Management and marketing things, not game design or anything, but every talent has its place.

I was worried, for the first few weeks after Emerson's grand gesture with the shelter, that everything would fall apart. After all, I have no idea what to do with a boyfriend. I don't know how to act or what to say. There were a few awkward interactions with my parents, but that was all on my parents' end. None of it was Emerson, and I managed to handle things pretty well, too.

Now we've been dating for six weeks, and everything has miraculously been smooth sailing. Even his grandmother seems to like me.

And three weeks ago, I found a new horse that needs my help. His papers say his name is Atlas Donatis, which is an ugly name, so for a barn name, I've chosen Adonis. He's pretty enough, with his sleek, shiny, dark coat. I specifically found a dark, dark bay.

Every single sorrel makes me think of Hottie right now.

Like most off-the-track thoroughbreds, Adonis has a spring to his step and a desire to move, which is an impulsion I usually find lacking in warmbloods. Unfortunately, his stride's short and choppy, and when I ask for more, he wants to give me a running canter. He's been watching the other horses in the ring flying over jumps, and he's curious. He's been eyeing them.

Today, we're alone in the arena, which is nice. He's so looky that when other horses are here, I spend most of my time just trying to calm him down. Soon, I hope, he'll learn that not everything is a race.

When I feel him pulling toward a jump, I steer him away. "Not for a while yet, sir." I pat his neck. "We need to get you moving into my hand better first."

"His contact does look quite a bit better already." Victoria's leaning against the arena rail.

"I thought you were busy today."

"Sorry about that."

I asked for a lesson, but she said she didn't have time. "Is everything okay?"

"Two new horses coming to the barn today," she says.

She's had a few more open stalls than she likes, so I think that's good news, but she looks inexplicably nervous. I pull Adonis to a halt. He dances around, because he's a young thoroughbred and that's what they do. "What?"

"You might want to hop off," she says.

"Why?"

"The trailer's pulling in now."

Adonis has only one real vice—he's a little spooky when trailers and new horses show up. "Thanks for all the advance notice."

"I just found out it was today myself."

I slide off his back.

But before I can lead him to the furthest cross-ties, Victoria takes the reins. "I've been thinking maybe he should be ridden through his nervousness."

"What if he bucks you?" I arch one eyebrow.

"You think I can't handle it?"

"I'm not saying that, obviously."

I've seen Victoria stay on horses that the rodeo would kill to have for their bronc riding. "I'm just not sure—"

"How about this? I'll work with him, and you go meet the trailer. Show the new owner to the stalls over by Peaches."

"Whoa," I say. "Whoever's moving in is a high roller, huh?" Those stalls are double the size of her usual stalls, which means they cost twice as much, too.

She shrugs. "They said they didn't care about the price."

"Must be nice."

The trailer that pulls up is a Four Star Center load, which is exactly the trailer I would buy if I were ever in the market. Victoria's been drooling over them for years. Whoever this is knows their horses. Thanks to the reflection of the sun, I can't see anyone in the truck, but it stops, and one of the horses in the back whinnies loudly.

"It's fine, fella," I say. "We'll get you out in a moment."

The driver's door opens, and a tall man I've never seen steps out. He smiles broadly. "Miss Perch?"

I shake my head. "She's on a horse, so she asked me to show you where to take the horses. Are you the owner?"

The guy shakes his head, his salt and pepper hair clipped short, but still blowing a bit in the stiff breeze. "Not me, nah. I'm just Mark the driver." He tosses his head as the passenger side of the truck opens.

Emerson steps out.

I blink a few times, because him being here makes no sense. Then I rub my eyes, but it's still Emerson. "What are you doing here?"

He smiles. "I bought a few horses, and I figured, what better place to board them than at your friend's barn? Only, I'm not sure she's giving me the friends and family discount, because the price she quoted me?" He whistles.

"Are you kidding right now?"

He shakes his head. "I know that to people on the outside, we look a little like Uncle Bentley and Lucky."

I can't help smiling at that comparison. Emerson's uncle still insists that he's only keeping Lucky on trial, even though it's been months. Even though Lucky has engraved food bowls. Even though Lucky has learned a dozen tricks, and Bentley hasn't traveled once since adopting her.

"He isn't a runner," Emerson says. "He never even wanted a dog."

"You never wanted a socialite, and you weren't much of an animal lover," I say.

"I'm learning to do better, slowly." He looks around. "But I'd like to fit in at the barn."

"So you. . .bought two horses?"

"Look," he says. "The lady at the horse auction said they do better in pairs. She said they get lonely when they're alone."

My boyfriend has lost his mind. "Oh, hon. Where did you find them, exactly? And why didn't you take me with you? I could have found you—"

But in that moment, Hottie's walking around the corner of the trailer, his back leg in a big old white and blue bandage. My brain stops working, and my heart explodes. Tears spring into my eyes. "What's—who—why's he here?" I can't speak. I can barely breathe.

"Hottie had an accident," Emerson says. "I bought him a few weeks ago, but he needed a pretty significant surgery, and I didn't want to tell you about everything unless he came through. The risks were pretty high."

I take three steps so that I can hit Emerson on the chest.

And Hottie starts to scream when he sees me. His nostrils flare, and he's pulling on the lead rope, trying to reach me. I run the rest of the way and wrap my arms around his neck. He curves his head around mine like he always does, and then he snots all over my neck and back.

Typical.

And it makes me bawl even harder.

"He came through the surgery like a champ, and now it's just six months of rehab and he should be all better."

I'm still crying, and I'm angry that Emerson didn't tell me, and I'm touched he bought Hottie for me, and I'm brokenhearted that he was injured. And I'm grateful that he's alright so far.

Mark hands me the lead rope and disappears.

"Wait, what else is happening?"

"Well, since Hottie was injured, I bought him for a song." Emerson's beaming like that's a coup.

"What on earth—"

"I had negotiated for a budget of a hundred and fifty, so even after the surgery, I had a hundred and twenty left to blow."

"Emerson, you're not making any—"

A snowy white angel horse prances around the corner, mane blowing in the wind, head tossing a little, her movement light and airy, like she's floating.

"Who's that?"

Hottie bumps me, like he's mad I'm even looking at someone else. But how could anyone not look at that grey? She's gorgeous.

"She was the nicest Grand Prix level jumper Victoria could find in your—er, well, in *my* price range."

I should have known my friends would be in on it.

"You won't be able to ride Hottie for a while, and I know Adonis is more of a project horse, so. . ." He flourishes one hand. "Marshmallow."

"Please tell me that's not her name."

Emerson scrunches his nose. "Isn't it a good one?"

I shake my head.

"Oh, come on."

"What's her real name?"

"Fine, if not that, how about Mäusespeck?" He lifts his eyebrows and beams. "Eh? Has a nice ring to it, right?"

"What in the world did you just say?"

"Hear me out. Holsteiners are German, and that's—"

"If you say that's marshmallow in German, we're having words."

His mouth snaps shut.

I roll my eyes. "Emerson."

"Fine. If you want the horrible, boring name on her papers, she comes from a cross of Ladykiller and Ramiro, who was apparently the stallion of the century."

"And her name is?" I'm actually impressed he memorized all that. I'm sure it's just stuff that Victoria told him, but it's still cute.

"Lansing Ramareah." He grimaces. "I can't tell if they were just trying to be cute with Ramiro and mare references? Or whether it's because they're German?"

I can't help laughing. "They usually go by a barn name, anyway. I'll have to think about it."

Emerson holds out both hands like he's releasing a wild bird and whispers, "Marshmallow. . ."

I roll my eyes again, like that might get him to stop floating such an ugly, long name. "Not a chance."

"Ah, well." He points at Hottie. "He's supposed to be in a stall all the time, except for when he's hand grazing. That can happen up to twice a day for ten minutes. This lasts for twelve lovely weeks."

How fun for him.

"I'll give you all the information on the rehab schedule later."

It takes us a bit to settle the two horses in, but Marshmallow—which is not a name I'll keep using, but I have to call her something—seems to *love* being out in the paddock. She really looks like she's floating as she prances from one end to the other. Eventually, she settles down and starts to graze. That's when I breathe a sigh of relief.

Victoria approaches. "Adonis was pretty calm. One tiny blow up and that's it."

"You're in trouble." I can't suppress my smile, though.

"Why? You don't like Marshmallow?"

"That is not her name," I say. "Don't use it."

"Oh, come on," Victoria says. "It's cute, and the guy who just bought her for you and prepaid six months of board likes it."

I have no idea why my friends insist on calling Emerson 'the guy,' but he doesn't seem to mind. "I do like that name," he says. "Have I mentioned that? Marshmallow."

"No," I say, but with less force. It's a stupid name, but it's also kind of cute how badly it fits her.

"And poor Hottie," Victoria says.

"I think he'll be happier rehabbing here," I say. "Maybe we can put Adonis nearby so they get to be friends."

"Oh, I like that idea," Emerson says. "Since I'm paying for the stalls, I think that's a good plan."

"Wait." My eyes widen. "These are *my* horses." He gave them to me.

"I have the paperwork coming," he says. "It's all in your name, but it takes time to process."

"No, but that's the thing." I should be the one paying for the stalls. "Crap, Victoria, I can't afford these stalls. They're twice as much." I don't even pay for Adonis. I work off his board, but there's no way I can work off the board for *three horses*.

"Actually." Emerson drops to one knee. I can't help noticing that he's kneeling in a pile of junk that someone hoof-picked out and didn't sweep up.

"What are you doing?" Did he drop something?

"Elizabeth Moorland, I know we haven't been dating long."

Victoria chokes, and then she whips out her phone.

"But I thought, well, what would Elizabeth want more than a big diamond ring?"

My breath catches.

"She'd want her horse back," he says. "Or, that's what I thought. So if you'll just agree to marry me, I'll pay for your board for all three horses. . .forever."

"I'm not sure I've ever heard a nicer horse-girl proposal in my life," Victoria whispers.

"No ring?" I put one hand on my hip. "Really?"

He frowns. "I just got you two horses."

As if on cue, Hottie swings his head over the side of the door and bumps my shoulder. He's right. He did do that. It is what I'd have chosen.

"Oh, fine." He stands up, and I realize that I waited too long. I should've said yes right away.

I messed this up.

"You drive a hard bargain, Elizabeth, but that's fine. I'm up to the challenge." He reaches into his pocket and pulls out a tiny little thing. He holds it toward me, and I realize it's not actually that tiny. It's practically grape-sized.

"This was *not* my grandmother's, though for the record, she did offer her ring."

I look up at him. "She knows you're proposing?"

He sighs and tosses his head back at the driver, who's holding a phone and smiling. The guy throws a thumbs up. Oh, no. She's on a live feed.

He mutters, "Please don't reject me on camera. In front of my aged grandmother." He drops to a whisper. "Did you hear her son just died?"

I can't help laughing. It's not lost on me that my future husband is making me *laugh* with jokes about his dead father. He's a strange guy.

But now, he's *my* strange guy.

Before I can say a word, Victoria reaches for the ring. "Fine. I didn't want to make things awkward, but if she's passing, I'll take it."

I slap her hand away and grab it myself. "It's mine, you greedy jerk."

The ridiculously large round rock is mine, and I can't stop staring at it. "This is going to get really, really dirty when I'm riding."

"You're not more excited about the ring than you are about me, right?" Emerson's half-smile is precious.

I drop my hands to my sides and leap toward Emerson. Luckily, he catches me, and I plant a kiss right on his mouth. "Not even close."

But when Hottie neighs, he turns. "What about that guy? Do you love him more than me?"

"That's a harder question," I say.

He shakes his head slowly. "I knew it."

"Emerson Alistair Duplessis Richmond," I say. "You are the kindest, loveliest, most reliable, and also the most surprising Toyota Corolla I have ever seen."

"You two are really weird," Victoria says. "So I have no idea why I'm so jealous."

"Did I mention that I have a brother?" Emerson asks.

Her eyes brighten. "Do you mean Jake—"

"He's a little immature for you," Emerson says. "But Killian's already pretty tall, and when he's finished with high school, he'll be a real catch."

Victoria laughs. Luckily, my friends seem to get my fiancé's bizarre sense of humor.

"So that's a yes, right?" Emerson whispers.

"It's a yeehaw, a yes, and a heck yes all at the same time," I say. "And thank you." I rest my head against his chest. "For knowing what I needed and for bringing Hottie back."

"You have a Hottie and a hottie," Victoria says. "It really isn't fair."

"A few months ago, I didn't have anything at all," I

say. "Chin up, girlfriend. Maybe you'll get your happily ever after next."

She snorts. "It's not like this is a Hallmark movie series."

"Too bad," Emerson says. "If it was, I'd get a free flannel shirt to wear as I realize that the world is a better place away from corporate America."

I shrug. "I've never much liked flannel, anyway."

"That's a relief," he says. "Because I'm just now figuring out that I'm a pretty good fit in corporate America."

"Please," Victoria says. "We're nice to your face because of Elizabeth, but we can't ever really accept you. You're *nouveau riche*."

"That's true," he says. "But when you have enough *riche*, people don't insult you to your face, and that's enough for me."

"What about that trailer?" Victoria asks.

"I bought that too," Emerson says. "I figured you guys might want another one."

"And the truck?" I ask.

He shrugs. "It took a little convincing, but Grandmother agreed that we needed a trailer and something to pull our new horses with. She's the one that insisted we go top of the line."

"You shouldn't have gotten me a ring," I say. "Now I feel bad."

"My biggest fear is that I have no idea what else I'm supposed to do around the horses other than buy stuff," Emerson says.

Mark has approached, and he pats Emerson on the shoulder. "My Uber's here. Good luck with everything. And don't worry about the horse stuff. All you really have to do is pay the bills and hold the lead ropes when they shove them your way."

"Is it really that easy?" he asks.

I feel a little bad about it, but I have to nod. "Yep, that's pretty much it."

"Ah," Victoria says. "A real-life prince charming." Then she hands Emerson a lead rope.

It's hanging on a hook by Hottie's stall, but he stands there and practices for a few minutes anyway. And that's how I know it's real love.

22

EMERSON

Mom didn't have much time off when I was a kid, and when she did, she was usually so tired that she just wanted to watch television, which meant I got to watch cartoons in my bedroom for the entire day. I was fine with that. But once, as we were both watching television in our respective places, Mom called me into the room with urgency in her voice, and I ran.

But there wasn't an emergency. She was staring at this scene on her show with a shining, smiling mother, who was tossing her child up in the air. Waves were crashing in the background, and inexplicably, Mom got it in her head that we had to go to a beach. She sat down and started researching where to go. On her next day off, we headed for the New Jersey beach that was reputed to have free parking and the most amenities, like public restrooms.

Unfortunately, that led us to Beachwood, which we didn't know also had the highest pollution. On the Saturday that we arrived, when Mom was all brushed and polished and ready to ask strangers to take perfect photos of us, the water quality was considered poor, and there were ugly flags up and down the beach warning that it wasn't safe to swim. Ignoring the warnings could result in stomach flu, rashes, pinkeye, respiratory infections, meningitis, and hepatitis.

The list was enough to scare even my mother.

As she debated about what to do, I saw something fascinating and crept toward it slowly. It was a dead fish that had washed ashore, and it was being attacked with great zeal by a huge flock of seagulls. They were loud, they were messy, they were aggressive, and they were ripping every single scrap of meat from that dead fish's bones.

As I've sat back on the sidelines and watched the wedding plans rolling forward, I keep thinking of those birds attacking that poor, dead fish, stripping its bones clean. I actually feel almost guilty for proposing to Elizabeth, in spite of how much I love her, in spite of how happy we are when we're together.

Because apparently my proposal turned her parents into seagulls, and my fiancée became a dead fish.

"It's fine," she says on the phone for the third time in seven minutes.

"If you don't like the flowers," I say, "just tell your mother that you want the stephanotis."

Elizabeth sighs and covers the receiver. "She's right that the stephanotis are expensive. Apparently they have to build up the inside of each flower."

"Which is why they look delicate, and that's what you liked about them."

"But daisies are cute too," she says. "It's still a pop of white, and maybe it's more my style."

So far, nothing about the wedding has felt like her style. It feels like she's just agreeing to anything to keep her mother happy. "Can I just mention again that if

things are costing too much, I could talk to Grandmother. I know a lot of the guests are coming from—"

"My mom would have a heart attack." She chuckles.
"It's been her lifelong dream to be connected to the
Richmond family or another family like them. She
wouldn't dream of asking Catherine to pay for so much
as a pickle."

"Wait, we're going to have pickles at the wedding?"

"Of course not," she says in her sing-songy-mimic-
her-mother voice. "Pickles? What, are you suddenly
Southern?"

"Well, if you change your mind."

"I won't." She uncovers the receiver and tells her
mom that daisies are great.

It's clear from her face that daisies are not great.

When I walk into work, there's a pigeon on the
windowsill of my office, which now reads "Director,"
and it's pecking at something. A beetle, maybe? But it
just makes me think again of that poor dead fish and
wish there was more I could do.

"What's wrong?"

When Grandmother walks in, she doesn't ask
whether something is wrong, like a normal person. She
asks *what's* wrong.

I spin around, doing my best not to look startled.
"Oh, I'm fine." Move along, nothing to see.

"Something is wrong." She sits in the chair across
from my desk. That's not something she would've done
two months ago. She's relaxing more every day without
even realizing it.

I sigh and sink into my desk chair. "I'm not allowed
to talk to you about it."

"But if you *were* allowed to talk to me about it,
would it have anything to do with wedding expenses?"

"If I wasn't allowed to talk about it, I wouldn't be

able to confirm or deny that excellent guess. I also wouldn't be able to mention that my lovely bride can't even get the flowers she wants and has to pretend that *daisies* are actually what she had in mind."

My grandmother doesn't say another word. She doesn't wink, or smile, or laugh. She whips out her phone and taps on the screen.

I hop up, quick as a blink, and practically sprint around my desk toward her, but I barely see the word *Moorland* before she's holding the phone to her ear.

I cringe and perch on the edge of the desk. I should have kept my mouth shut. I always thought I was made of stern stuff, but if I were being tortured, I'd clearly fold with one little dunking or one pathetic zap.

How disappointing.

"Betty." Grandmother's voice sounds weird, like she's. . .worried? Then she sniffles. Loudly.

"Catherine," Betty Moorland says, and I can hear it faintly thanks to Grandmother being half-deaf and keeping her phone volume all the way up. "What's wrong?"

"Oh, you know, ever since Alistair." Grandmother hiccups. "Some days are harder than others."

I'm actually a little worried, but then Grandmother holds the phone away from her face and winks at me. She's a real piece of work.

"This morning, I was interrogating Emerson for details about the wedding, and you know, he never gives me anything at all, the ungrateful boy."

"Oh, I'll tell you anything you want to know."

"But I realized today that, I'm not sure how much longer I'll be on this earth, and I've never planned a wedding, not once. I don't have a daughter, and I. . ." Grandmother waves her hand at my tissues, and I hurry to hand her one.

She blows her nose so loudly that I practically need to cover my ears.

"Oh, I'm so sorry. I'm just so. . .distraught."

I roll my eyes. There's no way that Betty's going to believe—

"Would you like to take over some of the wedding planning?"

"Oh, could I? Would it upset you?"

"Not at all," Betty says. "But I should warn you. My daughter's a real special girl, but she can be a little headstrong."

"I think I can manage her." Grandmother winks.

A few moments later, she hangs up.

"All the flowers, the meal at the reception, the hors d'oeuvres, the dress, the clothing for the wedding party, the transportation, the wedding hall, the table decor, the wedding cakes, and the music for the reception are now going to be handled by me." Her grin is pure Machiavelli.

For the first time, it occurs to me that my grandmother might just turn out to be another seagull.

"So, the thing is. . ."

She waves her hand at me. "I was acting, you know, but the best acting comes from an underlying truth."

"What is that, exactly?"

She stands. "I've always wanted to plan a wedding and never had the chance."

"What about your own wedding?"

"My father planned that, and it was just horrible."

I text Elizabeth. GOOD NEWS. YOU'RE OUT OF THE FRYING PAN.

WHAT DID YOU DO? she asks.

BAD NEWS: MY GRANDMOTHER IS A VERY HOT FIRE. MAYDAY MAYDAY.

She calls me, and I explain what happened.

Elizabeth sighs. "Oh, thank goodness."

"What does that mean?" My stomach's starting to hurt, and I'm not sure whether it's hunger—I skipped breakfast—or indigestion from stress.

"My mother's the worst, because we have no money, but it needs to look like we have money. I keep asking her if we can just be honest with your family about how we're broke, but she won't let me. So we go round and round, trying to spend as little as possible but make it look like we're spending a lot."

"And now?"

"Even if your grandmother has hideous taste, at least she has a black Am Ex."

Above all else, my bride-to-be is pragmatic, and I may love that about her the most. "Well, try not to let her push you around."

"I'm counting on my knight on a shining white horse to defend me."

I did try to get on Marshmallow once. I'm not sure whether she's upset because of the horrible name I gave her, or whether I just suck at horses. Even though Elizabeth was leading me around, Marshmallow still chucked me off into the dirt.

I haven't felt inspired to hop on any horse since then.

"Sadly, today I left my chain mail at home to be polished."

"I think we'll be just fine."

As if her words prove prophetic, at the cake tasting later, one of the few wedding events I've actually been looking forward to, Grandmother's wonderful. She doesn't even take a bite.

"At my age, just looking at this much cake is danger-ous." She sighs wistfully. "I swear, with one bite of sweets, my thighs expand an inch."

"Surely not," Elizabeth says. "You look amazing."

Grandmother tuts. "Enjoy it now, young one. Eat all the cake you can."

And we do.

"Chocolate mousse for my groom's cake," I say.

"With raspberry ganache," Elizabeth adds.

"And for the wedding cake?" the attendant asks.

"I liked the classic white wedding cake," Elizabeth says.

No matter what she says, I can't control my expressions.

"What?" Elizabeth asks. "What's wrong with that one?"

I shrug. "Nothing."

"Do you like the waterfall of roses?" She points. "Or can we do this one?"

The chef sketched a custom cake with animals chasing a bride and groom up the side of the cake. It's horses at the bottom, then dogs, then cats, and finally, two small Pomeranians near the top.

"It's cute," I say. "But don't you think it's a little *juvenile*? Our wedding isn't a kid's birthday party."

"Your future wife owns and trains horses," Grandmother says. "She saves the lives of tiny dogs and cats all over the state." She arches one eyebrow. "You think that's juvenile?"

"No." I sigh. "Look, what I'm saying is that—"

"If you're saying anything other than 'yes, dear,' then I have failed terribly." Catherine's basically glowering at me.

"Are you always going to side with her?" I frown. "Because you're *my* grandmother, and I did *not* tell you about the issues we were having so you could just come in and overrule me."

It hits me then.

"Wait. Am *I* a seagull?"

Grandmother sniffs. "I have no idea what nonsense you're spouting with the seagull, but if you have any opinions that differ from the bride's, you're the problem."

Well, crap.

The next day, we have a very full dressing room while I'm being fitted for a tux, and I know that next door it's even crazier, where Elizabeth's trying on gowns. Seren and Dave are allowed over there, even though I'm not, which seems monstrously unfair, and Elizabeth's parents are on my side, so as not to interfere with Grandmother's 'help.'

HOW'S IT GOING? I text.

I FOUND *THE* DRESS. Heart eye emojis galore convince me she's not kidding.

WELL, I LOOK LIKE A PENGUIN.

YOU'RE LUCKY THEN. I LOVE PENGUINS. LIKE TINY LITTLE MEN WITH BIG GUTS.

YES. THAT'S EXACTLY WHAT I MEAN. I BLAME ALL THE CAKE.

I LOVE YOU.

IS MY FAMILY MAKING YOU NUTS?

THEY'RE SO MUCH BETTER THAN MINE, she says. THE ONLY FAMILY BETTER IS THE ONE YOU AND I ARE GOING TO MAKE IN ONE MONTH.

And that right there is the focus. That's what I remember whenever I start to worry that either Elizabeth or I are turning into dead fish through this process of planning a one-day extravaganza celebrating our union.

It's because we're about to make our own family.

And we're going to do it right. We're going to do what my dad and my mom, and what her dad and mom, and what my grandmother all failed to do. We have Dave and Seren as our fearless guides, and we're going to make a happy, lasting family.

So when the day finally arrives, Elizabeth has the flowers she wanted—and the centerpieces and the altar flowers that she wanted. Our monstrously large cake is covered with tiny animals, all lovingly crafted, including Hottie, Adonis, Marshmallow, Floof, and Boba, all clawing their way upward to the adorable bride and the goofy groom.

The other friends and family we wanted to come are seated up front, and the ones we didn't want here are seated at the back. And all the faces we look out at are smiling. Plus, Elizabeth insisted on telling everyone to bring their pets if they wanted to, so there are dozens of dogs sitting on guest's laps. Which is really, really strange, but kind of neat, too.

Elizabeth's father walks her up the aisle, and as I reach for her hand, I realize that if I had followed any one of my plans, I would never have gotten here. Bentley was right that day when he forced me to exercise outside Elizabeth's place—sometimes plans are stupid. The best stuff just happens on the way to your existing goals.

After the priest finishes, he asks us for our vows.

"We have a strict pact," I say. "Elizabeth made me promise the same thing that she's made the family promise."

"Vows, toasts," she says. "They always get out of hand." If her grin is sheepish, well, it's still adorable.

"So we're getting one minute or less each."

The audience starts murmuring.

I'm not usually considered to be super hilarious, but I decide to run with my joke idea. I inhale a huge breath, and then I start talking as quickly as I can.

"The reason that I love Elizabeth isn't that she's gorgeous, funny, smart, and dedicated. No, the reason I love her is. . ." And then I slow down.

People get it, and they laugh, thankfully. Maybe it's pity laughter, or maybe they thought pretending to talk like an auctioneer in order to say more in my allotted one minute was actually funny. Either way, when I looked it up online, it said that making a joke before something serious makes it hit harder, and I'm hoping it's true.

"You don't know Elizabeth until you've seen her around an animal." I can tell from people's expressions that some of them already know what I mean. "It's like. . .seeing a seal on land, and then watching it jump into the ocean. When she's saving some helpless creature, she lights up, and it's beauty like you've never seen."

I take her hand in mine.

"As long as I'm alive, I'll care for you in the same way you care for all the helpless creatures in the world." I drop my voice just a hair. "All I ask is that you share a little of that great karma with me. You'd hate to leave me down there. . ." I look down. "And be all alone up there." I glance up. "Right?"

She laughs. "And, in a nutshell, that's why I love you, Emerson," she says. "You may have a strange sense of humor sometimes—what my mom might call an acquired taste—"

Her mom's shaking her head like she's embarrassed.

Elizabeth clears her throat. "She didn't say that about you, to be clear."

Everyone laughs.

"But all your jokes hit with me, and all your generosity toward me and your support of my goals hasn't gone unnoticed either. You're the kind of person who doesn't know or care about horses. . .until someone you love loves them. Then you love them, too. Not many people know how to love that selflessly, without reproach or timelines or strings. I promise that I'll try and be good enough to be worthy of the way you love me."

"And now I'd like to pronounce these two lovely humans husband and wife." The priest signals Elizabeth. My wife, being who she is, was absolutely insistent that we involve some animals in the ceremony today. After I face-planted thirty seconds into my first time sitting on a horse, she decided to nix the idea of riding in on her horses.

But, she's been working with Floof and Boba for weeks and weeks now, and she insists they're ready to bring us the rings. It took pounds and pounds of bacon to keep them on target for such a long distance, but my gorgeous bride in her massively fluffy, beaded, and sparkling dress calls them, and they come trotting up the aisle. One of the cutest things about Poms is how they always look like they're smiling.

Uncle Bentley's in the second row with Lucky, and unfortunately, once Lucky sees the fluffy beans racing up the aisle, she realizes something good is happening up here.

She slips Uncle Bentley's grasp and vaults to the aisle.

Within a beat or two, she realizes the pups are focused on Elizabeth's lowered hand, and she redirects, heading for the bacon reward like a heat-seeking torpedo. As she approaches, she leaps right over Floof and Boba, and lunges for my bride.

In a surprise move, Grandmother steps forward from the first row and body checks her, and I swear it looks like something out of a cartoon. Lucky abruptly stops moving forward and drops to the ground, stunned. I'm more impressed than I've ever been with my grandmother, until I realize that her arm's bleeding. Lucky's tooth or claw or something must have caught her skin somehow.

And sheesh, there's a lot of blood.

An alarming amount.

Chaos breaks out in the audience, with everyone shouting. Thankfully, I know my sister Ardath's here. I scan the front rows, looking for her face. When I finally find it, she lifts her eyebrows.

"Sutures?" I mouth and mime sewing someone up.

She nods big time.

Within twenty minutes, with more than five hundred guests watching, my sister has sanitized, numbed, and stitched up my grandmother's arm.

"You're one tough lady," Ardath says.

"You're not so bad yourself," Grandmother says. "Remind me what hospital you work at."

"Why? Are you planning to buy it?" Ardath's humor is quite dry.

Grandmother roars with laughter. "Maybe I should."

"Then let's just say it's St. Luke's, then." My sister's a baddie, and I bet my grandmother thinks twice about disparaging my siblings again.

"I like having a doctor on call," Grandmother says. "Now we can proceed with the wedding. Right?" She looks around at the gathered audience, and they scatter like errant children, scrambling back to their seats.

One pointed glance from my grandmother, and the band begins playing the march again, as if we're reset-ting to the beginning.

"No, no," Grandmother says. "They're just getting to their ring exchange."

The director looks confused.

"It's fine," I say. "Any music will do for me to tie this one down forever, just as long as no one else gets bitten, gashed, or maimed."

A moment later, after we've put the rings on one another, I've waited plenty long enough. I wrap my hands around my wife's waist, pausing for a moment to mouth that word. *Wife.* And then I pull her close, bring my lips right over hers, and whisper, "I am so glad you propositioned me when you did."

She slaps my chest, smiling her signature insouciant grin. "You wish."

"I love you more than you could possibly know, Mrs. Duplessis Fansee Richmond."

"Is this a good time to tell you that I'm planning to keep my last name?"

I blink. "Wait, you are?"

She laughs. "Not a chance. All your names are plenty confusing already, thankyouverymuch."

When I kiss her, I forget about all the people waiting. I forget about how we first started dating. I forget about all the dogs and horses who look to us, and all I think about is how I could do this forever and never have it be enough.

But I'm in luck, because we have forever.

A few minutes later, when all our family members start making toasts, for a brief moment, I wonder whether forever might be a little too long. Seren and Dave deliver touching memories about my first years with them, and they wish us luck, just as parents ought. My grandmother. . .well. She isn't the worst.

But Jake?

He's definitely the worst one.

"On the first day we met, Emerson had his head so far up—"

Bea grabs his arm and shakes her head.

"And to this day, he still has an army of soft-headed minions who will defend his every move—his every word." He snorts. "I have no idea how he does it. He has always been able to hypnotize everyone into loving him effortlessly." He nods slowly. "But the very most impressive move he has ever pulled off is this one." He shrugs. "Elizabeth Moorland, I hope you don't regret it, but you're surely the best thing that ever happened to my brother. Don't let him forget that."

Beatrice is quick to pop up the second he sits down, and I suspect she may have pulled him down. I'm not sure why my sister always feels like she has to make up for Jake's bullheaded rudeness, but it's been like that as long as we've had him around.

"Emerson and Elizabeth are everything that's right in the world," Bea says. "It's probably not a secret to most of you that all of us Fansee kids had a bit of a rough start in life, but Dave and Seren, whom we all call Mom and Dad, have brought us together, and their love has taught us where to aim. I'm not sure any of us thought we could find what they have, but." She claps. "Emerson, I think you found it." She starts to cry then. "I couldn't possibly be more happy for both of you." She sits, wiping at her eyes.

Her eloquent generosity actually makes up for Jake's idiotic diatribe.

When Ardath stands up, I'm shocked. She isn't the most talkative on a good day, but in large groups? Forget it.

"Emerson, you've always been a role model to me, and now you're still an inspiration." She shrugs and smiles. "I wish you two all the happiness that none of us had as children, and all the peace that none of us found until we met Mom and Dad."

When she sits, Killian pops up, like a mop-topped

daisy. It's like they all think if they don't make a toast, they'll earn demerits.

"Sorry," I whisper.

"Are you kidding? Did you hear my mom and dad?" Elizabeth asks. "Both their toasts were about Easton."

Those made me laugh. My new mother-in-law's a little distractible and once she realized she'd wandered off talking about how much she hoped Easton would find someone, she got flustered and thought she was out of time and sat down. Her husband tried to fix it by saying how many ways Easton had disappointed them, which just made the whole thing a bigger mess.

"You know, you'd think that by this point, I'd have realized that toasts are a bad idea." My fourteen-year-old brother tosses me a desperate look. "But I've never been someone who wants to be the only one not doing something, and I guess that applies to sticking my foot in it, too." He bobs his head a little. "But anyways, I guess I'm supposed to say how great Elizabeth is, but I don't really know her very well yet. Emerson's marrying her after knowing her like a week. What I do know is that Emerson has great judgment, way better than me, so if he loves her, she must be pretty amazing." He sits down abruptly.

And then everyone starts to clap.

"I'm pretty sure those claps are everyone's way of encouraging us to stop making toasts," Easton says. "But I just wanted to stand up and say that if everyone had a sister like Elizabeth, there would be way fewer sibling rivalry jokes. She has been. . ." Is *he* tearing up? "Just the best. Always the very, very best." Easton holds up his glass. "I'm sure you'll all join me in making one last toast, to Emerson and Elizabeth's happiness this week, this month, this year, and on to forever."

When people cheer this time, Lucky, Boba, Floof,

and all the dogs in attendance start to bark, too. Most people would have found it all far too chaotic, but I can tell with one glance at my wife that we just had the exact wedding she wanted. A cake with pets on it, stitches performed onsite thanks to dog idiocy, and an embarrassment of riches in the way of people clamoring to wish us well.

Nothing in our lives has been traditional, not how I grew up, and surprisingly, not how Elizabeth did either. Not our jobs. Not our goals or our manner of meeting. Certainly not our families.

But maybe that's what helps us recognize how special what we have really is. Because both of us know what it looks like *not* to have it. "Thank you," I whisper. "For being exactly who you are."

"And thank you, for being willing to change to make me happy," she says.

I figure, as long as we each remember our gratitude and our willingness to change, we'll do pretty well in our forever. I lean toward her, our lips barely brushing when people start chanting.

"Throw the bouquet!"

"Why do they want me to throw it now?" Elizabeth asks, looking a little annoyed. "We haven't even danced. We're certainly not leaving yet. Isn't that supposed to be the last thing I do?"

"Apparently a few people are leaving," I say. "It looks like Rhiannon—"

"Oh!" Elizabeth slaps her head. "Her mom has surgery tomorrow morning."

"Right. That."

"Alright." She stands up. "Everyone who isn't married, gather round."

At most weddings I've attended, it's a small but robust group of young women. This one, however, is massive. My sisters Beatrice and Ardath, and Elizabeth's friends, Victoria and Rhiannon. Plus a lot of people I've barely met.

"Wait," Mom says. "You should go over too." She nudges her best friend, whom we usually call Aunt Barbara, to join.

"No way," Barbara says. "Stop."

"You should go," I say. "It'll be fun."

Only, Aunt Barbara's pretty consistent in her refusal, so I let it go. The last thing we need to do is weaponize a silly tradition.

"Here we go." Elizabeth turns away from the gathered group, facing me. She's looking at me like I might give her inside information, and I realize she's mouthing something. I squint. . .and I realize she's saying Rhiannon.

Does that mean she wants Rhiannon to catch it?

I cut my eyes far right, which is the side Rhiannon's standing on, kind of off by herself. She definitely doesn't look inclined to dive for it, if Elizabeth's hoping for that.

But when my wife finally throws the flowers down toward the floor and then whips them back, she badly miscalculates, and they go sailing way past the women who are all lined up.

In fact, they almost bean poor Aunt Barbara in the face.

Her hands pop out as a reflex, and she catches them just before they break her nose. "Oh." Then, as if it's just registering with her what happened, she drops them with a horrified gasp. "Oh, dear."

"Oh, no you don't," Mom says. "You caught those flowers fair and square." Mom's smiling, but her best friend looks horrified. I hear her last marriage was a real disaster, so I can't blame her.

"You don't throw away the whole bag of potatoes just because one is rotten," Mom's saying.

"Oh, I disagree," Grandmother says. "Always throw out the whole bag."

Barbara looks like she wants to run and hide, so when we get up to dance, I lean over and whisper to her on the way to the floor. "Don't worry. The way you look is exactly how I felt right before I met Elizabeth. Something wonderful could be right around the corner."

"Or there could be an air conditioning unit, poised to fall from the upstairs window and smash me flat."

"Sure," I say. "Or that."

"Congrats on your happy marriage," Aunt Barbara says. "I hope there are no looming appliances waiting to flatten you."

It's funny how we all drag our own baggage around everywhere we go. When I gather my lovely wife into my arms and begin to dance with her, I think about all the oversized luggage she has helped me check.

"Thank you," I whisper, as our first song as a married couple ends. "For freeing me."

"All I did was point out your wings." Elizabeth stops in the middle of the dance floor and brushes off the shoulders of my jacket. "Now, let's fly off into the sunset together."

23

ELIZABETH

A year ago, Victoria told me that Hottie was ready to jump at the Grand Prix level, and I was elated. Clearly it's something I wanted.

I never got there.

Still, my heart's fluttering like it's the Grand Prix when Hottie and I enter the ring for our level two showjumping round. I think I'm more nervous than he is.

Three vets cleared him to jump.

And that was more than two months ago.

I still fretted about whether this was wise. At the end of the day, Hottie doesn't need to jump at all if it's not what's best for him. But as we move toward the start, he's eager, his eyes bright, and I realize that Victoria was right to urge me to compete on him again.

He needs this as much as I do.

Because the bond between a girl and her horse isn't just about staring into each other's eyes. It's about working together to become better than we were alone. Hottie trusts me, and I'm so proud of him for being here again. I'm proud of him for listening to me, for pacing himself as we clear our first oxer, and I'm delighted with the turns he makes, and the way he gives to the bit, even with people cheering and clapping.

We're about to clear the course when, on the last jump, his back leg knocks a pole. When we stop, I realize we also had a time fault.

"That was good, kiddo," Victoria says. "You know what I'm going to say, though."

"I should have gotten an add on the line."

She nods. "That left him strung out, forcing you to choke down around the big bend."

I sigh.

When they announce the horses who are advancing to the jump off, our names aren't on the list. My heart sinks a bit, but then it floats back up. My gorgeous husband's in the stands, waving and throwing his thumbs up, like he has no idea we were just cut.

Because to him, and to me, if I'm being honest, this loss doesn't matter.

The two men who do matter the most in my life, Emerson and Hottie, are both healthy and happy. I'm on my sweet guy's back competing again, and everything's going perfectly for once.

Even though we just lost.

The best parts of life don't require ribbons or championships or applause. The best parts are the people and horses we care about, showing up for things that matter. Two hours later, I watch as Victoria wins third in level nine. In its own way, it's as disappointing as my loss. But like me, Victoria pats her horse and smiles.

Life's full of wins and losses, but they aren't what

changes us. Emerson and all his siblings have endured hits that most of us can't even imagine. Like Hottie, they could've given up. If they'd called it, if they had quit, no one would have faulted them.

But they didn't.

They all got the care they needed, thanks to Seren and Dave, and they rehabbed, and now, like me and Hottie, they're getting back in the game. Even though I lost today, I count our run as a huge win. When I look back at my cheering squad—Emerson, Seren, Dave, Catherine, Bea, Killian, and Easton—I can't help smiling.

It's funny to me how often in life we think we've found the one thing that's perfect for us. I was sure that jumping Hottie at the Grand Prix level was it. I was sure that the fancy house next to the dump would be the perfect shelter. Sometimes we do the very same thing, but in reverse. I didn't think I would ever be good enough for someone like Emerson, and he thought he was a Toyota Corolla when I needed a Porsche.

Both of us were wrong about a few things.

Both of us were right about even more.

But when we believe the lie that we'll never be good enough, then we aren't. Because the ultimate governor on our own success is our belief in it. Thanks to Emerson, I have much more faith in myself. I may not have the exact life I've had in mind at various points, but in so many ways, it's better than I ever imagined. I have the original shelter I wanted, and it's got a new influx of people who walk past every single day, many of them hard-working, not-Posh people. And I'm finding that the people who *don't* have money often have more room in their hearts for the broken pets and people of this world.

I'm lucky that my sweetheart has room in his heart for me and all my broken animals.

If Emerson and I can find our happily ever after, there's hope for everyone else, too.

❦ 24 ❦

SAMPLE CHAPTER MINTED
BARBARA

Ten months ago, I saw my husband's favorite suit in the pile of our things that were earmarked for Goodwill.

"How'd you get in there?" I pulled it out, whipping it a time or two to free the wrinkles it had accidentally caught by being folded. I still remembered the time I spent haggling with the clerk—it was from the prior season, but it looked *amazing* on him. I managed to get the price down, down, down, until my husband walked out with the nicest suit I'd ever seen. . .for a price we could actually afford.

And now that same designer label was staring at me from the donate box. It felt significant for some reason.

"This almost got donated." I laughed as I handed it back to him. "Can you even imagine?"

Only, his chuckle when he took it and hung it on his side of the closet wasn't quite right.

A few weeks later, when I drop an earring and watch it roll across the floor of our closet and onto his side, I get down on my hands and knees and follow it.

When I stand up, my eyes are drawn to the rows and rows of suits hanging in his side of the closet. Plaid. Tweed. Grey. Tan. Striped. He has one of each, or in some instances, several. As a Brit, he can really wear almost anything and pull it off. Because he works in an office everyday—*our* office—he has amassed a metric ton of nice suits.

But the nicest one, the only designer suit he owns, is missing.

I wrack my brain to try and remember the last time he wore it, but I can't. I run my hand down the row, just in case I'm missing it somehow, but the one that I bought him for my mother's funeral's definitely gone.

I slide my earring in place, and I walk out of the closet to ask where it has gone. "Hey, is the suit at the dry cleaners?"

"What suit?" When he turns to face me, it's there again, the slight discomfort underlying his question. That's when I recognize what I didn't a month ago.

Guilt.

"Is something going on?" I ask softly, not sure I want to know.

Will my question cause a fight? What happens if it does? Do I really have the bandwidth to deal with a fight right now? I'm nearly ready for work. I just need to grab my jacket and slide my feet into pumps, but he's ready now.

It's not a famous designer, but his dove grey suit fits him just right.

That's not something anyone would say about me. Nothing really fits me right now. Actually, I had to buy a whole new wardrobe after Mom passed, and then again a few months later. It's been a rough year. But my husband looks *flawless*—my amazing, handsome, debonair husband.

The one who won't meet my eye when I ask him about a suit.

He glances at his watch. "I better head out. I have an early meeting."

"Wait, you're driving separately?" I arch one eyebrow.

He nods. "Plus, after dinner I have that thing. Remember?"

"The fundraiser?"

He nods.

"Right."

"Okay." When he turns to go, there's no hug. There's not even a peck on the cheek. He just heads for the door.

That's the moment that I *know*.

I can't explain why I know. I'm not sure how it can be true. It wasn't a single moment or a single day, but in *that* moment, it hits me like a mallet to the head.

My husband's having an affair.

There have been too many *things* lately. There've been too many early meetings. And the most condemning evidence of all is the mysterious suit. Being in the donate pile clearly wasn't a mistake. It was there intentionally, and I was too obtuse to parse out what it meant.

I wonder how many other *things* I missed.

I'm still not sure why the suit was cast off, but it's definitely symbolic. I chose that suit. It was the one prize that came from this miserable excuse for a year. But now that I've recognized something's off, I can't pretend.

That's not how I'm wired.

A moment later, I race after my fleeing husband, barefoot, no jacket against the cold. To add insult to injury, it's raining outside, and when he sees me racing toward him, instead of being worried, instead of having concern for me, my darling husband's jaw locks up. His eyes flash.

He's annoyed.

I wonder, in that moment, what caused it. Was it the weight I gained that changed his regard for me? Was it my chronic neediness over the last year, clinging to him like he was my oxygen in a hostile, unfamiliar atmosphere? Did I treat him like I treated chocolate, as a life preserver in a terrifying flood?

Did my mother's death destroy us? Or maybe it was my father's. If not that, is there something about me that would have destroyed us no matter what external factors had come into play to damage our bond?

The rain has plastered my hair to my forehead, my cheeks, and my neck by the time I reach his side. He still doesn't look concerned.

He looks *tired*.

"How many times?" I ask.

"What?" He's scowling now. "Barbara, what are you doing out here? Go inside."

"Just tell me how many times." Even to my own ears, I sound crazy. Maybe there's no way I could be sane in this moment.

"What are you talking about?"

My voice rasps the words, "How many times have you slept with her?"

I expect him to deny it. I expect him to lie, just as he's lied with every small action, with every meeting that didn't exist, and just as he's lied with every missed touch and kiss.

I expect him to lie straight to my face.

So when he doesn't, when he asks, "How did you know?"

It hurts.

I start to shiver then, as the rain sluices between my neck and my blouse, as my unprotected feet are sliced by the rough shape of the malicious gravel underneath them. "It's true."

He sighs, finally pulling out an umbrella and holding it over his own head, not mine. "How did you find out?"

"It was the suit." My lips are shaking as raindrops hit them and run down to my neck. "You donated the suit."

He laughs, but this time he's not even trying to mask his frustration. "I threw it away," he says. "It's what I was wearing when—" He cuts off in disgust. "It kept accusing me, just like you are now."

He was wearing *my* suit when. . . "We're over," I whisper.

In the movies, couples argue. Even cheaters fight for the love they've clearly abandoned. The heroine retains a shred of pride, because the guy pretends to care that he screwed up. But not my husband. He just nods slowly, turns around, and gets in his car. He has a meeting, after all, and later today, he has a *thing*.

What he doesn't have any more, apparently, is a wife.

No, I've clearly been all on my own for a while.

I'm just finally realizing it.

H ere's the blurb for *Minted*, which will be out just after Thanksgiving.

B arbara's year has not been going well. Both her parents died, she gained a lot of weight, and her husband left her. And now, she's stuck attending a million holiday parties for work. . .with both her ex and his new girlfriend. She's not feeling the holiday cheer, that's for sure.

Bentley, on the other hand, has realized that while his life is pretty good, he really wants to settle down with an amazing woman. Unfortunately, while he's a whiz at making money, he's not so great at choosing people to date. He and his old friend Barbara make a deal. He'll be her date to the dreaded holiday parties, and in exchange, she'll help him weed through the dross to find the shimmering treasure he wants to build a life with.

It doesn't take Bentley very long to realize that Barbara's the one he wants, but she's not as quick to believe that she's good enough for the handsome billionaire Bentley. Can he convince her that she's everything he needs in time to spruce up the holiday season? Or will her miserable year come to just as tragic a close?

MINTED
THE SCARSDALE FOSTERS
B.E. BAKER

ACKNOWLEDGMENTS

Biggest thanks always go to my husband. He's a rock star among men. And he's always my very biggest supporter.

Secondary thanks to my kids, as usual, for being so supportive and so patient with me while I hide in my room and write. Also, for always loving my books and reading and referencing every single one all the time. You guys are the very best.

My editor Carrie, I still love you.

And to my readers, my ARC team, and my fans-turned-friends. You guys keep me writing. Your excitement and support is EVERYTHING. I love you all so much.

ABOUT THE AUTHOR

I have animals coming out of my ears. Seven horses. Three dogs, three cats, thirty-ish chickens. I'm always doctoring or playing with an animal... and I wouldn't want it any other way. But Leo (my palomino) is still my very favorite.

When I'm not with animals, or even if I am, I'm likely to have at least one of my five kids in tow, two of which I'm currently homeschooling.

My hubby is the reason all this glorious madness is possible. He's the best parts of all the amazing men I write (although he's bald and his six pack sometimes goes into hiding because of cookies.)

I also love to bake, like to cook, and feel amazing when I find time to kickbox, lift weights, or rollerblade. Oh yeah, and I'm a lawyer, but I try to forget about that whenever I can.

I adore my husband, and I love my God.

The rest is just details.

The Setback

The Lookback

Children's Picture Book

Yuck! What's for Dinner?

B. E. Baker writes FANTASY ROMANCE and other stories with speculative elements under Bridget E. Baker (her real name!)

The Dragon Captured Series: (dragon shifter romance!)

Ensnared

Entwined

Embroiled

Embattled

The Russian Witch's Curse: (horse shifter romance!)

My Queendom for a Horse

My Dark Horse Prince

My High Horse Czar

My Wild Horse King

The Magical Misfits Series: (paranormal humor!)

Mates: Minerva (1)

Mates: Xander (2)

The Birthright Series: (urban fantasy romance)

Displaced (1)

unForgiven (2)

Disillusioned (3)

misUnderstood (4)

Disavowed (5)

unRepentant (6)

Destroyed (7)

The Birthright Series Collection, Books 1-3

The Anchored Series: (urban fantasy romance)

Anchored (1)

Adrift (2)

Awoken (3)

Capsized (4)

The Sins of Our Ancestors Series: (dystopian romance)

Marked (1)

Suppressed (2)

Redeemed (3)

Renounced (4)

Reclaimed (5) a novella!

A stand alone YA romantic suspense:

Already Gone